PRAISE FOR

GIRL IN SHADES

"An immensely satisfying coming-of-age tale and remarkable first novel."

— *Chatelaine*

"It's an engaging tale, and Maya is an always compelling character as she grows from anxious 1 2 to self-confident and, yes, mystical 2 0."

— *Booklist*

"For Maya Devine, growing up is more demanding and more intense than anyone can imagine. Her story holds messages and lessons about life, love, priorities, death and identity. Indeed, Maya's story speaks to the wanderer in all of us."

— *Guelph Mercury*

"An intimate, character driven drama, I was captivated by Maya's child-hood voice."

— Book'd Out

"There is a tenderness to Baggio's heroine that is reminiscent of a Judy Blume character — and as her home life unravels, Baggio articulates Maya's vulnerability with heart-rending effect."

— *Winnipeg Free Press*

"I enjoyed it . . . It would be a great read for a book club because there are so many layers."

— *Canadian Family*

"*Girl in Shades* is a whirlwind of a coming-of-age story. In a sea of coming-of-age stories, it manages to feel fresh and original. It has twists and turns that surprised and impressed me. Allison Baggio has told an incredible and layered story, and I can't wait to see what she writes next."

— Christa Seeley, Hooked on Books

"At times, *Girl in Shades* feels like Miriam Toews' *A Complicated Kindness* in that the impressionable protagonist is sharply observant (or some degree of psychic, in Maya's case) and is shaped by, and ultimately must break from, their dysfunctional families . . . Maya is truly an unforgettable heroine, and *Girl in Shades* a quick and touching read."

— Alison Postra, The Romantic.com

"Baggio manages to give Maya a voice that starts out as a young girl and develops into a woman, and that is no small feat, especially because it isn't noticeable until after the last page has been turned. Baggio's colorful writing and quirky imagery give life to the story as a whole, propping up even the direst of circumstances. And the absurdity of Maya's situation lends it a comical tinge. It's not outwardly funny, but quietly humorous, like the whole thing is an inside joke between the reader and the author."

— *The Weekender*

"There are no words I can use to adequately describe my love for *Girl in Shades* . . . [it] is an intense character driven drama that should be read by everyone."

— NicoleAboutTown.com

"There is no greater gift for a songwriter than knowing his words and music have inspired or touched someone. Allison Baggio's *Girl in Shades* is one such example."

— Corey Hart

IN THE BODY

A collection of short stories

and a novella

ALLISON BAGGIO

ECW PRESS

Published by ECW Press
2120 Queen Street East, Suite 200, Toronto, Ontario, Canada M4E 1E2
416-694-3348 / info@ecwpress.com

LIBRARY AND ARCHIVES CANADA CATALOGUING IN PUBLICATION

Baggio, Allison
In the body / Allison Baggio.

ISBN 978-1-77041-054-1
ALSO ISSUED AS: 978-1-77090-271-8 (PDF); 978-1-77090-272-5 (EPUB)

I. Title.

PS8603.A4413515 2012   C813'.6   C2012-902690-5

Editor for the press: Jennifer Hale
Cover design: Ingrid Paulson
Cover image: Nanduu/photocase.com
Text design: David Gee
Author photo: Bianca Fera
Printing: Webcom   5   4   3   2   1

The publication of *In the Body* has been generously supported by the Canada Council for the Arts which
last year invested $20.1 million in writing and publishing throughout Canada, and by the Ontario Arts
Council, an agency of the Government of Ontario. We also acknowledge the financial support of the
Government of Canada through the Canada Book Fund for our publishing activities, and the contribution
of the Government of Ontario through the Ontario Book Publishing Tax Credit. The marketing of this
book was made possible with the support of the Ontario Media Development Corporation.

  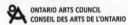

Canada Council Conseil des Arts
for the Arts   du Canada

Canada

ONTARIO ARTS COUNCIL
CONSEIL DES ARTS DE L'ONTARIO

PRINTED AND BOUND IN CANADA

MIX
Paper from
responsible sources
FSC
www.fsc.org   FSC® C004071

ANCIENT FOREST ™
FRIENDLY

For Tom, Noah, and Lily

You don't have a soul. You are a soul. You have a body.

~ C.S. Lewis

If anything is sacred, the human body is sacred.

~ Walt Whitman

CONTENTS

With Daddy

He comes to get me in the night. Or is it early in the morning? I don't know, but I think I might hear a bird singing from the tree outside my bedroom window. Just one bird. One is enough to create some music worth listening to.

He still has the key I guess, from when he lived with us, and Mom, well, she is fast asleep in her room I'm sure. He's been away since the day Mom said "go" and "now." It's a surprise to open my sleepy eyes and see him standing over me in the darkness of my room. My blinds are still pulled, which makes it hard to tell if it's time to get up or not. But I have a good sense from the clock that it isn't quite time. It says 5:08. That's a.m., morning, like we learned in school.

I'm not scared when I see him. It's been so long since I've seen him that it feels kind of like when I finally found my Polly Pocket under the couch, or when Mom holds me when I am crying.

"Daddy, what are you—" But he puts his warm fingers over my mouth and tells me to be very quiet. He says that Mom is still sleeping and that he wants to let her rest. He stumbles around in the dark, finding shirts and shorts to dress me in. And before we leave the room, I see him reach into my closet and pull all my jeans and sweatshirts down from the hangers. In one big swoop, he sticks them all in my Tinker Bell backpack.

"Daddy, where are we going?" I say as he loads me into the front of his stinky old pickup truck.

"You'll see," he says in a quick, quiet way.

I let him buckle the belt around me. I smell the cigarette smoke on his breath.

"What about my booster seat, Daddy?"

"Just be quiet now, okay?"

He slams the car door, and I realize that the whole street is still asleep. All of the windows are dark and the cars are still in the driveways. It's a lot earlier than I thought.

"I don't think it's time to get up yet, Daddy," I say while he starts the truck. Sputter, sputter, and then it goes. "Does Mom know about this, or is it a surprise?"

"You could call it a surprise," he says. Daddy's eyes look tired and his hair is all messy on his forehead. He's wearing a T-shirt that has a little greasy spot over his heart.

"I'm not sure I want to go anymore," I say, because I'm not. "I might want to stay. You can come back after the sun comes up."

"It's going to be just fine, kiddo," he says. "It's like a road trip, you'll love it."

I try to smile and be excited, but I'm not sure at all. As his truck pulls out of the driveway in one short burst, I turn my head to look back at my house. At that second, I see the light in the front window go on. Looks like Mom is the first one up on the street today.

I never wanted Daddy to move out. Even though there were times when he and Mom shouted, and when a blue vein on his neck stood up, I liked when he was there. More than when he wasn't. For one, it felt safer. Like if someone broke into the house, then he would be strong enough to fight the guy and make sure he never reached upstairs to my room. Also, sometimes Daddy would help me do my homework. Well, he did at the beginning of this year when I first started grade one. He was really smart at solving the questions Mrs. Clooney gave us, especially when he hadn't had any cans to drink.

Mom said that his beer was the main reason he had to leave. That it was the biggest problem. "That's ridiculous," I said to her. "Beer is not a problem; it's just a fizzy drink in a can." Daddy's cans just sat there on the table or piled up in the garage. They didn't say anything and they certainly didn't cause any problems.

"Okay, it's the beer inside your father that is the problem," she said. Which I still didn't understand, but didn't really feel like arguing anymore.

"When will I see him?" I asked Mom, and she said, "Oh, all the time, we'll work it out." I believed her about that, well, until it didn't happen.

The sun starts to come up as Daddy and I drive away. We go up the Don Valley Parking Lot (as Mom calls it) until there are no more tall buildings on the sides of the roads. We reach another highway and keep driving until we are surrounded by farmers' fields.

I must fall asleep because I wake up with my face bouncing off the door of Daddy's truck. It's bright sunshine out there now and feels like it's getting hot.

"Where are we?" I ask Daddy. He swallows hard and grips his hands on the steering wheel.

"Oh, we're just heading up north a bit. I thought you might like to visit Science North in Sudbury." His voice sounds scratchy, like mine does when I've stayed up too late.

"What's Science North?"

"Oh, it's this really cool place with all sorts of science stuff and IMAX movies. You like that, right? It'll be fun, just you and me . . . it's been a while, right?"

I try to answer both his questions with one nod.

"We needed this, Ash. It's about time that I get to be with you." Daddy has one of the beer cans with him. It's tucked between his legs and he takes a little sip of it after he talks to me. I think he notices me looking at it, because he moves it to the other side of him, near the door.

"That's just Pepsi," he says. "I just put a little Pepsi in there to help keep me awake for our road trip, that's all."

"Good, because beer is the problem," I say, and he makes a face at me like he just caught his finger in the door or smelled something rotten.

"Just be quiet now, Ashleigh. Dad is tired and I need to

4

concentrate. Here, I'll put some music on." He turns the radio dial and that song by Eminem and that girl comes out, telling each other they love the way they lie.

I think about how Mom was going to fill my kiddie pool in the backyard today, just so I could splash around and cool off. How I was planning to put one of her foldaway lawn chairs in there and lay in the sun with my feet still in the water. I wonder if Mom did it anyway. If she's out there right now sipping on an iced tea in her big black sunglasses.

That's when I notice I have to pee.

We stop at a gas station off the highway. It's got an outside door that leads into a bathroom for a boy or a girl.

"I'll just stand outside and wait for you," Daddy says. "Do you need help or anything?"

"Um, no," I say. It's only been a couple of months since Daddy has been away, so I'm surprised that he doesn't know that.

"Okay then, hurry up."

Daddy is fidgety. He keeps looking over his shoulder and jumping a little each time someone walks by. I wonder if it is because of the surprise for Mom.

The inside of the bathroom is gross. There is wet toilet paper stuck all over the walls and the toilet seat is dirty with even some pee on the seat. I pull off two strips of paper and lay them down over the seat like Mom taught me. Then I pull down my shorts and try to go really quickly without touching the toilet paper seat cover too much. I flush and the white strips go flowing down with my pee and the rest of the dirty water.

Thump, thump, thump. There is a knock on the door. I feel a

bit scared at first, but then I remember that it's probably just Daddy. "Ashleigh, hurry up," he says, and I wonder what the big rush is. I'm sure that Science North is going to be open until dinnertime at least. That's when my stomach reminds me that I haven't had breakfast or lunch yet.

"I'm coming!" There is no soap by the sink, but I run my hands under the cool water. It feels good. Daddy's truck is hot and I don't want to get back in.

"Here's a sandwich," he says when I open the door and see him there. It's one of those sandwiches with the thin white bread and flat orange cheese that is wrapped in plastic wrap.

"Thanks," I say, grabbing the sandwich and following him back to the truck. "A drink?"

"Shit. Wait in the truck, okay."

He puts me in the truck and rolls down my window a bit before he runs back into the gas station. While he's gone, I pull at the handle but he's locked it. I'm not sure where I would go if I was able to open it — I just have the urge to do it.

I close my eyes and imagine that my body is no longer a little girl. I morph into a tiny butterfly that can fold itself to fit through the slit he's left in the window. I am paper-thin with lovely designs on my wings — hearts and flowers in all colours. I'm gritting my teeth, willing myself into this butterfly that can fly high up in the sky where it isn't hot anymore. There are just cool breezes and my butterfly arms are light as hairs, taking me anywhere I need to go. I can flap, flap, flap in any direction I please, floating on breezes, inhaling flowers as I pass them. I can land on someone's shoulder — maybe a small girl like I used to be — and when I decide, I can flap myself away again. Soon, I see my house and I fall down through the air and into my kiddie pool. I wait a minute and let the water soak into my wings. When I see Mommy I fly back up, land on her hand, and stroke my tiny antenna on her skin . . .

I open my eyes and see that it's still my same old body — too big to fit through any slit, too heavy to fly anywhere. That's when Daddy opens his door.

"Here." He hands me a can of Sprite, which I hate. I say thank you anyway, because I know that Daddy is having one of those days when he might lose his frustrations at any moment. I crack the top and take a drink, wishing that Mom were here because she would have bought me a Minute Maid Orange Juice drink box instead. She knows me that well.

Sometime after lunch I have another small nap. We've started passing a lot of pretty black lakes, but they make me feel a bit sad because there are lots of kids splashing around in them, and I wish I could be out of the truck and in there with them. Maybe in an inner tube that lets me float and spin without having to worry about drowning or getting my head under the water for too long.

When I wake from my nap, I feel really grumpy. Daddy looks grumpy too, so I say that maybe we shouldn't go to Science North today. That maybe we should go back home and he can talk to Mom and set up another day. Also, that I'm a bit worried because I have a birthday party to go to tomorrow afternoon — for Jenny Paton, she was in my class this year — and that I'm not sure if we can go to

Science North and still have enough time for me to get all the way home, have a good night's sleep, and get ready for the party.

"I think you're going to have to miss the party," he says, almost like he doesn't care that it's Jenny Paton's birthday, or that I bought her I Can Be a Rock Star Barbie as a gift.

"But I don't want to miss the paaaarrrty," I say, and then my face gets all scrunched up and I start to cry, loud. I let all my frustrations out with this cry and Daddy doesn't say anything, just looks at me weird like I am annoying him, and turns the music up.

This is not the Daddy that I like. It must be because of the beer cans — it's the only explanation. I stop crying and decide not to talk to him until we reach Science North.

We aren't going to Science North. I know because I see the signs on the highway, "Science North 10 kilometres" and then "Turn here for Science North," and we don't turn.

"Where are we going really?" I say to Daddy. I notice that his face is red and sweaty, and there are also wet spots on his T-shirt.

"I told you, Ashleigh. It's a surprise."

"What if I have to pee again because of the Sprite?"

"Just hold it as long as you can, all right? I want to make sure we can get there in good time."

"What's good time?"

"In as little time as possible."

"Why, are we in some kind of race?"

"Sure," he says. "Like *The Amazing Race*."

"Are we the father-daughter team?"

"Yeah, father-daughter, that's it."

"Okay then, you should go as fast as you can. We could be the first father-daughter team to win."

"Maybe we will be."

"Dad?"

"Yes, Ashleigh?"

"Will we get a million dollars?"

"I don't think so, kiddo. But I wish."

We drive for a long time after that — it seems like hours and hours — without saying anything to each other. I keep pretending that we are in *The Amazing Race*, and even though Daddy doesn't believe it, that we *are* going to win the million dollars.

———

It's in the afternoon. Daddy says that we have to stop at the Walmart in a place called North Bay because he's realized that he forgot to bring my toothbrush and soap to have a bath and some stuff like that. I remind him about the Race but he says that we were just kidding, and why does Mom let me watch that show anyway when it's on so late? I tell him that she uses the PVR. That I watch it when I get home from school, but he doesn't really seem worried about my answer to his question.

We park really close to the front doors of the Walmart in the spot that says, "For Customers with Children."

"I'm only one child," I say. "Maybe this doesn't count for us."

"You count," he says, turning the key that shuts off the truck. "Trust me."

He makes me hold his hand as we walk in and tells me not to say anything to anyone.

"But what if—"

"Just zip it okay, Ashleigh."

Daddy's black running shoes clomp on the Walmart floor and I say that maybe he should get some sandals because it's so hot outside. He just tells me again to be quiet. To pretend that I forgot how to talk.

I follow him through the toothbrush aisle and he picks up a pink Disney Princess one, even though princesses are not my favourite anymore. He tries to grab some Colgate toothpaste, white mint, but I tell him that I usually have the kids' kind, the one with Winnie the Pooh on it. He grumbles something, but then takes the one I need and asks me if I need anything else at night.

"Just a glass of water before bed, but where are we going to sleep?"

"We'll find someplace," he says. "And I'm sure I'll be able to manage a drink of water."

While he's checking out with my stuff (he's also picked up some Johnson & Johnson lavender body wash "just in case"), I let go of his hand and close my eyes.

I'm a monkey, I'm a monkey, I think. A spider monkey. I'm no longer a little girl. I'm free! I use my long, hairy legs and gangly arms to climb up over all these racks of candy, and shirts, and cotton dresses and escape to the other side of the store. I'm scurrying under people's legs, weaving myself in and out of the racks much faster than I could move on my two little girl legs. People glance down at me and make scared faces, but they leave me alone. They know I won't hurt them. When I'm ready, I squeak up to someone, a kind-looking old lady, and tell her in my new monkey voice that I want to go home to my Mom and the kiddie pool. That my Dad said we were going to Science North, but he lied, and now I'm not sure where we are going at all. But wherever it is, there is not a million dollars waiting. A monkey. A monkey . . .

He's got the Walmart bag in his one hand, and he's waving me over with the other one. Then I'm back in the truck, we're driving again, and the sun is starting to look tired in the sky.

For dinner, Daddy and I go through the drive-through at Wendy's in some town that I don't know the name of. I'm getting really hungry by this time because one sandwich isn't enough for the whole day. Mom would have known that for sure.

When the lady hands Daddy the brown bag of food through the window, he doesn't look at her, or say thank you. He just grabs it and throws it over to my side of the truck.

"Thank wasn't very polite," I say.

"Just be quiet."

I do. But I feel crying in my eyes as we start to drive away. I try to forget about the tears as I eat my fries. But it's hard. I'm thirsty, but Daddy has forgotten to get me a drink again. I look at him and think that he looks like he wants another beer can. So I don't ask for anything.

I have had some good times with Daddy. There was this one time when he was home with us, and Mom wanted to go spend the day with her friends, so Daddy took me out for the entire afternoon. This was when I was really young — about four, I think — but I still remember.

We went to a little fair they were having out in the parking lot of the plaza, and Daddy let me ride one of those trains that goes around and around in a circle. You'd think it would have been boring, but I had so much fun. And after, he let me have Pepsi and cotton candy. I ate so much that I threw up in the car on the way home, but he didn't even seem to mind back then. He just pulled over and cleaned it up and wiped my mouth with a napkin.

"Oopsy," he said when he did it. "Too much junk."

I wonder what Daddy would do now if I threw up in his truck as we were driving more and more. Would he stop and clean it up, just say "oopsy" like before? Or would he get really angry? You never know with Daddy these days.

We are stopping at a motel along the road and Daddy says that we are going to sleep here tonight. There is a sign with the word "vacancy" flashing.

"But I don't want to sleep here," I say.

"You have no choice in the matter." Daddy is parking the truck behind the building. "I'm the adult, remember?" But that does not seem fair to me.

"I want to sleep in my bed." He hits the steering wheel with his hands when I say that.

"You are sleeping here, with me! That's it!" His eyes are almost closed even though he's still awake. Or maybe he is actually asleep and this is just his sleepwalking self who is yelling at me? Either way, I decide to pretend like I want to sleep at the motel, to make him happy.

"Fine, we can stay here just tonight. Tomorrow I want to go home to Mommy."

This seems to make him angrier. He grabs me by the arm and shakes me a bit. "No, Ashleigh. Just forget about her, okay?"

I really do start to cry this time. But he leaves me there anyway, locking me in. I wonder if he knows I could never forget about Mommy. Not ever.

We are in the motel room. It's dirty and stinky, and the curtains are stained, and there is black stuff in the sink when I wash my hands, and there is a brown line around the top of the bathtub. I decide that I will refuse to have a shower in there if he asks.

Daddy is lying on the bed with his hand on his head and his eyes closed.

I turn on the TV, but keep it really quiet so I won't wake him. There is nothing good on except this show about baby wolves walking out on the snow without their mother. They are taking tiny little steps, looking around, waiting for the mommy wolf to catch them if they slip. I'm afraid that their mommy is ignoring them, that the babies will fall, or slide far, far away and she won't be able to save them — so I turn the show off.

Daddy's cell phone is on the table and I grab it. I can see that people have been trying to call him because it says *21 missed calls.* That's funny, I never heard it ring once.

I decide to call Mommy to say hi and tell her I miss her. I start to punch in my number starting with the area code . . . 4 1 6 . . . 5 9 9 . . .

"What the hell are you doing?" Daddy says. He grabs the cell phone out of my hand.

"Just calling Mommy. I want to say good night."

"She doesn't want to talk to you right now," he says. "She's gone out with her friends tonight."

"Tomorrow morning then," I say. "When she's back."

"Look, Ashleigh," he says. He seems like he has a sore stomach or something. "I'm sorry about before, in the truck. I didn't mean to grab you like that. I was just frustrated."

"It's okay."

"It's just that I'm not used to looking after you on my own. I haven't done this at all since your mom kicked me out."

"I said it's okay."

I brush my teeth with my princess toothbrush and Winnie the Pooh toothpaste. I try not to look at the black in the drain when I spit out the white stuff. Daddy helps me change into my pyjamas, the Little Mermaid ones he grabbed from my room. I wish that he had grabbed the Barbie ones instead.

Daddy sleeps in one big bed, and I sleep in the other one. The room is very dark, and quiet except for the sound of cars swooshing by on the highway.

"Where will we go tomorrow?" I ask him through the dark.

"Farther," he says, which kind of confuses me. I try to convince myself that "farther" means, "all the way home" and then I try to make myself go to sleep.

In my falling asleep minutes I imagine that I am turning into a tiny slithery green snake — like the one Mom and me found in the backyard at the beginning of the summer. I am so small and slippery. I slide right off this big motel bed, across the floor, and right under the door. I slide through the parking lot, feeling the tiny pebbles on the ground push into my belly one after the other as if they were lined up waiting for me. I have no arms for anyone to grab, no hair to pull; I am bald and free to do what I want. No one walking by from their motel room could grab me if they tried; I would slink myself out of their hands in one instant. I decide to find some grass by the side of the road and dig my long body into the nighttime dirt. I find a groove and slowly start to make my way away from here. I'll just slither all the way home to Mom and—

When I wake up next, I can see that Daddy is sitting up on the corner of his big bed, and that he is drinking out of a beer can again. I can also see that he is all hunched over and that his shoulders are shaking a bit. This time, it's Daddy who is crying. I didn't know daddies did that.

I get up out of bed and walk over to him. He jumps a bit when I put my hand on his shoulder.

"It's okay, Daddy," I say. "I'm sorry we had a fight."

He looks at me, I can see the tears on his cheeks shining with the little bit of light that is coming in beside the curtains. He reaches up and grabs my arm over my pyjamas, squeezing me a bit but it doesn't hurt.

Then, he shakes his head like he's got a bug on his nose, saying,

"No, no, no." He turns and throws his can of beer at the wall. The beer flies out and lands all over the alarm clock that is beside his big bed.

He doesn't seem worried about what the people who own the motel will think. He wipes his eyes and looks at me.

"Look what you've done to me." He seems a little angry when he says that, but I don't blame him. He's probably going to have to pay to fix the clock when we check out.

"Put on your sandals," he says. "We're going now."

I do like he says, even though I know that it's still the middle of the night and I have even less of an idea of where we're going now than I did yesterday.

"I'll get dressed," I say.

"No," he says with a snap. "Never mind that, we have to go."

He pulls me out the door without even packing up my new princess toothbrush and Winnie the Pooh toothpaste. It seems like such a waste since I really do like the taste. I don't care much about leaving the lavender body wash.

We go out into the parking lot. The night feels cold. I'm still wearing the Little Mermaid pyjamas and my sandals. After I get into the truck, Daddy throws in a blanket that he took off of one of the beds for me to put over myself. That will probably cost him more too.

Daddy says nothing as we pull out of the parking lot slowly and start driving into the night. It's dark in his truck except for the little lights around his steering wheel. I bunch up a bit of the blanket and put it under my head against the window, looking out into the darkness.

I'm afraid to ask Daddy where we are going now. Instead, I

stare out into the night, trying my best to keep my eyes open. There are trees lined up beside the road everywhere, and giant rocks that look like they would be good for climbing. All the houses I can see have all their lights out. Every so often, another car passes and its headlights make me want to drop my eyelids.

I think about being a bird. That I could just roll down the truck window a bit with my little wing and fly up through the crack at the top . . . up, up, up, into the night and away from this. It's so wide open in the sky. The stars seem closer from up here, like I could touch them if I reached my wing up high enough. The tiny lights on the tips of the houses and in the street lamps below make little paths that are pointing the way home. The air is rushing up from underneath me, ruffling my feathers, reaching down to my birdie skin. My flying makes me forget what it even felt like to have feet. I don't need them when I'm up here. No toes trapped in my shoes, no legs to slip into my shorts, just tiny claws that swoosh through the air. I'm flying into the wind — the air is warm on my tired bird face.

A Canada goose flies by me — he's all alone too. We smile at each other. At least I do, trying to pull my little beak up in the corners.

"We're getting there," I tweet out to him. "We're almost home."

He flaps his wings and moves ahead. I turn and see that I'm flying into a cloud: a big, puffy white cloud that is inviting me in. It's so thick that I'm not sure if I'll ever get out . . .

When I open my eyes again the sun is up and I can tell from the way my body feels that I have been sleeping for a long, long time. I look around, searching for any sign.

We are on another highway, a big, fast one filled with cars. I know that this is no longer the highway to "farther." This is a highway I have driven on with Mom.

"We're almost home," I say.

Daddy just rubs his eyes, scratches under his skin, and smiles like he is really, really, tired.

I know exactly when we are almost on our street. Exactly which turn we need to take to be home, and he takes it. Our street is pretty quiet, even for the summer. It's Friday, which means that a lot of parents are at work and a lot of my friends are at daycare.

Then, I see Jenny. She's the girl I know from school, the one who's having the party today, and she's walking up the street towards my house. She is looking at the ground when she walks, like she's really sad or something.

"Jenny," I say softly, leaning towards the window to roll it down (it's so stuffy in the truck anyway).

"No!" Daddy says. "Don't talk to her."

"But she's my —"

"Just don't. Not yet."

When we pull up close to our house, I can see that there are a lot extra cars in the driveway. Strange. I wonder if Mommy is having her friends over this morning? Or if they stayed overnight for a sleepover?

I notice my Grandma's car, and Aunt Crystal's, and some others — there's a grey van I've never seen before.

Daddy stops the car in front of the house that is three down from ours. He leans over and pushes my door open, and I kick the hotel blanket off me and step out onto the curb. I tell him that I had fun with him, except that the motel was kind of creepy and the bed was hard.

He laughs and says, "Sorry about that, kiddo."

I tell him I love him and he says that he might not be able to see me for a while, but that he loves me too.

"See you soon," I say back, because sometimes I like to pretend that things aren't really true, even if they are.

I slam the truck door as hard as I can, and then I hear something. It's like a shrieking from where my house is. I look and see that it's Mommy. She's running down the sidewalk towards me with her arms out. She's got tears on her cheeks and her face looks like someone has really hurt her feelings. I turn to see if Daddy notices too, but he's already driven away.

Birthday Boy

When it arrived that February in 1970, Virginia wasn't at all surprised. She had read about the lottery in the paper before Christmas. She had known what to expect — but she still prayed something would change.

It was unbelievable. Out of 365 days in the year, the birthday of their nineteen-year-old son David — September 14 — had been chosen first. There had been some speculation by the statisticians that the lottery was not in fact random, but either way, it didn't help her David, not now.

"What are the odds?" Virginia said, shaking her head with her hand across her mouth, when she first saw his birthday written in black ink.

"One in 365, Ginny. Are you stupid?" Gilbert answered, to which she did not respond. "He's probably one of the few in

Fairborn, or in all of Ohio for all we know!" Gilbert was excited that day. And while Virginia rubbed her son's shoulder as he read the letter, her husband stood above them both, hands on his hips.

"Read it out loud, son," Gilbert said.

David looked up at his father, his eyes wide and his teeth clenched. He turned back towards the page and opened his mouth slightly. At first no sounds came out, only a squeak of air, but after a distinct swallow, he spoke: "Order to report for Armed Forces physical examination."

"Oh, Davy, you don't have to read this if you don't want to," Virginia said, putting her hand on his forearm. She noticed that the hairs on his skin were standing up like when he was a child. His plaid shirt was wrinkled (she'd been having trouble concentrating on the ironing lately), his walnut hair tousled, and his face had a little bit of stubble, like he was trying to hide himself.

"That's my boy," his father said. "Keep going. I like the sound of it."

David continued: "You are hereby directed to present yourself for Armed Forces physical examination by reporting . . ." Virginia hated how ugly the words sounded coming from her sweet son's lips. It was too grotesque to seem real.

David was going to Vietnam.

Virginia dropped to her knees in front of her son, grabbing his arms and praying silently. How could she ever let him go? She had to stop this, otherwise what kind of mother would she be?

"This will make a man of you" was what Gilbert said, before calmly re-folding the letter, putting it in his shirt pocket, and leaving the cool air of their farmhouse kitchen.

Virginia had chosen David's name even before he was born — a strong, plain name — in hopes of invoking an ordinary life. There had been complications leading up to his birth: high blood pressure, cramping, little spots of blood. She got scared if she didn't feel the baby moving inside of her. But after convincing Gilbert on two separate occasions to take her to the hospital during the night, her husband had announced that there would be no more dry runs. "We'll just wait until it's really close" was his justification, but his wife knew better.

When she felt the pains again before bed one night, Gilbert wanted to wait until morning, but she insisted that this time it was real. That their baby was planning to come into this world before midnight if they'd have him. So they went to the hospital, and this time, she was right.

When the time came for pushing, a nurse joked that her hand was almost broken from Virginia squeezing it. But soon, there David was — wrinkled, wet. Perfect.

Gilbert came in to hold his son while Virginia bled. And bled and bled. She bled so much that they had to remove her entire uterus. And afterwards, she lay on the bed like a hollowed out pumpkin, unable to move.

"At least this one's a boy," she said to her husband, who didn't seem to hear her. He nodded politely and turned to look out at the black night through the window.

"Just rest now, Ginny." He didn't look back at her when he said it. She could tell he was thinking of them again. The friends he lost when he was fighting overseas. But why then? She wondered what it was about a birth that made him think of nothing but death.

Ginny didn't care. She would not let him ruin that moment too. Because in her arms she held a baby that would give her life true purpose — tiny lips and curled toes that changed everything.

Virginia waited until David was sleeping before going to Gilbert with her suggestion. She crept around the corner into the living room while he was watching *The Tonight Show* with Johnny Carson. Multicoloured light from the television set flicked in the dark room — a muffled studio audience clapped and cheered. As she stood there, unsure, he yelled at her to "Just come in, why don't you?"

"Gilbert?"

"Say it, Ginny."

"I think we should send him to Canada."

"No."

"You won't even think about it?"

"This is what he needs."

"But I don't want him to go . . ." Virginia could feel herself starting to get weepy and felt frustrated that she couldn't say things as she had planned.

"Losing David in battle too, won't bring the rest of them back, you know."

Gilbert turned off the television and stood to face his wife. Redness had started to overtake his wide forehead, creating what looked like a throbbing beet underneath his grey hair. He towered over Virginia like he always had, but she felt it then more than ever. "You think I *want* him to go?!" he said. She was sure that David could hear him from upstairs.

"Gilbert, your voice."

"He's my son, Ginny. Of course, I don't *want* him to leave. But he has to go." He stopped and took a breath like he was trying to prevent himself from exploding all over her. "Look, Ginny," he said more quietly, stroking his jaw. "David's entire life has led up to this moment."

"Your entire life," she whispered, knowing that insinuating David was finishing his father's business could send Gilbert over.

"What did you say?" His voice boomed again and he put his hand on her thin arm, creating a long wrinkle in her white striped blouse. "So help me God, Virginia, if you even think about trying to send that boy to Canada, I will hunt him down like a deer. I'll bring him back any way I can."

"Don't say that." She took a small step backwards, but raised her chin to look Gilbert in the eyes and crossed her arms.

"And as for you Ginny — that'll be it for us." He squinted, looking right into her like a threat. "So choose, why don't you? Me or him?"

"You know I don't want to choose, Gilbert." She looked away then, feeling his hot breath on her face.

"Could have fooled me, missy."

When he passed Virginia to leave the room, Gilbert's meaty arm pushed her around to face the other wall. Virginia didn't think he did it on purpose — it's just that she was in the way.

The next day, David asked his father why he had to fight.

"You're nineteen years old, Dave. You should know why it's great to be an American."

"You haven't answered my question."

"You have to fight because you have the power to help protect a free democracy from communism. You have been chosen to do it and no one else. You owe that to your country."

"But, should someone really be forced into something like this?"

"You're not being forced."

"Says who?"

"You."

"No, I don't."

"David, this is not a friggin' debate!" A vein on the side of Gilbert's head bulged blue. David lowered his chin and looked at the floor, crossing his hands in his lap.

"But, I want to stay here. I want to go to college like I'd planned and study English. Maybe become a writer, or a teacher."

A pause from Gilbert, then: "That is not presently an option. Now, go help your mother with dinner, David."

And Virginia, listening and looking in from the kitchen, called out to her son to leave his father alone.

Gilbert had refused to celebrate David's eighth birthday. He told Virginia that he needed to work a long day in the fields before the corn turned too ripe, but Virginia knew he had picked it already. She wasn't stupid. She had been in the empty fields just the day before looking for David and had found him lying flat on his back staring up at the sky.

"Clouds can look like things!" he said when he saw her, and she smiled.

David had asked only girls to his party: Suzy, Mary-Jo, Grace, Nancy, and Joyce. Virginia still remembered their names because she was the one to make out the invitations.

You're invited to a party to celebrate David's birthday, she had written in her swirly handwriting.

Though it seemed a bit strange that David only wanted girls at the party, it was all right with Virginia. She accepted it; Gilbert didn't. He expected David to be playing flag football in the dirt, or trading baseball cards under the front porch. He told her this, loudly, when she let him know about the girls.

When David's eighth birthday came, it wasn't the happy occasion Virginia had hoped for. Upon seeing his father leave the house in the morning — without even wishing him a happy birthday — David pouted for most of the day. Even the pin-the-tail-on-the-donkey game and the chocolate cake didn't seem to cheer him up. Not really.

By the time Gilbert came back to the house it was already dark and David was in bed.

To show his displeasure at his father's behaviour, David had expressed his feelings to Virginia through a poem, which she found on her pillow when she turned down the covers that night.

Fathers are good.
Fathers are smart.

Except when they make you cry.
And wish you were someone else.

The poem made Virginia herself feel like crying. She kept it hidden away in her jewellery box. Despite what it said about Gilbert, she was proud of how well David had used language. She folded it into a small square and laid it flat under her mother's antique brooch. She knew it was somewhere that Gilbert would never look.

Gilbert and Virginia took David to his state-ordered physical examination. It was a Tuesday and Gilbert had taken the day off work. He told Virginia he didn't have to lie about the reason why. His boss at the car garage, where he'd worked since rootworms made his corn crops fail three years ago, understood that these kinds of things came first. Virginia went because she couldn't bear to have David go through it alone.

Before they left, David, dressed in the clothes he reserved for Sunday church, with his hair slicked back like his father's, said to Gilbert, "I hope I don't fail this thing, Dad. You know I've never been into sports or anything."

"You'll do fine, son." Gilbert puckered his lips and nodded like he was sure.

At the exam, David did everything he was told to. They weighed him, and measured him, and listened to his heart. Strong beat. Nice high arches. They made him run on a treadmill, but only for a short time, which David seemed to handle okay.

When it was all over, David stood with his parents behind a desk while his paperwork was processed. David was slouching and Gilbert kicked him in the shin, ordered him upright.

"Easy, Gilbert," Virginia said.

When David only slumped down further, Virginia looked him over. Her son's face seemed grey. His hand clutched his chest as he wheezed his air. She panicked inside.

"Gilbert, do something!"

"David, what's your problem?" his father said. The man with the thick black glasses and clipboard was looking away.

But David couldn't answer.

"For God's sake. Take a breath." Gilbert put his hand on David's back.

David continued to wheeze and began to wave his hand in front of his face, like he was trying to grab onto something, or say goodbye.

"Get out of here, David. Go outside right now." David did as his father said, bursting through the doors leading outside.

"Is there a problem with your son?" asked the man with the black glasses when he noticed David was gone.

"Just needed some air," Gilbert answered.

"Well, we're all done here anyway," the man said.

Virginia chased after David, finding him on the cement steps outside the building, gasping and heaving into the late February air.

When he got home, David went straight to bed. His mother brought him soup, the kind she made with lentils and peas. She watched as he sat up in bed and slurped it up with a silver spoon.

"Thanks, Mom, I just need to sleep is all. You don't worry about me, okay?"

She noticed then, with his shirt off, how broad his shoulders had become, and how muscular his chest. He had a tuft of hair between his pectorals. He wasn't her baby anymore.

"But you'll always be my baby, David."

"Ha! Tell that to my new army buddies and they'll eat me up."

She chuckled without planning it, but stopped herself. David grew serious again: "If this is what Dad wants, then I'll just have to do it."

"You know I wish things were different," she said, to which he just smiled weakly from the corner of his mouth, slumped back onto his pillow, and put his forearm across his eyes.

"I'll make it through this, Mom. I have to."

On a Saturday morning, days later, there was a knock at the door. It was Virginia's neighbour Sylvia from down the road and her son, Markus.

When Virginia opened the door, Sylvia was holding a pie wrapped in tinfoil, and she was clutching it against herself to protect it from the wind. Markus said he was going to go upstairs and see David. Virginia saw no problem with it; the boys knew each other from school. They had both graduated last spring. They'd worked together at Chesney's furniture store in the summer.

The pie was blueberry and Virginia cut out two thin slices for her and Sylvia to eat in the living room. She also prepared a pot of chamomile tea.

"So, he's really going to go then?" Sylvia asked Virginia when they had settled themselves on the couch.

"It looks like it, Sylvia." Virginia was not looking forward to the conversation.

"Believe me, I'm thanking my lucky stars that Markus was born on February ninth. He's safe for now."

"I'm glad, Sylvie."

"Ginny, this whole war is awful. I mean, I'm as patriotic as the next person, but when kids we know are coming home in body bags, something is wrong. Have you thought about sending him to Canada?"

"Who came home in a body bag?" Virginia said.

"The Patterson boy from in town. Same age as David I think — nineteen — such a pity. And to think, he volunteered to go."

"Volunteered?"

"The whole country is out of control if you ask me, with Bobby Kennedy gone, the hippies sliding around naked in the mud, the riots. When are we going to get to the end of it?"

But Virginia was still thinking about the body bag.

Then, yelling from above. Gilbert's voice. Markus shuffled down the stairs on lanky legs, his blond hair falling down over his eyes.

"Markus, honey, dear, are you okay?" his mother asked.

"I'll be outside," he said, but Virginia could barely hear him. The front door slammed.

Gilbert limped down the stairs, tripping over his bad leg. Fuming. He had nothing to say to either of the women, but his face was contorted, twisted, like he could barely stop himself from screaming.

"It's time for David to take this like a man," he said to Virginia after she followed him to the kitchen. He was hunched over, rubbing his sore thigh. "I expect him at the table for dinner tonight."

"Fine," Virginia answered without finding his eyes with hers.

"I'll be in the barn, Ginny."

Sylvia excused herself shortly afterward, which made Virginia glad, and David attended dinner that evening as his father had requested. Not a word was spoken throughout the meal — only eyeballs staring, and sighs, and the loud crunching of bread crusts.

The second letter, which arrived in May, was no easier for Virginia to digest than the first. Gilbert read it that time, out loud, so both his wife and son could hear.

"You are hereby ordered for induction into the Armed Forces of the United States."

Gilbert said the words slowly, giving each one a distinct emphasis that highlighted their importance. David looked away from his father, squinting and wincing like he was being punched in the stomach. Virginia glared at her husband, feeling anger for him growing inside her like there had never been before — like he had written the words himself.

The afternoon before David was to leave, Virginia washed and dried all of his underwear, folded them into small squares and packed them into a black duffle bag. She also added four bleached white T-shirts, two pairs of worn-out blue jeans with patches stitched over holes in the knees, a button-up flannel shirt, and three pairs of thick wool socks. She imagined they would give him most of what he needed, but figured it would be comforting for him to have something familiar. Before she zipped up the bag, she added a note.

My sweet boy. Every moment you are gone will seem like a million years to your mother waiting back home. Remember though, sometimes we have to endure unpleasant experiences to later appreciate life's true goodness. I will never forgive your father for making you do this. Come home to me.

She hoped the note would not depress him, but she wanted him to know that she was on his side. One hundred percent.

That night, Virginia insisted on tucking her son into bed like she had done when he was little. She sat on the edge of his bed and stroked his hair.

"Mom, you can go to bed now, really." But his blue eyes pleaded with her to help him.

"I want to support you through this."

"If only I was born a day later," David said. "Maybe I would be staying home to study instead. It's so frustrating . . . I've finally got the money saved."

"After," Virginia said, trying to make herself believe it. "There's always after."

"I don't know, Mom. I just can't shake this feeling that something really bad is going to happen."

"Of course it isn't, Davy."

"Maybe I should just leave tonight, go to Canada like you said." His legs were starting to fidget under his blankets, his arms flailing in the air as he spoke.

"He'd find you. I'm scared of what he'd do."

"Does he really want to lose his only son? Would *that* finally make him proud?"

"Go to sleep, David. That's all you need to do right now." There was nothing else she could think to say.

David collapsed back onto his pillow. As she stood up to leave, Virginia couldn't stop trying to think of a way out of this. The options wormed and circled through her head, making her dizzy.

Gilbert was already asleep. She could hear him snoring from the bedroom and the floorboards creaking as he moved from side to side on the mattress. His presence was like an ugly storm in the distance threatening to destroy a hundred farmhouses.

Like most brilliant inspirations, hers came in a flash. She saw the outline of her husband's gun case in the darkness of her thoughts. And before she could talk herself out of it, she had made her way downstairs and was standing in front of the real case. Guns on display like stiff sleeping snakes in a cage, lined up one on top of another. Guns used by Gilbert for hunting, and for protection, he said, in case they were ever threatened.

She opened the case. It was never locked. Gilbert didn't have the patience to fiddle with locks and keys. He liked to get in and out as fast as possible. She held the top rifle, heavy, and ran her index finger inside the loop of the trigger guard. Something about the way the gun sank into her forearm seemed right. She knew how to use it. She had watched Gilbert shoot cans with it plenty of times. Sometimes, he would only practise the motion of shooting, often in the house while he watched television. "The safety is on," he would tell her, "there's no danger." But she didn't know about that.

Going up, the stairs seemed steeper because of the extra weight. She knew the gun was loaded, and that made her walk slower, afraid that each squeak of hardwood would send a bullet into the wall, sabotage her whole plan.

Yes, she only had one chance to do what she needed to do.

She stopped at their bedroom door and looked in at Gilbert, the gun hidden behind her back. As she hoped, he was asleep under the quilt that she had pieced together after they were first married. Reds and blues and whites, triangles and stars, all interconnected in careful stitches. His hands were spread out, palms up, on either side of his head like a wounded bird and his lips were parted slightly. When he jerked his chin to the side, she clenched air in her throat. His grey hair hung loosely over one of his eyes, not greased back like when he was awake.

With him in such a vulnerable state, if she squinted, she could almost see the man who married her. The man she dated for six months after they met by the cotton candy machine at the town fair when she was seventeen. In his blue eyes and strong arms, she was sure she had found her future. And then he had gone to war.

It was 1943 and he was to be stationed somewhere in England, then Normandy, France. She wasn't going to give up on him though. He was her first — and to this day, only — boyfriend.

He wrote her letters. They came roughly every two weeks. Her mother used to hold them special for her on the windowsill.

When she came home from high school, she would take them out onto the front verandah to read. Hugging her legs up to her chest on their porch swing, she would tear the envelope open with her index finger, tuck her golden hair behind her ear, and read what her love, Gilbert, had to say. It was never anything exciting: what he ate for lunch, the prank he played on one of his friends, how he was euchre champion of his squad. Silly stuff like that, but it meant a lot that he wanted to share it with her.

Her favourite part about the letters was the way he signed them: *love and all that, yours, Gilbert.* This made her think that maybe he was hers, and maybe he did love her.

And then in the spring, his letters stopped. Instead, Gilbert's mother came by the house to tell her that Gilbert was coming home.

"It's over," his mother said to her, dabbing tears with her fingertips. "It's finally over, and my baby is coming home."

But Gilbert didn't come home. Not the Gilbert who had asked Virginia on their first date (a dance) with one hand rested gently on her shoulder, or the one who had looked into her eyes for one solid minute before he kissed her the first time. No, that Gilbert didn't come home, but someone else did.

His right leg had been hit by shrapnel on the beach, the bone shattered. He had a cast on and couldn't put down any pressure. When she visited him that first day, he stayed mainly in bed, looking out at her like an abandoned kitten.

"This injury is your greatest victory, son," his mother said to him, shaking her pointy nose back and forth. "This injury sent you home to me."

But Gilbert didn't agree with her. He just kept looking up at Virginia like he wanted to say something. And when he did, it was disjointed and slurred: "My buddies, Ginny . . . an entire squad . . . all gone like they never existed at all. I've let everyone down. It's over."

Virginia vowed then that she would not ever let Gilbert down. That she would help him see that it wasn't his fault.

And now, twenty-four years later, she stood looking at this same man as he slept in his torn paisley pyjamas, and her with a piece of deadly metal pushed against her back. She let the gun drop to her feet behind her.

He opened his eyes. Just like when he returned from war, his words were mumbled, almost like he wasn't consciously saying them: "I'm sorry, Ginny. So sorry. We'll make it through this." His eyelids were droopy and he seemed to be looking right through her.

She felt a wave of nauseating guilt rush over her. "Go back to sleep, Gilbert." She put her hand on his arm, warm, and he touched it with his fingers. "Everything's okay." In a breath, he was snoring again.

A clock ticked in the hall. Her thoughts jumped.

Nervous adrenaline pumped through her insides. Fear. She had to act fast. She was already very close to talking herself out of what she had to do.

She stood outside David's room with the gun in her arms. Her heart thumped violently in her chest.

Soon she opened the door, slowly, and was somehow surprised to see him sleeping there, curled up into a ball like when he was inside her. In her mind, she apologized to David for what she had to do. She also asked Jesus to forgive her and give her the strength to endure her husband's inevitable outrage.

"Son, sometimes we have to endure unpleasant experiences to later experience life's true goodness." She moved her lips over these words, without making a sound. He would see it someday.

And Gilbert would understand — he knew about being injured. Maybe she could say she was only trying to scare David, teach him a lesson, toughen him up. She could pretend it was an accident — a stupid mistake.

And like she was there for Gilbert, she'd be there for David, every step of his recovery.

She quietly cursed war and reached down to the bed. She peeled the quilt up carefully around David's left ankle. She lifted the rifle, steadied its heavy stock on her bony shoulder and pointed the barrel at her only son's foot. She took a long breath to try and stop her hands from shaking.

Then she closed her eyes and pulled the trigger.

Spilt Milk

The lion doorknocker tried to bite his hand when he reached to grab it, trying to provoke blood in exchange for the blood that he himself had spilled. He waited five beats before he heard them fumbling with the lock on the inside. And as he took two long breaths inward, the door swung open, and they were in front of him.

"You must be Aseem?" the woman said, the corners of her mouth reaching out towards her ears, the wrinkles around her eyes dancing on her ivory face. "Do come in."

The man stood behind her, with his back leaning up against the banister that led upstairs. He crossed his arms across his convex belly. His red mustache appeared to sprout from his nostrils like tiny flames.

"Excuse the mess please, Aseem. As you can understand we've been a bit preoccupied."

Aseem nodded and walked through the door. The house was immaculate: marble floors that shimmered, wooden coffee tables like mirrors, nothing out of place, not a sweater on the back of a chair, not an empty coffee cup, not a pair of empty shoes.

"I'm sorry it took me so long to come see you," Aseem said to the woman.

"You don't worry about that, hon."

"I know they gave you my name right off as the one who was driving the car. I stayed in hospital for a while with injuries, because of the seat belt."

"You are here now, and that's what counts. We knew you would come."

The man, Mr. Barber, had still not spoken, only taken Aseem's jacket and led him into the sitting room. Aseem sat down on a couch surrounded by a collection of six-foot Roman statues: naked, white, missing arms and tips of noses.

"Interesting artwork," Aseem said. He wondered whether he should have come.

"Now, what can I get you?" the woman, Mrs. Barber, asked.

Aseem said "nothing" and as she left the room, he added, "thank you." He and Mr. Barber were left alone. Mr. Barber's eyes looked tired, with redness in the corners and skin puffing up underneath.

Mr. Barber sighed, and seemed to let the words curl out on his thick breath: "Was it your fault?"

"Huh?"

"The accident. Was it your fault?"

Aseem felt two invisible hands of guilt and regret reach around his neck, choking him. He cleared his throat, shook his head, and said the words he had practised: "Sir, it is hard for me to remember what happened. Things are fuzzy in my mind about that day. It was so busy. I know that your daughter and I were heading west on Bloor Street when something went in front us — a bicycle, a person, a small car. I don't know. As I said, it is mostly a blur to me. I regained my consciousness in a hospital bed."

"So it wasn't your fault?" Mr. Barber's eyes were squinted to slits.

"No, sir, I don't see how it could have been."

"Cheese curds!" Mrs. Barber shouted then. She had returned to the room with a silver tray with orange cheese bits piled in the centre.

"Mrs. Barber," Aseem said. "Mrs. Barber, I'm sorry about the loss of your daughter."

"I appreciate that," Mrs. Barber said and sat down on the chair opposite Aseem. The chair was covered in plastic and made a crunch as her bottom end hit it. "Beatrice was very special to us. We had high expectations for her life, what with her cello playing and her ability to knit scarves without ever looking at her fingers."

"It must be horrible for you now without her."

"No use crying over the milk glass that has already tipped," Mrs. Barber said and both her eyes looked down at her own nose in reflection. "We are looking forward as much as possible."

Mr. Barber turned his head down and to the right like he was checking to see if his armpit had created a wet mark in the corner of his golf shirt.

"Mrs. Barber, if there is anything I can do . . ."

"In fact Aseem, have a cheese curd first."

Aseem popped two of the greasy curds into his mouth. "They

were Beatrice's absolute favourite snack. But of course you would know that."

"I would?" The cheese had lodged along the sides of Aseem's throat.

"Well, of course, since you two were an item." She created finger quotes around the word "item" and winked and wiggled in her seat.

"Mrs. Barber, I can assure you we weren't . . ."

"No need to be coy, Aseem. I know you two were driving together when it happened. Where do young people go on dates these days anyway — the cinema? It took my daughter twenty-one years to lose her virginity and even though I have only known you a few minutes, I can honestly say I'm glad it was with you instead of one of those geeks in her music program."

"Virginity?" Aseem's cheese throat began closing up, building lactose bridges across his esophagus. He was shocked by Mrs. Barber's assumptions, but afraid to make things worse by telling her the truth.

"And don't think that Mr. Barber and I are ones to worry about differences in culture. We are just happy to hear that she got into bed with anyone at all." Aseem fell silent, caught between honesty and respect of the departed. "The good news for you, Aseem, is that all is not completely lost," said Mrs. Barber.

"It isn't?"

"No, as you probably know, Beatrice has an older sister."

"She does?" Aseem shifted on the couch and held air in the upper parts of his cheeks.

"And I know what you're thinking: 'Would it be right for me

to be with Beatrice's sister after her own tragic death?' The answer, I can assure you, is yes. Beatrice idolized her sister Laverne. She's only ten years older. That's not too old for you is it, Aseem? You look like you're in your late twenties."

"Twenty-five."

"Close enough, Laverne is thirty-one. She's the perfect age to marry and move away from our house. You've heard about older women, huh, Aseem? Grace and maturity like a finely aged wine."

"Excuse me, Mrs. Barber, did you say marry?"

"With your culture, you are probably used to marriages being arranged. Just think of it like that."

"I do not agree with arranged marriages, Mrs. Barber. I think love should be the only deciding factor in a relationship."

"Somewhere along the line though, I'm sure there were plenty of successful marriages in your family this way; your mother and father perhaps? What's one more, especially when it would do so much to refill the empty cup of happiness around here."

"Mrs. Barber, I'm sorry to have to tell you this, but I can't marry your daughter. I feel terrible about what happened, but I just can't."

Mr. Barber spoke then like lightning that sizzled: "You owe it to us."

Aseem, hit with Mr. Barber's bluntness and buzzing with his own guilt, was forced to reconsider.

The girl was resting her cello against her hip. Raising one hand in the air as if signalling an old friend, he knew she was trying to make him look at her. At first he ignored her — angling his head down to fiddle with the metre on the dashboard. He resented the idea of waiting as she loaded her instrument in rush hour traffic. She waved again. Was she trying to make a sound with the moving air? Then she opened her mouth: "Hello! Over here, please! I need a ride!"

The driver's side window was open — he heard her all right. With the light green, he reluctantly turned the steering wheel and pulled over to the curb where she stood.

He tapped his foot on the brake pedal and watched her face in his rear-view mirror: round bumps for cheeks, a tiny cluster of pimples on her chin, thick eyebrows growing into one.

"Thanks for pulling over," she said in a whisper, her hands drying themselves by smoothing out her knee-length skirt. "I'm going home. Nine Vermont Avenue, please."

He only nodded and punched out a grunt that grew from the back of his throat and hovered in front of his mouth before disintegrating. He hated his job. Days full of complaints, silences, body odour, and huffs aimed at him. He hated this city. Crowded, busy, tense, noisy, rushed, calculating, superficial. Toronto left him in a cold shadow, especially after the news he had just received.

He longed for the countryside of his boyhood. Taking in the moist smell of dirt during monsoon season and absorbing the dusty sun like a leaf when it came. During his shifts, his thoughts often rested on what he left behind in India — to give him strength — wrinkled old aunts draped in colourful saris, incense burning in every room. Priya. But he couldn't let himself think of her now, not with things the way they were. His thoughts flipped back to his new life. Back to necessity, responsibility, privilege.

"Avoid Bathurst Street if you can, please," said Beatrice from the back seat.

"Whatever," he mumbled.

"Try to go up Palmerston. It's fastest."

He wondered why passengers saw him as a miracle worker. Could he prompt steel to rise up over the other cars? He pushed his elbow into his horn, letting up when, in the rear-view mirror, he saw the girl with two fingers stuck into her ears like carrots, foolish.

They were wedged on Bloor. Buried within rush hour congestion in a taxi cab coffin.

———

Light woke him, pushing medical brightness through the ache in his face.

"Hold still, Aseem. This won't hurt if you relax." Needles pinched holes in his veins, tubes plugged his nose, and nausea swelled his insides.

He twitched when he remembered. Was the taxi okay? Would he have to go back to India? He'd made a mistake. And then one final thought that pounded mercilessly into the top of his spine: *What about the girl?*

———

A slow-moving figure in the darkness of the bedroom. Her. Emerged from the washroom. Laverne. Beatrice's older sister. Aseem's new wife.

The wedding had been arranged within a month with Aseem an unimportant part to every manic detail. Aside from making time for Aseem and Laverne to meet awkwardly in the Barber kitchen over two large glasses of chocolate milk, Mrs. Barber had little use for Aseem in the preparations. Mr. Barber served only as Enforcer, to watch over Aseem when he was at the house and inflict nighttime phone calls to his dusty apartment to make sure he hadn't changed his mind.

"A deal is a deal," he reminded him. "You do this for us, and we will forgive you for what you let happen to Beatrice. You can live free of guilt."

Aseem moved through each day before the wedding as if fully immersed in cloudy water. He felt lucky to still have his job with Downtown Taxi and a brand new cab to drive. He deserved it. Accidents happen after all. He began opening doors for riders, getting out to lift heavy packages, and waiting while they said sloppy goodbyes to their lovers. He overlooked Toronto traffic, and smog, and pretense, to embrace what he saw as his best opportunity yet: the chance to become a Canadian citizen, once and for all. He would not be the first to marry a girl for whom he felt no desire.

Mrs. Barber insisted he call his parents in India and inform them of the engagement. He told her he did but no phone call was made. Better to tell them once the wedding had taken place. It would be easier then to deflect their attempts to direct him instead towards a complacent Indian girl in Brampton. Easier to tell them that instead of attending university next September, he would be marrying the sister of a girl who rode in his taxi for only a few minutes — minutes that just happened to take place immediately before her death.

The April wedding took place at City Hall with only Mr. and Mrs. Barber present as witnesses. Photos were snapped by a homeless man in Nathan Phillips Square under a sky of grey clouds. The man grasped the disposable camera Mr. Barber had given him between his greasy fingers, told everyone to smile, and took nine pictures of Aseem and Laverne standing in front of a small flower garden surrounded by cement. Aseem did not smile, nor did he lift the bride in the air when it was suggested. Not that he would have been successful if he tried.

"You make a wonderful couple," Mrs. Barber said. "I knew this day would come, Laverne. To think of all the nights you cried." Mrs. Barber took her daughter's hand in hers. "At least we know now that your sister didn't die in vain."

A small reception was waiting for them when they returned to the Barbers' house. Finger sandwiches that reeked of tuna, grapes floating in a punch bowl filled with red liquid, white balloons already staring to deflate.

Aseem forced a grin at each person who congratulated him. He saw the pity swimming in their eyes, but tried to ignore it. Worry battered him from inside his head. The moment he dreaded most about the entire arrangement was approaching — he would soon have to take Laverne back to his apartment to sleep.

Lying back on his pillow, Aseem blinked through the black of the bedroom, his pupils fighting to take in the light from the bathroom down the hall.

"I'm ready, Aseem," she said from beside him.

Anxious to delve into his future, to accept his penance, he turned the knob on his bedside light.

Rippling arm flesh led down to the sheer nightgown draped over her large hips. Her lace-lined thighs touched almost to the knees, overgrown toenails pierced the air, red nail polish chipped itself into nothing on toes that hooked inwards like claws. Her hair was pulled back off her round face, which looked much more weathered without makeup and in the dim light.

"Do I look okay?" she burped, staring down at the stained carpet.

"Just fine." He turned off the light.

She peeled back the covers and inserted each leg under until she lay beside him. He wondered then if he had taken things too far. I should never have agreed to this, he was about to say but stopped when he felt her hand on his bare chest. The pulse from each of her fingertips burned through his skin. She moved her hand down over the hair on his stomach and into the mass of pubic hair living under his boxer shorts. He pinched his eyes tight. My wife, he reminded himself, it is only my wife who is doing this. He knew that life came with sacrifice. He knew that mistakes carried retribution. He knew that a husband must come through for his bride.

Before long she was moving her hand up and down the length of his penis — slowly at first and then accelerating to a clumsy swiftness, pulling and pinching skin with each stride. He swatted her hand away and rolled on top of her, pushing in to find the warmth between her heavy thighs. He rocked until he spilt himself while she moaned a language of her own creation.

After it was over she grew quiet — bringing her body into a fetal position at the end of the bed. He ignored her for a while, trying to will himself to sleep, but soon, noticed that she was also crying into her hands, her hushed sobs pushing their way into the darkness around them.

He rubbed her back with the flat of his hand.

"You regret this," she blubbered. "You don't like me."

"That's not true."

"You wish I was someone else."

"We'll make it work," he said. "It just takes time. We hardly know each other." She turned towards him in the dark and wrapped her limbs around him. Her touch was unfamiliar and left him feeling like he should be sneaking out and going home.

Her snores, when they finally came, kept him awake in the dark. Her hand was still resting on his stomach and he tried leaving it there for a while, testing himself, willing himself. But eventually, he pushed it away and she turned over in sleep until she was facing the other way.

He brought his hands up behind his head and waded through memories of his life back home. In India he had worked in a printing shop — small pay, long hours, but he had three people under him who clamoured for his respect. He loved a girl named Priya whom he met at college, skin calm like brown milk, sullen eyes, delicious wrists that wrapped round his face. Because their families did not know about their relationship, they met secretly when they could. He remembered hot afternoons, sweat licked from skin, spice from fingertips.

When Aseem's parents convinced him to leave for Canada,

Priya cried round tears that took forever to fall. But she promised she would wait for him while he earned enough money to send for her, and she did. She waited for two years.

And on that day picking up the girl in his cab, Aseem had a letter crumpled beside his seat. Opened that morning and in Priya's handwriting: "It's been too long. Forget me. I'm engaged to someone else." Her words sucked the hope from his cells and injected despair into his heart. The distance between them did not dim his sorrow. It grew when his taxicab got caught in traffic, and erupted with the girl in the back seat who wouldn't stop nagging.

The car ahead had moved up to give him space. He took it but wanted more. His foot squeezed down on the gas pedal and his hands spun the wheel, veering off the road, over a curb, halfway down a side street and finally up onto the sidewalk. People screamed and scattered. Metal and glass crunched itself into a light post, throwing him forward, but saving his life.

He remembered the girl. From the back, into the front windshield, and onto the seat beside him. Her final air slipping from her lips in what sounded to him like a sigh of relief.

Face Like This

Ingrid spends most days trying to distract herself from unhappiness, and on Sundays she shaves her legs. On the first Sunday of every month, she walks cautiously to the country store down the street from her house and buys a new package of razors and a fresh can of aloe vera shaving cream. She shaves herself from ankle to bikini line — hoping someday to have a lover who will notice. With her twenty-ninth birthday threatening, she needs this sort of hope.

Going to the store is hard for Ingrid because of her face — she always feels like people are looking at it. Since age thirteen, Ingrid has dissected her own beauty, concentrating on her nose and the ugly way it bloomed during adolescence. She has her father's nose. He always said that his own was a lot uglier than her slightly irregular, much smaller version. But she only remembers "slightly irregular." As Ingrid sees it, her nose is crooked, bulging, full of veins and much, much worse than slightly irregular.

She uses a red cotton scarf to hide herself in every season, even when it's hot. She always wears the scarf when she walks to the school where she works as a janitor. Despite the morning scrubbing of toilets, she enjoys the job because it is private and doesn't take long — which gives her lots of time to paint.

Today, Ingrid leaves home at one o'clock. She walks up the narrow laneway in front of her house, careful not to step on jagged cracks in the concrete. Her scarf is draped daintily around her neck. It darts up and down in front of her features as she walks, but she tries to look as natural as she can. The smell of damp pavement fills her nostrils and weaves its way through her sinuses.

At the store, Ingrid drops her razors, shaving cream, and two tubes of crimson oil paint onto the counter. As she reaches into her pocket to pull out a crumpled twenty dollar bill, her scarf drops and she catches a glimpse of herself in the reflection of the cash register. Crooked, bulging, veiny nose. It seems to be pulsing in and out, taunting her. She holds the scarf back in place with her left hand and pays the bald man behind the counter. He smirks at her from his spot under the cigarette cartons and in front of the Trojan latex condoms.

"They say it's going to rain all day," he says.

"Yeah, they do," Ingrid says. She smiles politely from behind her scarf, only her big, watery blue eyes showing. Unsure how to continue the conversation, she scrunches up her toes in her running shoes and looks towards the door. The bald man smiles as Ingrid grabs her brown grocery bag. *I sound so stupid when I try to make small talk*, she thinks as she runs from the store.

Blinking through the rain, Ingrid reaches her house and stares briefly at its crooked foundation: three rooms leaning strangely to the left, white siding yellowing along the bottom, and ancient chimney crumbling. With the lake just down the road, her house used to be someone's summer cottage, but now serves as the fragile borders of her own secure existence. She goes inside. Safe behind the walls of her imperfect palace, her black wood stove burns continuously in the centre of the room, like her own furious heart.

The phone rings and before she answers Ingrid knows who has dialled her number. Cassie calls every Sunday to tell her what she did on Saturday night. Sixteen years of friendship and she still hasn't realized that Ingrid doesn't really care. Unlike Cassie, Ingrid recognizes the imperfection in her own life. Everything reminds her, especially the mirror.

"Hello," says Ingrid into the green receiver.

"Ingrid, my dear, hi! How are you?"

"I'm doing fine, considering that it's raining today."

"Ingrid, you'll never guess what happened to me last night — it was absolutely hil-ar-i-ous!"

"Really, Cassie, what happe—"

"Well, I met Peter at Biagio for dinner and I ordered the steamed sea bass with a side of mussels, and it was delicious, and we were having such a wonderful time celebrating our three-week anniversary, and Peter looked absolutely gorgeous, and you'll never guess who walks in — Jason! So we're sitting there and I lean over and tell Peter that I am just going to hide behind my menu for a while because my ex has just walked in and he is like, 'Cassie, we have nothing to hide,' and I am like, 'Ahhh, Peter, you are so incredibly sweet,' and in the end, Jason didn't even end up seeing us, and we had an amazing crème brûlée for dessert. Ingrid, can you believe it?"

"Unbelievable, Cassie," Ingrid says picking blue paint from under her fingernails.

"So what did you do last night?" Cassie says, knowing perfectly well Ingrid stayed home.

"Oh, you know, I just took it easy. Relaxed."

"We really should hook up one of these weekends — it's been ages! I found a great guy you should meet; he loves girls with brown hair and eyes."

"Sounds good, Cassie."

"Ingrid, what's wrong with you? You sound so down."

"Nothing."

"Are you sure you're not worrying about your nose again? Like you did in high school?"

"No, I'm not."

"Good, because it's perfectly fine. Really, I can't notice anything wrong with it."

"Thank you, but I'm not worried about that."

"Great, because it's ridiculous."

"I know."

"So anyway, it's been great talking with you, but I have to get my beauty sleep. I have an early meeting with a client. Why don't you touch base with me next week and we'll set up a time to get together, okay? Ta, ta!"

Click.

Click.

Ingrid runs the tips of her fingers over her nose and gazes at her latest painting, which is sitting on the easel her parents gave her last Christmas. Her mother had said, "Maybe if you invest a great deal of time to painting, you could start selling pieces and make some real money." Ingrid had felt momentarily ambitious, but then embarrassed by her mother's dry laughter.

Ingrid paints only for herself. She ripples with pride over what she created on the canvas last night. With straight lines and soft strokes, she has painted a perfect female face — unassuming, naive, and pure. She traces her hands over the energy of the eyes, nose, and jaw line — all delicate and symmetrical. Colour has sprinkled off her brushes and onto the ground around the easel. Splotches of blue, yellow, and orange cover the black floor.

Ingrid abandons her painting to shave her legs — knowing she won't be able to concentrate until they are done. On her way to the bathroom, she stops in the kitchen and chooses a tarot card from the deck lying in a neat pile on the table. She bought the Universal Tarot deck last summer at the local occult shop, hoping maybe the cards could tell her what she should be doing with her life. Mostly they just confuse her. Today, the Hanged Man stares back at her, his face looking lost and desolate. She reads the meaning of the card out loud, "Mind at the end of its tether, trial of courage and faith, surrender, a great transition taking place, the brink of enormous awakening of spirit." She leaves it face up as a reminder.

Ingrid drapes one scrawny leg over the side of the tub. She runs the water, squeezes some shaving cream onto her calf, lathers it up, and starts to carefully bring the razor from the bottom to the top.

Slow, steady strokes leave bald skin instead of pink shaving cream. She nicks herself on the shin. An I-shaped cut fills with blood. She wipes the blood away with a tissue, and it comes back, again and again. The blood keeps returning, until she covers it with a Band-Aid and can't see it anymore. She switches legs and does the other one.

After she finishes, she stops as usual in front of her mirror. Rusted around the outside, she is only concerned with her own reflection. Her heart pumps an extra fast squirt as she realizes once again — *I definitely have the ugliest face of anyone I know*. She sighs to greet the familiar fixation and splashes cold water from the tap onto her greatest enemy. Looking at herself through squinted eyes, she wonders if she will ever get married and if she does, how she will handle walking down the aisle with everyone looking at her. With a face like this, she does not foresee a proposal anytime soon. Anxiety races up the back of her throat, burning her as it goes. She swallows to deter it.

As she's gathering her garbage, three strong and diligent knocks clunk down on Ingrid's front door. Her body tightens.

Opening the door, Ingrid sees an unfamiliar face. The woman, in her fifties, has wrinkles sprouting around her mouth and in the corners of her eyes. Ingrid's imagination draws lines in the folds of her skin. The woman's nose sits small and pert with a subtle upturn at the end and there are tiny veins escaping from the sides. She wears a long blue skirt, white blouse, gold cross hanging proudly around her neck, and flowered vest — the kind Ingrid would never choose. A Bible sits snugly under the woman's right arm.

"Hello," Ingrid says, looking at her nose instead of her eyes. Now that she looks closely, she realizes the stranger's nose might be only a little smaller than her own.

"Beautiful child, my name is Camilla and I have a very important question to ask you."

"Go ahead," says Ingrid.

"I just need to know . . ." says Camilla.

"Yes . . ."

"Dear child, have you welcomed the Lord Jesus Christ into your life?"

Ingrid stands dumbfounded. "Well, I don't know if I have. I never really thought about it. I guess I have because I pretty much welcome anyone into my life if they push hard enough. I actually let people walk all over me. But no, I haven't been to church in like, seventeen years, if that's what you're asking."

"There is a salvation like no other," Camilla says, "waiting for you within the pages of this book." Camilla holds her Bible proudly in the air and does a heavenly dance, shifting her weight from one plump leg to the other. Her head flies back and Ingrid examines her nose hairs, thick and black sticking out of each dark opening.

Though she is flattered to have someone take time to try to force their beliefs on her, Ingrid looks past Camilla to a white mutt walking by on the sidewalk. The dog hobbles along with one front leg missing, his tongue flopping out of the corners of his mouth. Each step looks like a struggle but the dog doesn't care. He seems more interested in a squirrel up a tree or the crumpled-up candy wrapper stuck to the sidewalk. She's fascinated by the fact that the dog doesn't seem to realize that he is different, imperfect. If he does realize, he's not smart enough to know that it really matters.

She turns back to her visitor and smiles with her hand resting on her nose as a disguise. *I'm so ashamed of the way I look.* She thinks about how simple it would be to have one book that would make everything feel right. To be able to hold that book in the air and believe everything it says. Every single thing.

She doesn't know what to believe anymore.

"I like to use tarot cards sometimes," Ingrid says to Camilla. "To give me some guidance about what my life means."

Camilla stops for a second but doesn't respond to her. Instead, she opens her Bible to a specific page and uses her wrinkled finger to point out a passage that she says she believes might give Ingrid strength.

"And your fame spread among the nations on account of your beauty, because the splendour I had given you made your beauty perfect, declares the Sovereign Lord," she reads out, but Ingrid feels nothing special when she says it.

"I'll be back," Camilla says as she shuts her Bible. "Just think about what I've said."

"I'll try," Ingrid says, but she's already thinking about her nose again.

Her front door safely shut, Ingrid squeezes red blobs of paint onto her palette and decides to use her fingers to apply it to her canvas. Thick oil-filled air floats into her nasal passages. She strokes subtle red smudges across the cheeks of the face she created last night — expensive blush, or warpaint maybe. She looks deep into the picture, concentrating, and gets caught in the feeling of stroking on the paint with her fingers. Soon, she has applied so much red that the face is covered up completely. She's relieved to see the face hidden on the canvas. She puts the painting on the ground and lays her cheek against it. She finds herself dragging both her hands down the picture and then across her own face and over her nose. Her fingers slip over her skin, covering her up.

She stands and walks to the bathroom mirror, looking at herself. Like the girl on the canvas, she has also been hidden and the sight of her red skin gives her another strange sense of relief. She wonders if she could paint her face every day like this to relax, but hates to waste the paints. She squints and imagines that the red is actually blood — that her face has exploded and she is hiding under the remnants.

I'm gone, she thinks. *Just like that, I've disappeared and am no longer a stain on the earth.* It feels too good to think that. Too good that she knows she is dipping further away from where she needs to be to be healthy — where she needs to be in order to go to work, have friends, see people, hold face-to-face conversations.

It has been exactly one year since she decided to stop talking to the therapist that her mother had recommended. Three hundred and sixty-five days since the day she convinced herself that she had finally escaped. *It's better*, she thought. *I'm ugly, but I can live with it.* A rush of energy bolts into her body again as she remembers. She panics, searching frantically for a way to bring the feeling down again.

She sees the package and remembers, just as her breathing is starting to make a sound, her chest starting to contract in the centre of her.

Ingrid reaches over and grabs a fresh razor from the pack on the counter. She removes the cover and holds the blade up beside her nose.

It would just take one fast swipe to change things. Her hand shakes. *If I push hard enough on the bridge of my nose, I could probably even shave some off. The blood would certainly come.* She thinks she might be in love with her bloody face — a pain that everyone can see: her mom, Cassie, strangers on the street — but is it real love? She moves the razor a bit closer, like she's daring herself.

She holds her breath, waiting to see. Her vision goes blurry, her hand continues to shake as it brings the blade towards her face . . . steady, steady . . .

And then like it was planned, a wave of wind blows in through the open windows of her house, causing her tarot cards to flutter like pigeons in the corner of her vision. She releases the air in her lungs and feels that her vibration has settled once again — like it always does.

She brings the razor back down, sets it on the counter, and turns on the taps, putting her hands in the stream so the cool water tickles her fingers. Then, she leans into the sink, bringing up her hands, letting the water wash the paint away until the porcelain is stained red.

Cross to Bear

The mahogany of the confessional booth traps him like a prison cell. He considers ducking out — away from the priest breathing behind lattice — through the fog of incense and out until light pokes his eyes. But he doesn't. His mother stands outside the door, waiting like she always does, which makes it difficult to escape.

"Lucas, tell me your sins."

"I cheated on my school test."

"And how did you do that?"

"I wrote the answers on a small piece of paper and hid it inside my shoe."

"Is there anything else?"

"I spoke harshly to my three younger brothers."

"Uh-huh."

"And my six older sisters."

"Anything more?"

"No."

"Your penance is one Our Father and three Hail Marys."

Lucas welcomes the redemption. They have been happening more often and getting clearer. The thoughts. Like the split second of a horror film splashed across the inside of his forehead. Real enough to make his hands numb and his heart pound like a fist banging against his chest — from the inside trying to get out.

"Lucas, sit up while you say grace," his mother says. His fingertips kiss in front of him, elbows on the table. He sits up. She hits him on the back of the head with a baking spoon. *Smack.* And he sits up straighter.

"Eat your beef," she says. "Your father works hard to give you that meat. You think all families in Rivière-du-Loup have hearty cow to eat? No. You should be thankful for that. With this economy. You should thank God."

Lucas sucks a string of fat under his lips, holding it there while his siblings swallow. He squeezes his eyelids shut, trying to cut off the images.

At night, while his brothers sleep around him, Lucas lies on his back and begins his penance silently.

Our Father who art in heaven. Please get rid of these nasty thoughts. Hallowed be thy name, and make me stop acting out inside my head.

Thy kingdom come. I'm sorry for being a sinner.

And soon out loud.

"Mother Mary forgive me, Mother Mary forgive me, Mother Mary forgive me." Seven syllables to each prayer, all of them fading into oblivion, chasing him into sleep, smothering that which keeps bubbling up.

He kicks his bare legs against André's.

"What?" André says from beside him in the bed.

"Too much milk with dinner," he whispers through the black air. "Let me out."

André lifts up his legs so Lucas can roll himself over and onto the ground. Then he creeps across the wooden floorboards and down the stairs to the kitchen.

The rosary curls itself like a snake on the windowsill.

His mother's kitchen rosary, the one she moves through her fingers when she prepares meals, ingesting holiness with each prayer she says, each bead she passes.

He takes it in his hand, wrapping the beads around his wrist and clasping the cross in his palms. He brings it to his lips.

"For Thine is the kingdom, the power, and the glory."

He kisses it again.

"For Thine is the kingdom, the power, and the glory."

He kisses it again.

"Forgive me, Jesus."

His hands sweat. A rock grows in his throat and thumping invades his ears. He brings up the rosary so that it hangs in front of him, and in one quick swoop, whips in down over his shoulder and across his bare back. The pain fills him. He whips it again. Again. He thinks that there must be red lines on his back by now. Satisfied, he brings the tiny Jesus back to his lips, letting its outline whisk him into sedation.

Two more times that night he comes down into the dark kitchen of their farmhouse. Each time he holds his mother's rosary, kissing the cross and saying the words, still feeling the throbbing from the lines on his back. The third time he also weeps, wondering if you can ever escape a chasing dragon that never sleeps.

———————

The next day, Lucas tells him mother that he is sick and must stay in bed. His back is aching under his shirt.

"Lucas, you don't look sick to me," his mother says. She has her rosary in her hand. She's saying her prayers like she does every morning. "You will go to school today."

"But I might throw up. That's how sick I feel."

"Just look to Jesus to help you — he will make you feel better."

"Sometimes I wonder if Jesus even loves me," he says then, to which three of his siblings cover their mouths with their hands, afraid of what is coming next.

His mother gasps and looks to his father, who drags him into the yard and dumps a bucket of cold water over his head. Then he tells Lucas to go get ready for school.

———————

At school, he tries to find out how closely God keeps track of him. He puts up his hand in class.

"Yes, Lucas?" Brother Côté clutches a Bible.

"Brother Côté, may I ask you a question?"

"Please stand, Lucas."

He does. "Brother Côté, tell me please, can God hear my thoughts?"

"Why yes, Lucas. God is everywhere, even inside your head." Tears fill Lucas's eyes as he looks towards light flooding through a window.

"Why do you ask, Lucas? Do you have impure thoughts?"

"No," Lucas answers, knowing that it is this or a strike across his palms. "I just wanted to know." He sits down and pretends to read his spelling workbook.

When afternoon lessons are finished, Brother Côté takes him to the corner of the classroom and asks if he needs private counsel, away from the rest of the boys.

"Now is the time to sort things out, Lucas. Once you turn thirteen and start to work on your father's farm, you will have less and less time with the brothers."

Lucas hesitates but speaks: "Sometimes I don't like what I see in my head."

"So you *do* have impure thoughts?"

"I don't know if they are impure, Brother Côté. Just scary."

"As an example, what?"

"Sometimes, I think that the shoes or jacket I am wearing were stolen from one of my classmates."

"And were they?"

"They are my shoes, Brother."

"And your jacket?"

"I haven't stolen but I'm afraid that I have. I can't stop it."

"I see. And what else?"

"I take the Lord's name in vain in my head sometimes."

"Do you do it out loud?"

"No, only in my head," Lucas says. "And there is something else."

"Go on." Brother Côté wrinkles his eyebrows so they touch across his forehead.

"I see dead animals in my thoughts and I am afraid that it was me who made them like that."

"I am sure you have seen animals slaughtered, on your farm."

"Yes, but sometimes the animals have real faces. Sometimes they are the faces of my brothers and sisters, and my mother and father."

"So you think you will kill your brothers and sisters? And your mother and father?"

"I don't want to. I am afraid to break my vow not to kill." Brother Côté pauses, glances at the Bible resting on his arm, and then says, "Lucas, these thoughts are clearly from the devil."

Brother Côté then makes a suggestion. "Go directly to church on your way home from school today, sit in the pew, and pray for your soul."

St. Patrice Parish sits empty, a Wednesday afternoon. Lucas climbs the staircase leading up to the peaked door that splits to let him in.

The air inside, stale and thick. The ceiling tall and expansive, the Holy Spirit looking down at him from up in the cross beams. And far in front, candles burning, a marble altar, and the flame where Jesus lives.

A nun kneels in the sixth row, silently praying. She turns her head to nod at Lucas as he slides into the pew across from her. The black and white of her habit makes his heart rattle against the inside of his ribs.

He pushes himself down onto his knees, scratching his skin against his wool pants. He places the fingers on his right hand on his forehead, heart, and each of his shoulders — "Father, Son, and the Holy Spirit."

And he prays for his soul.

As he lets the holy words pass through his mind, the sinful thoughts keep trying to fight back. He grits his teeth and squints his eyes hard to try to focus on becoming redeemed. His stomach churns, his back continues to ache.

When it comes time to leave the church, when anyone else would feel completion, holiness, Lucas can't make himself leave. The air suffocates and invigorates him all at once. Instead of going home, he runs to the altar and kneels down. He lowers his lips to the shiny marble and whispers the lines he learned at Mass.

"Domine, non sum dignus."

The words come out in a voice lower than his own, and he follows them up with what he knows they mean.

"Domine, non sum dignus. Lord, I am not worthy." He keeps saying the words, trying to make the feeling of wrong somehow feel right. He uses his fingers to keep track of the number of times he has spoken the words, aiming for thirty-three.

And then after the sixth time, he hears, "Lucas, does your mother know you are here?" Father Dubois stands beside him, looking down from what seems like heaven.

"No," Lucas says, holding his index finger as a place marker.

"I suggest that you run home, Lucas. Your dinner will no doubt be on the table by now. Your prayers can cease for this evening."

"I can't," Lucas says, his words small in the air of the cathedral.

"Of course you can, Lucas. Get up!" Father Dubois grabs him by the shoulder of his school shirt and hauls him to his feet. Lucas is certain his feet leave the ground.

"Father, I can't," he says, but turns and walks away anyway, down the aisle, towards the door leading outside.

At the threshold, he lowers his face to the cement steps to suck in the footprints of priests and nuns. Then he stands up to stick his warm lips to the handrail to ingest the palm prints of the holy. Frigid steel pulls at his smile when he finally leans back.

He refuses to eat dinner. None of the beef in gravy, none of the corn or strawberry jam on bread. He refuses, and when his father threatens to put him on an iceberg and float him into the St. Lawrence, he chews the food down as small as he can, spits it into his hand and drops it under the table. He's careful to spread the pieces so as not to create one noticeable pile, only a dirty floor. He does this all because of something his mother once told him. *A brain cannot work without a good meal.*

Sun sets and soon four male noses hum a symphony of snores through the house. Lucas leaves his bed before even trying to close his eyes.

He sneaks into the barn in his flannel pyjamas, dust and hay between his bare toes, cows breathing from their stalls. He sits down, cross-legged, on a pile of swept cow dung that has hardened. There he feels comfortable. There he feels just outside of things enough to belong, for the moment.

Light pricks him. Morning. He has fallen asleep in the dung and someone is opening the barn door.

"Lucas?" His father, looking surprised, at least the parts of his face Lucas can see under the shadows of his brimmed hat. "What are you doing out here?"

Cows are mooing and stirring. They want to be milked.

"Papa, I'm sorry," Lucas says, still groggy, his cheek smeared with dung. "I'm sorry for sleeping out in the barn."

His father removes his thick gloves, squats beside him in the dung and takes Lucas onto his lap. Lucas smells cooking from the kitchen and feels the warmth from the wood stove still clinging to his father's chest.

"What is wrong with you, boy?"

"I have thoughts." *There, I said it.*

His father laughs, a laugh that sounds like crumpling paper and fades out like a bouncing rubber ball.

"Of course you have thoughts. I should hope my boy has thoughts."

"Yes, Papa, but my thoughts are sinful." Lucas stands then and tears drip from the corners of his eyes. "And I can't get them to stop." Lucas reaches his tiny hands out to his father. His father's face straightens out. No more laughing.

"Impure thoughts can lead you in a bad direction, Lucas."

"I know, Papa. I know."

"Have you not listened to the words spoken in Mass?"

"I have, Papa. I have listened until my ears ached. I have listened until my mind is throbbing." His father rises to his feet again.

"Lucas, you know the difference between sinful thoughts and pure thoughts. I suggest you choose to clean yourself up before you are led too far off course."

Lucas nods slowly like string is pulling his head up and down.

"Now get in the house and wash your face. And I do not want to find you sleeping in the barn again."

"But, Papa . . ."

"Come help me with the milking once you are cleaned and fed." His father disappears into one of the cow stalls, leaving Lucas alone in the frosty mist of his own rapid breath.

———————

Sunday comes again. Mass at St. Patrice. Lucas's father, mother, and nine brothers and sisters are inside the church. Lucas walked last in the line of them, but couldn't follow them in, couldn't pass through the arched doors. Instead, he kneels on the church steps, running his hands over and over the jagged concrete until his palms start to bleed. They haven't noticed he is missing.

———————

The days Lucas is in the hospital seem to join like one long, dark train — with each twenty-four hours representing another dusty, uncomfortable boxcar.

He sleeps a lot, his head resting on a foreign pillowcase provided to him by the nurses. He wakes only to take the pills that are fed to him and to prop himself up while the doctors listen to his heart, take his blood pressure, and tell him that there has been "little change to his condition, which is good."

His mother is too busy to visit past the first day. "As if, after all that God has given to us, we need something like this as well!" she screamed when they found him passed out on the stairs after Mass, his nose and lips streaked with blood from rubbing his wounded palms over his face.

His father comes three times in four days, his face painted with a look that makes him almost unrecognizable to Lucas. He sits at the end of Lucas's bed and strokes his leg tentatively through the blanket, telling him that he will be back home with his brothers and sisters soon.

"God willing," he says through a tense mouth, which makes Lucas close his eyes. He can still smell the barn smell on his father, even when he can't see him.

"I'm sorry, Papa," Lucas says finally, feeling himself drift away again. As he looks out through sleepy eyes, he struggles to focus on his father's morose expression.

"Rest," is all his father says back to him. "We'll see you again soon."

Next time Lucas opens his eyes it's night outside and he feels someone standing over him. Lucas's heart constricts. He wants to run from the room.

"Lucas?" the man says. Lucas can't bring himself to respond, but manages to nod, his fingers clutching onto the bedding by his sides.

He finds the nerve to look up and that's when he sees the long dark cloak, the white collar that seems to glow like a beacon.

The priest raises his hand in the air and brings it down on Lucas's arm. His eyes close and his mouth starts to move quickly over invisible words, sentences, prayers. The holy man is wrapped in the darkness around them. It is only the glow from the full moon outside that allows Lucas to see the features of the man's face, his hands, the neatly combed hair on the top of his head.

"Who are you?" Lucas asks.

"Shh. It's okay, Lucas. Your parents know I'm here." The man's voice echoes through the room like they are in an empty tunnel together, the hum of his murmurings absorb into Lucas's body — up his little arms, down his legs and into his toes, then back up, past his heart and into the spot between his eyes.

"What's happening?" he whispers.

"Shh, Lucas."

When the priest is finished, he crosses himself with the tips of his fingers — head, heart, shoulder, shoulder, Father, Son, and Holy Spirit — and leaves. Lucas is suddenly more awake than he has been in days. He sits up in bed, looking around the room, trying to make out the shape of anything he can to feel real again: a small table, a locked cabinet with medicine, a water basin sitting on a shelf with one small empty cup beside it.

When he feels like he may be starting to forget the God feeling — the one the priest showed him, when he's clean and whole and good — he closes his eyes to help himself remember. With no one around, maybe for hours to come, he thinks that maybe things can be different now. That perhaps he can finally stop the thoughts that come without warning and change him, and instead, go back to being as he once was. A happy boy. A boy who loved his parents, went to church, ate, drank, played, lived . . .

Without meaning to, as he is thinking, Lucas rubs his fingernail over one of the scabs on his palms and starts to pick.

Saving Katie

We rented a house on the beach in Maine. I found the place on the internet, on a site called "New England Getaways," and put a deposit over the phone after only seeing a couple pictures. I can't say why exactly we decided to go there, but as soon as we justified to ourselves that this would be the best thing for Katie, we both knew we had to go to someplace where the air was breezy and there were large spaces between the suffocating voices and staring people. You could see for a long, long way, out into the ocean and down the beach and that made it seem like there was always a way for us to go. I think though, that it's the colours I remember most: blues of the sky and water, pure white sand, and the brightly patterned shapes on our beach towels.

On the drive out from Ottawa, Ethan was silent as he controlled the car and all of us in it. Katie was asleep for most of the ride, which meant we didn't have to spend any time trying to encourage or support her. Our support had exhausted us. Our encouragement had dried up like a faucet in a sink that no one used anymore.

We didn't know what else to say. But we knew we had to be with her.

I tried to play the radio in the car for a while but Ethan was having none of it.

"You'll wake her up," he told me.

"Ethan, she's fine. She's asleep to the hum of the car; a little music is not going to—"

"No!" he said, putting his moist hand on mine. "It just doesn't seem right." We rode together almost as if the teenager in our car was back to the sweet, smiling baby we used to drive around the town at night, hoping she would fall asleep. We spoke in hushed voices like maybe if she woke up, we might not be able to get her back down again. And when we got to the rental, Katie rose, walked inside, and curled up on the bed we told her was hers.

"Talk to you in the morning," she said. It was late, but we had hoped that something about the place would inspire her, woken her up, brought her out.

While she slept, Ethan and I sat on the porch in the dark looking out at the waves, each one seeming to get larger than the next, bringing something else with it.

In the morning she was awake before we were. I rose from my bed and walked straight onto the porch, looked out over the railing and saw her sitting on the beach. She sat so still, like a jagged piece of rock partly buried in the sand. I was surprised to see her wearing a tank top, because she never did at home. The bones in her shoulders were pushing out towards the sky, welcoming the sun onto her translucent skin. I stood there looking at the back of her — her spine, the way each little knob worked its way down her back — and tried to resist the urge to go down there and pick her up and bring her back into the house, cradling her like a young child. I was certain I would have been able to lift her. I may have been almost fifty, but a small body like that, I could have wrapped her around me and taken her in, held her until she wouldn't let me anymore.

"Is she up?" It was Ethan from behind me, his voice groggy and probing.

"She's down there. But just let her be for a while. She looks like she's thinking."

"Make her come inside, make her eat."

"Shh, Ethan. I will, in a minute." We both stood there looking at her. A few strands of her hair got caught in the breeze, seconds before they were pushed back behind her ears with her bony fingers. We were scared to disturb her, about what that might mean next for the morning, for all of us.

"I'll cook the breakfast, Samantha," he said to me. "Bacon and eggs sound good?" I nodded without looking at him, still stuck in the trance left by my daughter's presence, at having her all to ourselves. When she turned her head towards the house, her face was straight and absent of any expression that I could identify. I raised my arm and motioned to her.

"Breakfast, honey!" I yelled like this was a normal thing for us to say, like I expected her to want to come. She looked away again and her square shoulders rose and fell like she was sighing. Then she stood and turned towards me. It was almost shocking to see how small she was across — barely able to block out the sun hanging low in the sky. I looked away as she walked up, like she had undressed and was coming towards me, only she was still wearing her jean shorts and tank top. When she got to the top of the stairs, she crossed her arms across her chest in defiance.

"You're not going to make me eat that," she said, motioning to the kitchen. The smell of Ethan's bacon and fried eggs had filtered into the early-morning musty smell of the beach house.

"Just try . . ." I said.

She tsk-ed and shook her head at me, her lips pursed into a look of disgust. "I've told you I can't—"

"For me," I said. "Try."

We were all seated at the kitchen table together, looking at our plates. Ethan had two fried eggs, five strips of bacon and two slices of buttered toast cut in half to make four pieces. I had one egg, two bacon strips and one slice of toast. Katie, as Ethan had prepared it, had one egg yolk, poached, and half a slice of non-buttered toast. There was a long pause between when Ethan put the plates down and when he got the nerve to take his first bite. The anticipation of the meal was huge, considering we hadn't eaten with Katie for almost two months, not since she had been gone. I looked away from her and instead at my husband's grey hair and the wrinkles around his eyes that seemed to be setting deeper each day. I examined his thick fingers wrapped around his fork, the first morsel of food entering past his lips into his mouth, the way he chewed with his mouth just slightly ajar.

"So, what kind of stuff did they feed you at the centre?" Ethan blurted out to Katie. She still had her arms crossed and was staring past her plate down at the floor.

"Milkshakes and apple slices," she said. "Oh, and an iv drip." Ethan kept chewing, not sure whether she was joking with him or trying to shock him.

"Ethan, she doesn't want to talk about that," I said. "The whole point of coming here is so that we can escape all that. Try something new, right, honey?" Katie shrugged, and I continued, "I imagine the stress of being at home with everyone watching you, that can't help things."

"That's not the fucking problem!" Katie said with quite a bit of conviction, which made me want to switch to a new subject. This kind of energy was not what we wanted to create around her. This was the kind we wanted to forget.

"Katie, I'll appreciate if you watch your language," Ethan said. His plate was empty by that time, but Katie and I hadn't started. "Do you girls not like my cooking?" he said to us.

"Are you friggin' serious right now?" Katie said. Her jaw was clenching so that I could almost see every muscle in her face and her cheekbones cutting below her eyes. "Do you honestly think that . . ." She let her voice trail off in a sarcastic sigh.

"Katie, your father is just trying to make conversation," I said. "There is no need to—"

"I'm done with this," she said, standing up and pushing away from the table. "I don't even know why you brought me here. It's not going to help anything." As she walked out, she glanced our way again and then picked up a banana off the counter before she walked out of the room. "See? I'll have this. No biggie," she said, waving the banana in front of her face. When she was gone, I picked up my fork and looked down at my plate. I took my first bite of food.

"This is very good, dear," I said. "Thank you for making it." Ethan was still looking towards where Katie walked about.

"So much for trying something different," he said.

"Give it time," I said. "With time, who knows?" I looked at him and made a weak smile, but he wasn't looking at me. He was staring out the window towards the water. Katie had gone back to the beach.

———————

Ethan and I were playing a board game on the deck. Monopoly. He had Park Place and that other blue one, which made the whole exercise fairly meaningless.

"Roll, Sam," he said to me. "Don't give up yet." He had a bit of a mischievous tone to his voice, like he was actually having fun. I remember thinking that all this sea air and time away from his desk must been having a good effect on him, clearing out the cobwebs that had gathered over the last two years when our only daughter was fading away to what she had become —

I rolled the die, still glancing occasionally down the beach to where Katie had walked off.

"Oh, I'm in jail," I said, moving my little thimble.

"At least pretend like you're having fun," Ethan said.

"I am, dear," I said, putting my hand on his arm. "It's just that . . ."

"You're worried more about her than me?"

"That's not true."

"Something like that though?"

"I'm worried about her, that's all."

"And you think I'm not?"

"Ethan, I never said—" He stood up. He was looking down to where I sat in the wicker chair that came with the beach house. There were sharp little wicker ends sticking out randomly, poking me when I tried to get more comfortable.

"Forget it. Let's just forget about trying to enjoy this at all, then." He turned away towards the beach. "The first vacation I've had all year, but let's just stay gloomy and depressing like we are at home."

"Ethan, you know why we're here."

"Yeah exactly, let's be really sad and mad all the time and see how that helps Katie. See if she ever comes back from her walk to wherever she went — if her body even has the strength to make it back."

"Don't say things like that, Ethan."

"You just stay here, Samantha. Stare out there and wait for her and let her ruin us as well."

"No one is going to ruin us," I said, but Ethan had walked away before I finished, back into the house and away from me. I sat and wondered if it was true what he said — if maybe I felt guilty about feeling anything good simply because she wasn't.

I decided to walk along the beach myself. I took off my shoes and took the path that the water defined in the sand when it lapped up against it. It was still cool outside for late June, and the water nipped at the undersides of my feet when the waves touched me. I kept my eyes to the ground, hoping I would find one of Katie's leftover footprints to give an idea of where she had gone. I heard a voice and looked up. It was someone standing on the porch of a neighbouring beach house, waving. I waved back and tried my best to smile. It was exactly the behaviour I had been trying to escape by coming here. The sympathetic smiles as Katie and I walked into the grocery store, the shaking of heads when they thought I wasn't looking, the probing concern of the people I had worked with before I had quit. These are the things I was quite sure would not help my family recover from what we were going through, would not help Katie start eating again.

It was her anger that baffled me the most. I wondered who exactly she was mad at. Was it really me, or Ethan? Or her friends, her teachers, the television shows she watched, the fashion magazines she read, that girl Tracey who had bullied her in grade six, or herself? The thought that she was mad at herself was the most difficult to deal with. No one wants that for her child.

The winds had started to pick up a bit and some clouds were rolling in so I decided to head back. I passed a man walking his golden retriever, its paws sandy and tongue hanging out happily. The man was lost in thought so I didn't even make the effort to look up and waste a smile on him. I got back to our rental just in time — the rain started pounding down on my shoulders as I hopped up the steps. I couldn't stop thinking: Was she cold? Did she bring an umbrella? Had she found any shelter wherever she had gone to?

Ethan was in the living room when I got there. I stood in front of him, shaking off my hair with my hand, peeling off my sweatshirt. He was playing with the rabbit ears on the television, trying to get it to work.

"Any sign of her?" I asked him. He shook his head and kept fiddling with the rabbit ears. "Should we go out looking? With the rain and all?"

"She'll come back," he said. "And if she doesn't, well then she'll just have to fend for herself. We've tried everything, done everything, said everything, taken her everywhere. Maybe the only one who can fix this problem is her?"

"I'll never give up on her," I said shaking my head.

"Not give up, Samantha. But step back. We need to encourage her to take some responsibility for herself. She's seventeen. If she wants to walk off in the rain just because I made her some breakfast, well then we'll let her."

"Maybe she walked to town. That little one we passed on the way in, with the blue chip truck on the highway."

"Are you even listening to me, Samantha?"

The room was quiet, except for the sound of rain hitting the windows outside and the waves crashing up against the beach. "It's getting pretty nasty out there, Ethan."

"It's time we accept that we've lost her." I felt my eyes start to drip and my throat tighten when he said that, I think mostly because I knew he was right. "We can't make her do anything; she has to want to do it for herself."

"I know that. I just think that with enough love from us . . ."

"You're delusional, Samantha. She doesn't want it."

At ten, when it was pitch black and I was drinking coffee at the kitchen table, there was a knock on the door. Ethan was in the bedroom — apparently sleeping — so I went to open it. It was a police officer: tall, blue uniform, hat wet with rain. He was standing beside Katie: drenched, still in just her tank top, looking at the ground.

"Does she belong to you?" the police officer asked like he was bringing back an orange tabby. I scrunched my eyebrows at him and wrapped my arms around Katie. She stayed flat, then she pushed me away. "Found her shivering under the pier in town. She said she was lost."

"It's quite likely," I said, putting my fingers around her stick arm and pulling her over to me. "We're not from around here you know." I grabbed an afghan and put it over Katie's bony shoulders, shooing her into the living room. "Thanks for bringing her back, officer."

He looked at me with suspicion, like he was really chewing on his words before letting them come out.

"Ma'am, I don't want to overstep things here . . . but the girl looks like she needs to eat something." I looked at him, horrified, and crossed my arms in front of me.

"Well that, officer, is the understatement of the century."

When I returned to the living room, the wet afghan was balled up on the floor and Katie had closed the door to her bedroom.

"What was that about?" It was Ethan, sleepy-looking, standing in his pyjamas in the hallway.

"They found her, that's all," I said. "She's back."

"But for how long?"

"I don't know."

"And should we let her stay?"

"Ethan, she's staying." I was folding up the afghan as I spoke. "She's our daughter, and she's staying with us until she's better." Ethan sighed and shook his head.

"I'm going back to sleep then. I imagine you'll be sleeping out here tonight, to make sure she doesn't leave again."

"If I want to, yes."

"More bed for me," he said and went down the hall and into our room, and at the same moment that our door shut, I noticed that the tiny space that was left in Katie's doorway closed shut too.

I took four steps until I was standing outside the closed door, listening. I thought maybe I could hear her breathing from inside, and then, shifting on the bed. I lifted my knuckles to the door.

"Katie, open up," I said as I rapped lightly. "I want to talk to you."

Silence.

"You can't avoid me forever, dear. C'mon." The door slid open just a touch and I could see a sliver of her through the space. Her face was turned away from me. "Can I come in?"

I saw her shoulders shrug. I went in and sat on the bed. I opened my mouth a little but she started talking before I did.

"I know what you're going to say," she said. Her voice was so familiar and comforting, like it always lived inside me somewhere.

"You're going to say that if I would just start eating again everything would be fine."

"Obviously it's not as simple as that. Or else you would." She looked at me, the skin around her sunken eyes almost grey.

"You're right."

"So what else can I do?"

"Leave me alone."

"You know I can't do—"

"I'm serious, Mother. It's over. It's bigger than me."

"I don't believe that."

"I give up."

"I'll never give up on you."

"I'm serious. Just let me be."

"It's not in my biology to do that, as a mother." She turned and was looking out the window at the beach. "Do you want to take another walk or something, Katie?"

"No!" She whipped her body around and threw a hand-sized shell that was sitting on the window sill. It hit the wall behind me. I turned and leaned down to pick it up. "Just leave it! Leave me!"

"I told you Katie, I can't." How many times could I say it?

"Get out then." I brought air into my lungs and held it there, wondering if any more words would escape from my lips. They didn't. I turned and left her like she wanted, feeling exhaustion seeping into all my body's cells.

I walked down the hall and into the bedroom where Ethan slept. I peeled off my clothes and let them drop to the floor, sliding on a cotton, knee-length nightgown that I felt around for in the dark.

I slipped myself between the cool sheets with Ethan. He was

breathing in a silent way that let me know he was still awake. I reached my arms out towards him, pulling my body into his warm spot. With my fingers almost touching him, I heard his voice, hushed and jagged in the dark: "We can't help her if she doesn't want help."

"But we made her." I brought my hand down his warm back, tracing his shoulder blade with my palm.

"We'll have to bring her back to the centre and that's all there is to it," he said, shaking me off him and inching away from me on the mattress until there was a decided gap between our half-naked bodies. His movement made me feel like he had vanished from the bed entirely.

"How could you suggest that, Ethan?" I said, "Didn't you hear what I said?!"

"Why don't you get the hell out of bed if you are going to scream at me, Samantha!"

"Stop being such an asshole!" I threw my pillow at him in the dark and he grabbed it, lifted it over his head and threw it at the door. Then, he stretched back out and put his own pillow on his head.

I grabbed a blanket from the end of the bed and stomped over to the door, tip-toeing down the hall and into the darkness of our unfamiliar living room. I lay alone on the prickly summer couch in the sunroom. It was dark enough that I could no longer make out the faded floral pattern on its fabric.

I supported my head with the folded-up afghan I had wrapped around Katie. As I relaxed further into the couch, I let my tired mind examine the possibility that Ethan was right. Maybe this whole trip was pointless; we should never have taken her from the treatment centre. Maybe she didn't need to be here with us at all; in fact, maybe she needed less of us to make this work for her. As I drifted to sleep I resolved that I would sign her back into the centre as soon as we got home next week and wouldn't visit her for at least a month, force her to face this, take responsibility for—

I opened my eyes again to see her frail body standing over me.

I could see from the porch light coming in the window that she had been crying, that in fact, her shoulders were still bouncing with the waves of tears falling down her face. The sight made my own chest contract. I sat up.

"Are you okay, honey?"

"You and Dad were fighting?"

"I'm sorry, Katie, it's not your fault."

"I'm scared, Mom." She whispered like she might wake me again, the darkness providing a shield between us.

"I know, honey, I am too." I hated how formal my words sounded, even though they were true.

Scared to disturb the moment of calm between us, I lifted up the blanket that lay across my lap and invited her in. She crawled in and I pushed my back closer to the couch so she could fit. She was dry and dressed in her usual baggy sweatshirt and sweatpants — freshly laundered by me, smelling of that lavender washing soap that was on sale at the grocery store downtown. She snuggled in to me with her back up against my breasts. I could feel her backbone, see the angles of her body catching the moonlight from outside, but I couldn't see her eyes.

I reached out and wrapped my arms around her again and felt a wave of sadness as I pulled myself into her thin frame. This time she didn't pull away. I kissed the back of her head, her hair still fresh with the breeze off the ocean. I smoothed my hands over the bony parts in her shoulders and rubbed down her arms to warm her. She grabbed my hand with her cool fingers. I squeezed back, and together, we slept.

One Too Many

"I don't understand," she says putting her coffee mug back on the kitchen table and running her fingertips through her long brown hair.

"Let's finish our breakfast first," he says back. "I don't want to fight about it." He places both hands on his left thigh, one on top of the other. She covers her lips with her fingers.

"But, Theo. Your own leg?"

"I know it comes as a shock." His heart is pounding under his skin, propelling him to reveal what he needs to.

"Losing your job has pushed you over the edge." She won't look at him.

"I just have more time to think about what's really important to me."

"You're in denial."

"Alice, I told you, I don't care about the job," he says.

"Are you going crazy?" She stands, both palms flat on the table in protest.

"I shouldn't have told you."

"Maybe you shouldn't have."

"This has been going on forever."

"What?"

"My desire to get rid of it. From the time I was a boy, I never felt right having the left one. I never wanted it. I would pretend my mom's brooms were crutches and hobble around my backyard."

"Why on earth would you do that?" She crosses her arms, but then catches herself and lets them fall to her side.

"Walking on two legs has always been foreign. I felt happier pretending." He takes a long inhale and holds it under his lips. She walks over to him and wraps her lanky arms around his broad shoulders, resting her head on his chest. "What is this for?"

"I'm going to help you, Theo. I mean, I'm going to get someone to help you."

"But I don't need help. I just need to find a surgeon."

"What are you talking about?"

"Someone who will amputate this left leg."

"Are you kidding me?" She stops hugging him.

"I'm sorry, Alice. I thought you would understand."

Through her weeping: "Has the doctor heard of people feeling this way before?"

"Yes. There are others like me."

"And what causes it?" Her chin hangs down after she asks, leaving her mouth open in a dainty *O*.

"Something to do with your brain. You know my mom did those

strange things and my uncle couldn't stop swearing or twitching through Thanksgiving dinner. Maybe it's like that." Relief from his disclosure spreads through his cells like a comforting jelly; he searches her face for some sort of compassion.

"If other people have it, there must be a way to talk yourself out of it."

"I have been trying my entire life to talk myself out of it. I don't want to anymore. I just want to be whole."

"But you wouldn't be whole. You wouldn't be whole at all." She releases herself onto the floor, her white nightgown floating up around her waist to reveal her handsomely smooth legs, her face hidden under her hair, her knees turning pink against the ceramic tiles as she rocks herself back and forth.

"Alice, please get up. You said you would support me no matter what." He reaches out for her delicate wrist and she pushes his hand away before it lands. Moist paths on her tanned face lead from the corner of her eyes to her collarbone, all curving down on different angles.

"What about the wedding?" she says, looking up at him.

"What about it?"

"Are we still getting married?"

"Why wouldn't we?"

"How will you get down the aisle?"

"Crutches."

"And that will make you happy?"

He nods and she lets her forehead fall to the ground.

"My wedding day with a cripple," she mumbles from the ground. He winces and she stands up again.

"I won't let you." She holds his hands in hers. "I won't let you do this. You are having a hard time and as your future wife, I have to protect you."

"You don't need to protect me, just support me," he says. She turns her head from side to side. He stares straight ahead out the kitchen window.

"It's absolutely disgusting, heinous," she says, her unpainted fingernails tearing at her cheeks.

"I promise, I'll still be me, just better. You don't know how hard this is for me—"

"Stop it, Theo. You are sick and I have to look after you." She takes him into the bedroom and forces him to lie down under the blankets of their ornate floral-patterned bed. She tucks up the lace edge of the comforter around his neck, hiding his whole body.

"But I'm not . . ." he says, but the resolve in her gaze frightens him enough to stop his denial. As she bends over him, her breasts partially exposed, her pupils dilated and anxiously taking him in, he decides to momentarily surrender. "Maybe you're right, Alice. Maybe I should think about this for a while. It is a pretty huge decision." He avoids her hazel eyes.

"Now you see, Theo." Her scrawny shoulders drop and a small stream of air escapes from her nostrils. "I will take you to a psychiatrist tomorrow. He can help you find the truth about things, you'll see. He's just what you need."

"You know we can't afford that, Alice."

"I'll use the wedding money if I have to."

"Alice, I don't want you to have to do that."

"It's okay, Theo. We can fix this." She crawls into the bed beside him, snuggling into his ribs. He feels entirely suffocated by the pressure of her body.

On Theo's first day of grade three, his mother had packed his lunch full of items that began with the letter *T*: tuna sandwich, tabouli salad, tomato juice, and Tootsie Rolls for dessert. She liked to do things like that for him, but its odd assortment had embarrassed him as he unpacked it onto the lunchroom table and placed the items among the jam sandwiches and apple juice drink boxes of his friends. Theo hated how all of the kids in his class were asking questions about his tabouli salad in the Tupperware with the red lid. He hated that Amanda Pilgrim kept asking to have one of the Tootsie Rolls. He hated being even more different than the rest of them.

He tried to pretend they didn't exist, by closing his eyes and humming the theme song from *Star Wars*.

After lunch, that day in grade three, they had to draw pictures of themselves to put up on the bulletin board. They used pencil crayons and glued on tiny pieces of yarn for their hair. Theo looked so hard at the paper that the rest of the room seemed to go blurry while he worked. He almost lost himself in his need to create himself. When he finished, he carefully placed the brown yarn bits on top of his head and brought the artwork up to his teacher, Mrs. Jamison.

Her face lifted upon seeing his picture, eyes wide like he was wearing a distasteful Halloween mask.

"Theo," she said. "Why on earth would you draw yourself like this?"

"That's how I look, Mrs. Jamison."

And as she turned the paper around, even Theo himself was surprised. He hadn't planned it, and in fact, would never have chosen to share his biggest secret — it just came out naturally.

Without even realizing it, he had drawn a picture of himself without his left leg.

"I'm going to have to talk to your mother about this," Mrs. Jamison said. On the paper, she had drawn a large red circle around the missing limb, with a perfectly shaped question mark, and the words, "Call me."

"Now, make sure your mother sees this," she said, putting Theo's picture into his bag. The rest of the kids' pictures were carefully tacked up on the bulletin board beside each student's name. Beside Theo's name, there was nothing. Emptiness.

When his mother came to pick him up after school like she always did, they walked hand in hand by the train tracks towards home.

He felt his picture burning in his knapsack. His back almost felt warm from its presence. He wanted to take it out and rip it up before she had a chance to look at it, but she kept such a close eye on him.

"So tell me about your first day," his mother said.

"Fun."

"What did you do?"

"Met friends and found favourite furniture."

"Ah, so we are talking in *F*s today are we? How did you like the tabouli?"

"It was okay," he said, kicking at a stone on the ground. A train approached.

"Did anything go wrong? You seem upset."

"It's just that I don't look right," he said, trying to explain.

"It's okay, Theo. We all have things about ourselves that we would change if we could. For example, that's why I got my eyebrows drawn on, and my lipstick tattoo. That's exactly why."

He looked up at his mother's animated face, blinking his eyes in the warm autumn sun.

"I wish that—"

He had been silenced by that passing train and lost his nerve as the metal cars whizzed past them. His mother reached out and pulled him back towards the trees, and they fell onto one another in the dirt.

"That was close," she said. When they got home, Theo ran to the washroom, still wearing his school knapsack. He closed the door and locked it.

"Theo, do you need anything, dear?" he heard his mother yelling from outside the door.

"I'm fine. I'm fine."

He quickly unzipped his pack and took out the picture, pausing once more to look at the image of himself.

"Perfect," he said, as he tore the picture into snowflake-sized pieces and sprinkled them into the flushing toilet.

In high school, he didn't go out on Friday nights. He was too consumed with what he had to do to make himself feel better. He would lock the door of his room.

"Theo, darling. Dinner is outside here if you want it," his mother often said through the door. Sometimes she cooked all orange foods: sweet potatoes, peppers, and fake veggie meat with an orange tinge, and sometimes it was an all "buh" feast — "burgers, bananas, bacon nibblers." He often heard her whimpering from the kitchen, but his guilt was not loud enough to distract him from what he needed to do.

He had several red markers, Sharpies, permanent ones because that's the way he liked it. By the time Friday nights rolled around, this was the only way that he could settle himself enough to even try to go out on Saturday night. Last week's red would almost be worn off under the weight of seven showers when he pulled down his pants. Sitting in his underwear, by the light of the Darth Vader lamp that he should have gotten rid of years ago, he would start to carve. Red Sharpie on the skin, around his left thigh where he felt it should go. The thick red mark soaked into his leg quite well, and if he squinted his eyes, he could pretend that the red marker was blood and that the rest of the leg was gone. Gone from the thigh, back to where he felt like it belonged.

The ritual took most of the evening — over and over the red line on his skin — and he usually collapsed in his underwear with his hand clenched to his thigh, welcoming sleep in a haze of frantic relief.

At his mother's funeral seven years later, Theo leaned down and whispered into her cold ear as he passed the casket.

"I want to cut off my leg," he said. She didn't flinch and he felt glad. He was tired of keeping it from her, of bathing in her potential disappointment of him.

When he wakes, darkness engulfs their room. Alice lies silent, her exposed chest expanding and shriveling beside him. Under the sheet, his shin brushes against her soft calf and he jerks it away. Invisible spiders crawl up the inside of his head, causing hair all over his body to rise. He drops one leg to the floor and pushes himself out of bed, being careful not to disturb her.

I can't live like this, he thinks.

He shuffles his bare feet across the hardwood across the room. She kicks in bed and rolls onto her other side. He walks into the bathroom adjoining their bedroom and shuts the door. The click of the lock causes her to stir but she stays sleeping.

He sits on the toilet in his underwear, thinking about when he first met her. His job at the plant was so depressing before he saw Alice. Everything he did was methodical and repetitive: push a button, check for leeway, lift a tire, spin a tire. It numbed his brain just enough to allow his thoughts about his leg to gain intensity. He didn't talk to many of the other workers. In fact, he stayed so inside himself that it was like he wasn't there at all half the time.

But the day he first saw her, his entire outlook changed.

He wasn't supposed to be in that part of the plant, but he's certain now that it was her pulling him there — like a beautiful magnet. He limped over, because that's usually the way he got around; it calmed him. She was sitting behind her desk, him grimy from working on the floor, hoisting around car tires, and her, perfectly polished, shiny and pink-sweatered at her computer.

"Do you have an HR issue?" she asked him, but he was too busy staring at the shine in her hair and the soft blond hairs on her wrist.

He fumbled his way through an introduction — "Theo, my name's Theo" — and faked that he had an issue about his paycheque.

"GM policy is that paycheques always go out on the same day each month," she informed him with a small smile outlining her reply.

"Oh, yes, yes, that's fine," he said, staring.

"Is there anything else?" she said, dropping her ear towards her shoulder.

"No, no, that's it," Theo said, shuffling his steel toe boots away from the desk. "Guess I'll get back to the floor now."

"Guess you should," she said, resting her petite chin on the heel of her hand.

It had taken him three more weeks before he talked to her again, in the parking lot that time, and then another week before he asked her out. He caught her on the way up the stairs, resting his hand gently on the sleeve of her cashmere sweater.

He proposed quickly — in terms of time passed, and not the speed at which the words emerged from his mouth. It was only six months after they first met, and when she said yes, he insisted that she move in and start planning her wedding all at once. He had never met, let alone been engaged, to someone like her.

In the thrill of newfound love, he found himself worrying less and less about his extra appendage. He even stopped marking it up at night — a habit that had stayed with him since high school — or staring longingly at a jigsaw in the factory, fantasizing about the blades slicing through skin, tendons, and bones.

But after she moved in, and the newness began to wear off as she combed through bridal magazines and spent long hours on the phone with her mother, it started again.

He found it particularly hard to cope when he was at work — when she was tucked up in her office and he was on the floor, hauling things, fixing broken fittings, and inspecting car axles.

It was in the monotony of those moments that the desire to get rid of it swelled stronger. His only outlet was to go into the men's washroom and look at himself in the full-length mirror screwed to the wall on the other side of the urinals.

He squinted his eyes and stared at it, trying to pretend it wasn't there. Sometimes, he would fold it up and hop on his other leg like it was his only option of getting around. It was at those moments that he received some relief, feeling at last like he had the body he was meant to have.

He was in that exact position, experiencing that relief, on the day that everything began to change.

"What the fuck are you doing, Theo?" His supervisor, Malik, shouted at him.

He put his leg down. "Um, nothing, just looking . . ."

"You look gorgeous, weiner. Into my office, now!"

Malik's office overlooked the factory floor and wasn't clean and almond-smelling like where Alice sat. It was rough, dirty, and had a rusty desk and ripped chairs.

"I've been watching you," he said. "I know how many times you go into that washroom."

"I don't know what you're talking about," Theo had said, looking around the room like a little bird trying to find a way out of a net.

"It's really none of my business what you do in there," Malik said, rubbing the stubble on his chin. "But today, today it is my business because you missed a malfunction in the automatic welder. Two cars are toast because of you, and that costs us all." His face was seriously straight. Theo knew what was coming; what he didn't know was how he was going to tell Alice.

She was waiting for him when he got home. He had gone to the bar near the plant, hoping for a bit of time to formulate a plan. No doubt she was upset when he finally walked in, but not about his beer breath, or what had happened with Malik, she was worried about where he had been.

She hugged him tight when he came through the door, digging her sharp nails into the fleshy parts of his arms, resting her head on his shoulder.

"I didn't know what happened to you."

"Oh, I doubt that," he said.

"I didn't know where you were . . . I was worried about you."

They were still hugging then, and the warmth of her made him collapse a little further into her arms, holding tight to her the way she was to him.

"We're going to figure this out," she said. "I have savings, and I know you'll find something else soon . . . at one of the other plants in town, maybe. They were stupid to let you go just for taking a bit of a long lunch one day. It's not your fault."

He swallowed hard, feeling the truth rising like bile in the back of his throat.

"Job or no job, I will be there for you. We are in this together now, Theo. I will support you, through good and bad, sickness and health, and all that. It is your soul, your spirit that I am in love with, not anything on the outside."

It was those last words that had stuck with him the most. The idea that she was with him for life — that she was in love with who he was on the inside. This actually made him believe that she would understand what he had to do next. Understand how he was going to use his time off work, his desire to start his job search again as an amputee.

It was at that moment, in her arms, that he made the decision to follow his dream once and for all, because — he thought — he had found the girl who would actually stick by him through the long and difficult road to his real self.

That was then, and this was now, sitting alone in the bathroom of their apartment, staring at his left foot and wishing it would disappear. And all at once, he has a new plan.

It starts raining a bit when he finally reaches the tracks. He had trekked through the brush out behind their apartment building, sucking on a bottle of whiskey as he limped through the dirt.

There are absolutely no lights, just darkness. He looks up. Clouds are moving fast with the wind, parting to reveal a smattering of stars — so many points of light that seem visible only now. He stares at them, hard, his eyes crossing and blurring a bit under the effects of the alcohol. He tosses the empty bottle against the rails and it shatters into a collection of jagged pieces, landing around his feet.

He thinks about his mother: her warmth, her obsessions, her desire to have the best for him, and through his alcohol fog he can see that there is only one way to make this stop.

"It'ssssss okay, Mom," he says out loud. "This is it. This is going to work." *This will be so much cheaper*, he thinks. And efficient. They will have no choice but to get rid of it.

And then he thinks about Alice: her tiny rose-shaped lips, her strength, her aching for a perfect life. "We'll get through thisss, Aliccccccce," he slurs. "Nothing can defeat usssss!"

He considers how good it will feel to reach the end of this suffering, and then gently, lowers himself down onto the ground. He pushes his boot against the hardness of the rail, tapping it like he doesn't believe it's really there. Then, he leans himself over and slowly rolls up his sweatpants, positioning his left leg at the exact point he wants it gone. The track is cold against his skin, a sharp kind of chill that signals to him how momentous the moment is. He lays his body back onto the ground, his arms above his head, and his eyelids droop closed, blocking out the stars above him, welcoming in the black behind his eyelids.

He pictures how her face will look when she finds out, furrowed, but relieved: "At least he's alive," she will say. "At least he's still with me."

And finally he hears it, the roar of the early morning train in the distance, barreling towards him on a path of no return.

Lucky Ones

I can tell a lot about a person by how their feet look. For me, it's like a secret peek into someone's personal life. Like having someone tell me their dream, thinking I'll just laugh, without knowing I know exactly how to interpret it, and what it says about them. Clean cuticles, dirty toes, pointy nails, unkempt, calloused, rough heels, scaly skin. Every little part of a foot shows much pride you have, how much time you have, and just what kind of a person you are.

My husband Quan's feet for example, are amazing. No matter how hard things got at home in Vietnam, he always took care of them. That included skin creams and buffing, the full bit. He even did it when I was over visiting with him and his family: polishing and scrubbing, poking and scraping, really, right in front of me. And it wasn't just his feet; he took care of all his different parts the same way: face, hands, chest hairs. It was very unusual for someone his age who didn't have much money. And it is this concern for his own appearance that first attracted me to him. Rather, it was his desire to take care of himself that made me believe that he would take care of me just as well.

And then we came to Canada.

It wasn't easy to leave our families, our homes, everything we had grown up with as children, to come to Toronto. It wasn't easy to adjust to the wintertime, to perfect our English, to find Quan a job, and a cheap enough place for us to live. It wasn't easy, any of it, but we did it. And when the rent on our two-bedroom apartment was past due, and the fridge was empty except for some Sriracha sauce and a yellow onion, we gathered our stuff and moved somewhere else.

You see, the plastics factory had laid Quan off after only six months. And despite my desire to stay home and create my own Canadian baby, I soon found myself working in the nail salon owned by my cousin Trai, who spent his days sitting in a vinyl chair in the waiting room "supervising us" and doing crossword puzzles in his bare feet.

The new apartment Quan and I found near Spadina and Dundas was cheaper. It was also smaller, smelled like rotting potatoes and had mice nibbling through the cupboards. It was almost a relief in the morning to leave Quan — doubled over in front of the classified section spread out on our Thrift Store coffee table — and head out to my job at the nail salon. It took a streetcar, then the subway to get out to the Beaches where the nail salon was and I thought about Quan the whole time. I thought about how excited he was to come here, how the thrill had worn off so quickly, and how we could never, ever go back to Vietnam.

When I arrived at the salon, my friend Binh was often the first to greet me. She would wave coyly from a side table as I stepped through the door and my head filled with the smell of sweaty feet and nail polish remover.

"Morning, Kim," my cousin Trai would mumble as I passed, engrossed in the page in front of him. His pencil was usually poised and his smooth feet on the coffee table — dusty toes in the air like they hadn't moved since last night. Trai's feet were too smooth and spongy to be respectable — they made him look nothing but lazy.

So that Saturday in early May, she was my first customer. Rushing, I guess, because she probably couldn't stop, even on the weekend. She had shiny skin, red lips, and was wearing a seriously fancy business suit — you know, the kind with pinstripe pants that flare out and a matching blazer on top of an impeccably ironed white blouse. Her blond hair had been carefully shaped into a graduated bob and she was wearing yellow stiletto heels with bare feet. And if I hadn't been so consumed with Quan and how he was probably at home flirting with suicide, I might actually have said hello to her. Said hello and asked her how she was today, like I usually did. But I was thinking so hard I only waved with the flat of my hand and nodded. Then I shoved the tray of nail polish in front of her and she picked a shiny blood-red polish. I led her over to the footbaths where she collapsed onto the polyester seat, flicked off her shoes, dropped her keys into her oversized Gucci bag, and sunk her feet into the whizzing water.

We stared at each other while she soaked, and honestly, I couldn't bring myself to make any words. After five minutes, I motioned for her to raise her feet up out of the water so I could start my work. I dried her gently with a towel while she studied a spot on the ceiling that was obviously more interesting than my face.

You could see from her feet that she put a lot of effort into her image — although they were a bit wrinkled from being stuffed into the pointy toes of her shoes. Her toes were long and thin, and the big toe curved a bit over the next one, with a slight callous on the outside like she had been walking around a lot in heels. There was already polish on each toenail, pale beige, which told me that she was looking to turn it up a notch by adding the new color. Maybe she was going on vacation or had a secret lover, or both.

She had no idea that as I massaged her pads and heels I was getting a complete read on who she was as a person, and maybe even, where she would end up. Kind of like a palm reading, only she had no idea I was doing it. That's what made the pedicures fun for me, or at least more interesting. She leaned back in the reclining chair, letting out a long sigh and doing what looked like mathematical calculations with her right pointer finger.

"I really needed this," she said then. "You would never believe how much I worked this week. Hours like that should be against the law, and now, I've got this out-of-town client to entertain today." She opened her eyes and looked at me, waiting for me to be impressed.

I said nothing, only looked down and smiled, although I wanted to tell her I had my own problems to worry about.

"Oh, you poor thing," she said with her head tilted away from me. "You have no idea what I'm saying, do you?"

And as she said that, her cell phone rang. It was one of those piercing, loud, mechanical, "I don't care who this interrupts" kind of rings. A ring she obviously wanted other people to hear. Her phone was in her bag, which she had dropped close to her on the floor. She leaned her body over to retrieve it, dropping one pasty arm in like a Caucasian fishing pole. She managed to pull the phone out and flip it open in one fluid motion. It landed on her ear and clunked against her diamond stud earring.

"Yes . . ." she said into the receiver. "Bonnie Blake here."

A tap on my shoulder. It was my cousin Trai who had somehow managed to remove himself from the chairs up front and make his way on bare feet to my station. He whispered in my ear in English. "This lady a big tipper . . . kiss up," he said, puckering his lips and dabbing them with the tips of his fingers. His breath reeked of garlic and it was only 9:13 a.m., which meant it must have been from something he ate last night.

Again, I only nodded as he hobbled back to the front in his black jeans and white T-shirt. I was biting down hard but still trying to smile on the outside. Quan and I needed the money, so I should probably have thanked my cousin, even though I wanted to cuff him.

"This is a fine time to talk," Mrs. Blake said into her cell. "I'm getting a pedicure. Oh yes, treating myself — I deserve it!" I cringed at her fake laugh.

"There's no one here except my Asian beautician and the poor thing can't speak a lick of English." She made another insincere gurgle as she glanced my way. "Why come here if you can't even communicate?"

I let my smile disappear, but tried to hide the sneer.

And then the fake laughing stopped.

Bonnie Blake's face went incredibly serious. Straight. Empty. Like she might puke or punch someone all at once.

"Are you sure it was him with her?" she asked, her eyes narrowing. There was a pause while she listened and clenched her lips.

"That bastard," she said finally into the phone. She said it with such seriousness that it came out as one word — *thatbastard*. I looked down at her feet to avoid her glare and began smoothing off her toe polish with a soaked cotton ball. She was breathing like it was difficult, mostly through her nose. She was tapping hard on the arm of the chair with her free manicured fingernails. *Tap, tap, tap,* like a ticking clock, or a time bomb.

"But I don't understand," she said. "I mean, c'mon . . . how selfish can you be?" Her broken sentences were laced with panic. I finished removing the polish on the last of her toenails, the baby one, until they were all bare.

With anxious force, she jumped out of the chair with a bolt, ripping her feet out of my hands.

"Where is the washroom?" she said to me, clicking her phone shut without saying goodbye or good luck to whomever was on the other end.

I just stared at her.

"Oh never mind, I'll figure it out," she barked. She slid her feet into a pair of those paper slippers we keep in a basket on the floor and hobbled towards the back of the shop.

When she was gone, I noticed that she'd left her bag. Without deciding to, I grabbed it with my foot and dragged it closer to my chair. I was wearing sandals. My own toenails were unpainted and a bit overgrown, a silent reminder of my desperation. The leather bag felt soft against my big toe. I imagined its contents: makeup, probably, to cover things, some red rouge and liquid foundation to hide the bags under her eyes, most likely some gum or mints, a condom maybe. And of course, a wallet. A fancy, busy, overstuffed wallet.

And then, my leg moved again without my telling it to. It reached out on its own and with one quick motion kicked her purse under my table. I looked down and glared at it. It was one thing to look, but who was I to . . .

I dipped my hand into the bag. It was open on top, the zipper undone like she hadn't had the time to close it. My fingers went right to what felt like an alligator-skin wallet. I stroked the smooth scales that probably once flourished on the back of some poor doomed creature.

She wouldn't even miss it, I heard my secret voice say — the one that taunts me when I think about going to community college or criticize Quan for not being able to find a job. I thought about how easy it would be to deny it. I can't even speak English as far as she's concerned. How can you accuse someone if they don't know what you are saying?

I closed my eyes — just long enough to see my father's face, his serious gaze, and the dignity he wore as a mask. I opened my eyes and he disappeared. A little piece of myself weakened inside of me.

I snapped open the wallet and ran my fingertip over the jagged line of credit cards. Before I could tell myself to stop, I had caught something. I closed it in the palm of my hand, its edges digging into my skin.

I glanced down to my lap and saw the word "Visa" on gold, and then with a sly jerk, it was in my pocket.

I placed my guilty hands flat on the table in front of me, staring at my own ratty fingernails, chewed down, blood on the cuticles.

With my chapped, unpolished toes, I kicked the bag back beside the footbath where she had left it — the card now smoldering in my pocket.

I noticed then that Binh was looking at me, eyeing me like she knew my secret, like she wanted in on it. But she couldn't have seen. She was too busy working on an old lady's cuticles to have noticed what was going on under my table. I waved to Binh and pouted to throw her off. *Another boring day*, I seemed to be saying as I shook my head. She nodded back and looked back at the lady's fingers.

I thought about what I would do after the woman paid, with cash hopefully: I would leave early and take the subway downtown to a fancy department store — what's that one where they put all those displays in the windows at Christmas? I would find the most expensive clothing I could, or small appliances, or better yet, jewellery. I would gather up as much stuff as I could and take it to the counter. I would hand over the card long before she even noticed it was missing, and after I signed her name (matching the signature on the back), I would take everything and head for home. I'd trash the card in some random garbage can in the subway station, and before I knew it, I'd be sitting with Quan trying to figure out who to sell the stuff to.

"She had it coming," I'd say to him. "She got what she deserved." And we'd figure out which bill to pay first, and how much to send back to our parents. We'd make love then because of the pure joy of no longer having to worry about how our next dollar would find us. We'd finally be two of the lucky ones.

When she came back, I looked into her blue eyes. She was still upset and was clutching her cell phone angrily in her hand. Her mascara had run and had been wiped up. There were faded black lines on her white cheeks.

She sat back in the chair. Her face drooped hopelessly between the diamonds in her ears.

"*Xin lỗi,*" I said in Vietnamese. I'm sorry.

"My marriage is falling apart," she said, as if by accident, because she stopped herself. And when I put my hand on her shoulder, she brushed it away and snapped back into something else.

"You'll never know," she said as she shoved her bare feet into those yellow heels and grabbed her bag from where I had kicked it. I focused on the colourful polish bottles on the table — creamy orange, baby pink, feeling-sassy red. I tried to distract my mind, forget about that crinkle I saw between her eyebrows, the one that asked, *Why is this happening to me?*

I watched her leave. I saw Trai nod to her and then turn to scowl back at me. I felt the sweat gather between my own eyes, feeling the card in my pocket like a five-pound weight.

Then I heard my other secret voice — the one that tells me I need to send my mother a letter that gives her hope, or rub the bottoms of my husband's feet so he can relax — and I chased the woman into the street.

The sun was hot that day and it hit my face quite unexpectedly. I squinted my eyes as I ran up behind her.

"You forgot this!" I yelled out and she turned, tripping over her own feet.

I held out the Visa card, its golden tints glittering in the sun.

She looked at me, confused, and her wounded face morphed

into a grimace that wrinkled her upturned nose. "Typical," she sneered, snatching the card from my hands.

"*Xin lỗi,*" I said again, trying to smile.

"Fuck you," she responded and turned to trudge away from me. Soon, she was gone completely.

Before I went back into the salon, I stopped and thought about going home after work. There, I would find Quan, sitting motionless on the couch in the living room, the glow from our twelve-inch lighting up his solemn face in the dark.

"Any leads today?" I would ask.

"Leave me alone, Kim," he would say to greet me.

Remission and Other Tragedies

It seems silly that even though my name is on the mortgage, I waited on the front steps of my own home for almost an hour that day. I made some use of my time though. I scraped a piece of gum off the walk with my car key, patted down some soil around one of my potted gardenia plants and sorted the day's mail into piles: bills, junk, and personal.

It hurts to admit, but if I had my imminent death to do over again, I would do things a bit differently. Not to say that we don't all do the best we can, but perhaps if I had acted more rationally, I would not have found myself at that difficult moment, inhaling the smell of burning hamburger patties as I hid outside of my own house like a zombie back from the dead.

They were in there — all three of them — which was why I couldn't put the key in the lock and open the door. Unfortunately for us all, my planned scenario was coming to beautiful fruition. Be careful what you wish for I guess, especially now that I knew I was going to be all right. Damn it. Ida didn't deserve to get messed around like this, not at her age. Not when she was such a kind and unassuming person.

And my dear Milo, he must have hated me for what I tried to do to him. But he was such a good sport, going for afternoon coffees with Ida, pretending to give it a go when he obviously wanted me to stay. But I knew it would be worse for Ida, poor woman, to have her hopes so high, and then cut down. I'm evil. That's why I couldn't make myself go in the house.

It was their first day spending time all together. They were going to watch a Disney movie with Emma (*The Jungle Book*, I think), and then have a barbeque afterwards. Milo was "going to give it the old college try" — that's what he said to me before I left for my doctor's appointment that morning. I put my hand on his shoulder (like a good friend) and kissed him on the cheek when he said it, but I knew he was only acting it out for my benefit. He wanted to grant me my last dying wish. He was being the committed husband and putting up with my obsessive craziness one last time. He had no idea I was off to receive my most recent scan results. It had seemed cruel to give him hope.

How can cancer just go away? If you ignore it, does it get bored? If you accept it, does it scream out, "Psych! Gotcha!" Well, the joke's on me. Despite my doctor's previous confidence while handing down my death notice, my inevitable demise was not meant to be quite yet. All my tears — and Milo's, and Emma's (bless her little heart) — were for nothing. I guess miracles happen, even when you're not expecting them. Maybe they happen *mostly* when you are not actively hoping for them. It's not that I wanted to go, but after I got myself together, there were bigger things to worry about. Emma. It was all about Emma. My enchanting, darling, nine-year-old daughter and my wish for her to grow up with a proper mother.

I'll admit that I'm a tad controlling — even about my own death as it turns out. I have an incredible desire to make sure that everything goes exactly as I have planned it: vacations, holiday parties, casseroles. Of course this is never the case. So why you ask, did I not just go into my house, hand Ida her crocheted daisy purse, and pop back into my familiar place with my family? I guess you could say I was embarrassed. Ashamed that I made a mess out of preparing for my own afterlife, that I had bullied my husband into a situation he thought was ridiculous, and most of all, that I had taken advantage of Ida. Poor, sweet, virginal Ida.

I chose Ida because I wanted Emma to have an attentive, intelligent female role model in the house. And so Milo too, would have someone to talk to. Ida was one of the best listeners I had ever met, which Milo deserved to have.

I also chose her because she worked in a library. Which meant: she knew about a lot of different subjects, would offer great homework help, and knew how to be quiet when the situation called for it. I had also appreciated how interested Ida had been in Emma's life when we talked. She asked about things that others didn't, like Emma's ballet lessons.

"So what did she learn last night?" she would ask. "I bet Emma looked so sweet in her tutu, you must be so proud."

When I told her Emma was sick, Ida would offer to make her some homemade butter tarts to cheer her up. And though I would remind her that sugar was not helpful for a cold, I appreciated that she took the time to think about her. Ida could clearly see that children were the most important parts of us, and that's why she would have made a perfect mother.

All the years I had been going to the library downtown, asking Ida for help, chatting about town festivals, gossip, and our lives, I had never once heard her mention a boyfriend — past, present, or in the beginning stages. This seemed odd since she was in her mid-forties and had expressed to me that she *was* interested in getting married and having children. She was open to it, but "just couldn't find the right guy" — to which, one is just supposed to nod and say, "Isn't it true!" But it's not true for all of us. I found the right guy: calm demeanour, striking nose and blue eyes, always asks if I am cold, or hungry, or needing a break (from studying, or working, or caring for the baby). I had found my *one*, and he had given me a new part of myself — Emma —and that had changed everything.

Ida had never been in love. She actually told me that one afternoon shortly after we met. I was hunched over a table near her desk, trying to get a handle on my thesis. Although it was her job, it was difficult for Ida to help me because I think my subject matter, the cultural history of a woman's orgasm, made her a bit uncomfortable. It was after she sheepishly brought me a book entitled *The Big O, Finding the Pleasure You Need*, that I told her it was nothing to be embarrassed about. "It's not about sex," I said. "It's about love, really."

"Well, I don't know much about that" is what she said, which I assumed meant that she had never herself experienced what it was like to fall in love with someone. "I consider myself asexual these days actually," she said. "You probably find that unique in this lust-driven society."

It was at that moment that I began to like Ida even more. It had always been comforting to see her big green eyes, long brown hair, porcelain-white skin and tall, lanky limbs behind the desk each time I arrived at the library to work. She greeted me so warmly, saying my name and looking right at me when she smiled. That was rare in a person — authenticity. I started to look forward to seeing her for no other reason than I knew she would find me a quiet, empty cubicle to work in and make sure I was not distracted by anything. It was so hard to write or read with Emma and Milo around, and if I was going to finish my master's, I needed to concentrate. Ida, only a few years older than me, acted as my surrogate mother and guardian when I was there. She looked after me, in so many ways, which is strange to say about someone who is really only an acquaintance, but she did. And I began to trust her, immensely.

Since she'd told me, I'd always felt a bit sad about the fact that Ida had never been in love. Here was a perfectly lovely person who was maybe destined to be alone, simply because she was a bit shy and socially awkward. I had always thought how nice it would be to help her somehow.

When I found out about the cancer, Ida was the first person I told. It's always easier to tell difficult things to people you don't know very well. I just hoped that by sharing the information, I was not bringing our relationship to a level that would supersede the anonymity we had together. We bumped shoulders as we were coming out of the washroom that day.

"Oops, so sorry, Elizabeth," Ida said, placing her long fingers briefly on my arm. She was taller than me, and looked down at me when she spoke.

"It's no problem, Ida," I said, surveying the frayed section of orange carpet below our feet.

"What's the matter?" she said. "You are not your regular chipper self?"

"No, no, I'm not," I said through my sudden blubbering.

We collapsed together onto the ground, right there outside the washroom, where I told her the whole story: how I had found the lump, the biopsy, metastasis, how little time they predicted, all of it. I shared with her my most intimate and most terrible news, though she hadn't really even known me that long. Maybe it was too much to dump on her, too unfair to make her deal with it all, but at that point, I didn't know what else to do.

"You have to tell your husband," she said. "He is a good man who loves you and he deserves to know." And I knew she was right.

───────────

It's not that I didn't want to tell Milo I was sick. We typically share with each other when we have something on our minds. We have a date night once a month; we make love every Friday night; we talk, a lot. Of course this was something I wanted to share. It's just that he was away in China for work when I went in with the lump, and only came back when I was waiting for the results. I figured that no one should hear bad news when they are away in another country — makes for long, terrifying nights in a strange hotel room — and by the time he came home, well, he just needed to relax. He didn't need to worry about something that wasn't even confirmed yet.

But when I heard for sure, I found a different excuse. I didn't have the heart to put this kind of blemish on our otherwise perfect marriage together. How could I tell him that he and Emma were going to have to live the rest of their lives without me, that his only daughter would no longer have a mother? So I suppose that is why I went to Ida first, looking for insight from the impartial observer — from someone who, apparently, had never been in love herself, which really, I found hard to believe in a woman her age.

But I couldn't avoid it forever. Eventually, I had to sit Milo down and give him the bad news: the big C, stage four, my bleak treatment options, all the cliché things that had ever been said about it. I think he was shocked at first, unable to process it. His blue eyes narrowed in concern and he crossed his arms like he was trying to keep himself in one piece.

"I'm sorry" was what I said to try to help him, though I don't think it did me any good to apologize. My real apology would come much later and would have to be much more thorough and convincing if it were ever going to stick.

It was at that moment that I began to hatch my horrible and misguided plan. I have no idea where the idea came from, or why, but one morning, I opened my eyes and I knew what I had to do next. How I was going to protect my family. Flash forward a couple months, and things were so much better, and much, much worse than I ever could have imagined.

So that was the reason I camped out on my front step for an hour before going in to deliver the positive, wonderful, perhaps life-shattering news, depending on your perspective. After only one round of chemo and radiation, some manageable nausea and hair loss that could be easily covered with a stylish scarf, my cancer had stopped. I was not going anywhere. Everything I planned could be forgotten — *as you were, people*. But I felt guilty. So, instead of rushing to tell my family the news, I parked my car at the end of our shady street, walked home, and stood outside — immobilized and in total fear of what was about to take place.

I wasn't worried about what Milo would say. Of course, I knew he would be relieved. He had flapped his pointer finger in protest when I first told him what I wanted him to do. "You're not gone yet! How am I supposed to pretend you are? And with this woman? It doesn't make sense," he said, his eyes all watery-like.

"But this is what I want, for Emma. She needs a mother, and you will need someone. You will," I said, almost pleading. I cried then, and begged dramatically, "This is my last wish as a human being walking on this planet. I need to know that things are going to be okay."

I made *him* feel guilty and slowly he gave in (or pretended to anyway). And now, I'd like to say it was the drugs they were giving me that caused me to act so irrationally — *imagine, putting him in that situation.*

But no, it wasn't him I was worried about facing; it was Ida. Oh, how I had pleaded with her as well. "Please, Ida, as a friend, I need you to do this. Be there for my family."

"I want to help you Elizabeth, but, it just seems, so . . . inappropriate," she had said, her big eyes confused and wounded. But after the initial shock, she had warmed to the idea. After all, she *was* the epitome of compassion. She was always so patient with those who forgot their library cards, and quick to call a cab for the old ladies and single mothers who couldn't make it home in the rain. I told her this was me paying her back, for all the times she had located the right book when I was researching my thesis or the most fitting colloquialism to help me make it through the day (some of her favourites were "God doesn't give us anything we can't handle" and "Today is the first day of the rest of your life.") Yes, eventually she took what I was offering her as a gift, the chance to have her own husband and daughter — *mine*.

After their first date I had called Ida on my cell phone, sitting on the picnic table in our backyard so Milo wouldn't hear, pulling out loose strands of my own hair and dropping them into the grass.

"So, how did it go?" I asked her.

"Oh, Elizabeth, thank you!" she said, almost breathless. "He was a perfect gentleman." This I understood. I knew Milo would never have been attracted to a reserved woman like Ida. He'd always liked a bit of spunk in his women — look who he married. But attraction wasn't really necessary. In fact, I figured that I would rest more peacefully knowing there wasn't any funny business going on between them.

So Ida was excited. And she stayed that way for the next few weeks, throughout the coffees, the hayride date, and right up until the day when she was going to come over to the house and meet Emma for the first time — casually, of course. Things were going perfectly, until my own healthy cells ruined it all.

I imagined what would happen after I told Ida that the plan was off — that she could step aside now because I was in remission and had many years left. I imagined her eyes bugging right out of her head, her lanky arms and legs turning into ropes wanting to strangle me, fire screaming from her mouth. And I pictured the other possibility. I saw her erupting in tears over her failed life, over the fact that the only chance she had to honour a husband, cherish a daughter, had vanished.

So as I sat outside my home that day, I stayed very small and quiet. When I got tired, I rested my head on the tacky garden gnome that Milo's mother had sent us last summer. I rubbed my hand over the silk of my crimson floral headscarf and imagined poor Ida breaking apart at the thought of her dried-up ovaries. I saw her collapsing, tearing at her own face in agony — trying to slit her wrists with her car keys.

I wasn't ready to tell her how my own well-being was set to destroy hers. Yes, just when she thought it couldn't have gotten any worse, I had ruined her life beyond recovery.

As it turned out I didn't have to go into the house at all. After an hour of me lurking in the bushes, dodging squinty glares from the neighbours, and sifting potting soil through my fingers in anguish, the front door opened.

The scene as I saw it: Milo standing with muscular arms crossed over white polo shirt, nodding politely with his eyes fixed down on his daughter. Emma was happily demonstrating the new light-up skipping rope that Ida had brought her that afternoon, her honey brown hair flying up as she jumped.

And Ida, with one hand on the doorknob to leave and another

hand gesturing wildly in the air like a giant paisley tree branch in the wind — "Thank you, thank you, what a wonderful time!" she was saying. And on her face, the most tragic look of contentment that I had ever seen expressed by another woman.

"Ida," I said, like I was surprised to be running into her.

She just smiled in a timid way and nodded in my direction. I got the distinct feeling that I was now officially someone she preferred to avoid. And rightly so . . .

Because at that moment, I abandoned any sense of tact or respect that I had left. I didn't think about Ida's feelings, about her future, or what a good friend she had been to me. Instead, I thought only about myself as I blurted out the good/emotionally devastating news for all to hear.

The first thing I felt afterwards were Milo's arms around me. He was crying, his gentle sobs muffling into my shoulder, his fingers clutching the back of my neck.

"Does this mean you are going to be okay?" Emma asked then, and as I pulled away from Milo to look down at her, I noticed that Ida — probably overcome with shock, embarrassment, and life-altering devastation — had already disappeared down the street.

Sum of Her Parts

Aggie's first appointment was on a Tuesday afternoon, four o'clock. Frank was excited when he saw it in the book, giddy even. He put on cologne at three o'clock. And at three thirty he did fourteen push-ups and a bunch of crunches on the floor of his office. Even though seeing Aggie as a patient wasn't the first date he had imagined, he'd take it. It had been a while since he'd allowed himself time to have romantic interest in any woman. His heart was beating fast under his white lab coat.

She was right on time; after she knocked on his office door and he opened it, she just stood there for a couple of seconds before coming in. She was wearing a soft cashmere sweater, which fit snugly over her curvy shape. Her face was impeccably made up, shiny, almost like he could see himself in her lip gloss. She had a beautiful glass beaded necklace around her neck. It hung down between her breasts.

"Thanks for seeing me, Frank," she said once she was seated. "I knew there was a reason we met the other day. It wasn't just about being overcharged for car parts." She smiled and he nodded. He'd never before been at a loss for words during one of his consults. That first meeting was usually all about the possibility of what he could do for women who hated their bodies. How he could make them love themselves again.

"It's my pleasure, Aggie," Frank said finally. "Of course, I was never implying that you needed work done, but I'm glad to help you if I can." He was looking down at his desk as they talked, instead of looking at her.

"It's just that, my ex-husband is dating a woman who is a great deal younger than I am, and I feel . . ."

"No need to explain, Aggie. I've heard it before."

"And she's probably more fertile as well." Aggie's eyebrows were wrinkled together when she said this, as if in physical pain.

"Aggie, you mustn't talk like that." He scanned the chart he had created for her. *Aggie Sutton. Age forty-six. Concerns:* "So what exactly are you looking to have done?" He hated to ask, though he knew he had to.

"These," she said, grabbing her breasts in her hands. "Also, my eyes lifted and my nose shaved down. I have always hated the way it bumps up like this."

"Aggie, I know we've only recently met but are you sure you want . . ." He stopped himself. "Anything else?"

"Well, I would like something done with this double chin, if you can." She flicked at the skin under her neck. "Can't you suck the fat out of there or something?"

"I could, yes, although maybe you would opt for something less invasive."

"Such as?"

"Botox."

"In the neck?"

"Sure." He couldn't believe he had actually suggested a less expensive option. He wondered if the exhilaration of plastic surgery had stopped coursing through his veins — or if it was just because of her, how she was.

"No," she said, her eyes squinted up a bit. "I've got my husband's alimony money. I think I'll go for the whole shooting match."

Frank had sat closest to the window in the waiting room at the car garage because he really couldn't stand the smell of car fumes. The air was stagnant like it was just released from the inside of a can of gasoline. She came in after he had, checked in briefly at the counter, and sat down in a chair opposite him. He looked across at her. Frank wasn't usually one to notice women when he was out places — after all, he spent every day examining their parts at work — but something about this woman was making Frank want to stare at her. Perhaps it was the roundness of her face, the surprisingly smooth skin on her cheeks, the gently wrinkled folds in her neck, the way her hair fell softly onto her shoulders. Maybe it was something different entirely, one of those things you can put into words, can't dissect, or —

"Have you been waiting long?" she asked him, folding her fingers into each other, turning her lips into a cordial smile. He stuttered his words on the way out, like he'd been distracted by his thoughts about her.

"I, um, yes, well, it's been almost half an hour for me."

"Not too bad, considering how these things usually go. I've got brake problems with my Corolla — had a terrible grinding and screeching this morning."

He smiled and put his BlackBerry back in his suit pocket, adjusting his frameless glasses on his nose. "Oil pan," he said. "I've got a leak in my oil pan."

"No good," she said. "I'm hopeless with these things. My husband Teddy used to handle all this stuff before we separated." Unsure what to say Frank nodded again and then surveyed the magazines that were set out: *Popular Mechanics*, *People*, *Maclean's*. He picked up a Sears catalogue and flipped through it. "Do you handle everything for your wife?" she asked next.

"Wife? Um, no, I've never been married."

"Oh I see," she said. "Not often you meet men your age without wives; do you mind me asking, are you gay?"

"Gay?"

"Oh I'm sorry, was that a horrible question? I have a tendency to speak before my brain has processed whether it would actually be an appropriate thing to say. Who am I to make judgments when I myself have reached this age without having any children? People might try to make assumptions about me for that."

He laughed a bit at the way her cheeks had reddened, and how she was wringing her long slender fingers in front of her. "I'm not gay," he said. "I'm a doctor, so I've been devoting a lot of time to my clinic over the last fifteen years; makes it difficult to have a social life sometimes."

"Anderson!" A voice rang out over the loud speaker. "Tabitha Anderson, your vehicle is ready."

He looked up into her face, expecting recognition, but was secretly pleased when she didn't look towards the desk. A woman in her twenties came in from just outside the doors and went up to the counter.

"So you have a clinic?"

"Yes, plastic surgery. For women mostly."

"How interesting," she said, her hand rising to her face. "And is business good?"

"Consistent."

"I suppose that's why you're driving a Porsche," she said, motioning to his key chain. He looked down and then tucked the symbol into his fist. "What made you choose that as a career?"

He had never been asked that question, and had to think about it before answering.

"My father," he said finally. "My father was the one who wanted me to be a doctor. When I was a young boy he read me medical textbooks before bed and took me to tour hospitals in grade school. I guess you could say that he ingrained a love of medicine in me from quite a young age."

"So is he a doctor as well?" she asked.

"No, no. He's from Iran — he didn't have these types of opportunities growing up."

"And plastic surgery?"

"My way of being creative I suppose." Frank tried to say this casually, implying that what he did was something that could be considered in a light way as well. Really though, he knew there was nothing frivolous about cutting women open to try to make them feel more valuable. He knew there was nothing flippant about people's absolute distain of themselves and the way they would go to any lengths to change—

"Is everything okay?" she asked him, and when he looked up to see her concerned eyes he realized that he had sunk into some sort of daze. This was part of the reason he was still single after all these years. Even when he found a woman interesting, he couldn't seem to hold his concentration on her long enough.

"Fine, fine, I'm sorry. Look, I'm Frank." He stood up from the plastic red chair and walked across the aisle, reaching out his hand to her. She shook it, and her hand was soft, and he probably held it for a little longer than he should have.

"Doyle!" the loudspeaker said out. "Agatha Doyle."

"That's me," she said. "You can call me Aggie."

"Aggie," he said, noticing that he was staring. She gathered her purse from beside her and stood up. He reached into his suit jacket and removed one of his business cards, holding it out in the air to her. "Listen, Aggie, perhaps you'd like to give me a call sometime."

She stuck out her bottom lip and moved her head back in surprise.

"Are you saying that you think I need—"

"No, no! I just thought that maybe . . . well, whatever you want."

"It's fine," Aggie said. "I'm starting a new chapter in life, so maybe I could use a pick-me-up." She took his card and tucked it into her purse.

"I really wasn't . . ." Frank said. "I just wanted to . . ." He felt frustrated by his own lack of clarity.

"Agatha Doyle!" the voice boomed again.

"It was nice meeting you, Frank. My Corolla is calling!"

He sat back on his chair, uncomfortable from the sweat in his armpits and the knot of nervousness in his stomach. When he looked up again, she was gone.

When Aggie's surgery day arrived and she was prepped for her procedures — dressed in her little paper hat and gown, waiting on the stretcher in the pre-op room — Frank made a point of going to her when he knew the nurse would be out.

"So, you're sure you want me to do this? I mean, you can always change your mind or wait a while, or . . ."

"No, Frank," she said. "It's time for me to take my life in my own hands."

"Umm, hmm."

"I want you to do it."

"Okay, Aggie. Before you go under, I just want you to know that . . ."

"Yes?" She looked up at him. She was tapping her fingertips on either side of her on the bed, like she was playing miniature pianos.

"I'm going to do everything I can to make you into your best self," he said like he was reciting a script.

"I'm glad to have met you, Frank. Maybe after all this is done, we could get together without all the uncomfortable distractions." She looked away towards her IV drip machine, blushing slightly.

"I'd like that." He held her hand for just a second. Her fingers were warm.

"I think you're a special woman," Frank said, but stopped himself from saying more, instead, taking out a black Sharpie from his pocket. "Now, I just have to make a few markings."

He prepared to make the pre-surgery strokes on her skin like he had done to so many other women — tiny scratches to lead him where he needed to go. He looked down at her chest and she nodded. Trying not to smile or even worse, swoon, he carefully opened her gown to expose her bare breasts. He clenched his teeth and leaned himself towards her. Then, he softly made some lines to ensure symmetry. They smiled shyly when he was done. Finally, he made the dots under her chin where the liposuction rods would go in and some black lines on the sides of her nose and around her eyes for the lift.

"I think you're all ready, Aggie."

"Thank you again, Frank," she said, her face marked up like a Raggedy Ann doll's. "I think you are a special man too, and I . . ."

She fell asleep mid-sentence. The sedatives had taken effect.

As he stood over a sleeping Aggie Doyle on the operating table, Frank felt nervous for maybe the first time since before he had started his residency. He had to concentrate very hard to even bring himself to the part of the surgery he had reached. *Wash hands at sink. Enter operating room. Consult with anesthesiologist. Prepare for first procedure.* He was stuck at the point where he had a scalpel in his hand and was preparing to make an incision on the first of Aggie's breasts. *Ask the nurse to pull back the gown. Make incision.* He looked down at her breasts, her small light nipples, the gentle curves, thinking about what it would be like to have the weight of them in his hands. *Make incision.* He asked the nurse to wipe his brow, and looked towards his anesthesiologist for him to acknowledge that everything was all right. He did. *Make incision.* He noticed that his hand was shaking a little bit, probably not visible to anyone in the room but he could definitely sense the slight wobble in his fingers. He dropped his head downwards, looking intently at Aggie's body, wanting to shake her awake, to tell her to get up, go out for lunch with him, anything to avoid having him do this to her.

He'd stood over hundreds of sleeping faces before, almost every day, but for some reason, he could not make his hand move. Could not do what he needed to do to make Aggie feel that she too was beautiful, that she too had value in this superficial world; he just couldn't—

"Dr. Ganji, are you okay?" It was his nurse's voice. It seemed as though a couple of minutes had passed without him making any moves. Aggie's gown was open and her bare skin exposed.

"Yes, yes, I'm okay." He cleared his throat beneath his mask. "I was just thinking about, how, maybe, well, there is more information I need from this patient. I'm not sure I feel confident enough to perform this surgery."

"Not sure?"

"I don't . . . no, I simply cannot perform this surgery at this time." Frank put the scalpel back on the tray and the nurse just stared down at it, not speaking. "Well, what are you waiting for? Tidy up!"

The nurse's eyebrows were crinkled and her blue eyes wide. She looked at him a couple seconds more and then leaned down to close up Aggie's gown. "Yes, yes, sir," she mumbled.

"Bring her back, Roger," he said to the anesthesiologist, who nodded and put down his fishing magazine. "Let me know when she's awake." Frank flicked off his rubber gloves with two defiant snaps, reached down and rubbed his bare finger across one of Aggie's cheeks, and left.

The clock on the wall of his office was ticking very loudly as he waited — he wondered if it was broken, if perhaps the sound was louder than usual. He fidgeted in his seat for a while before standing up and making tiny laps around his desk. His phone rang two different times but he didn't answer it. He pushed the mute button and then he chewed on the fingernails on his pointers like he used to do when he was a little boy. Finally, there was a knock on the door.

"She's awake," the nurse said, her mask gone but her suspicion remaining. "She's in room three."

"Thank you." His voice was formal and almost in a whisper like maybe he had something to hide. "I'll be right there." Before he went to see her, he turned back into his office briefly and pulled open the drawer of his desk, popping a Tic Tac into his mouth and swiping his tongue across his teeth.

Her eyes were still closed when he reached her bedside. He placed his hand on her arm softly and said her name like he was waking a child. He held his breath as her eyelashes floated upwards.

"Frank," she said sleepily. "It's all over?" He nodded. His stomach was churning so much he was afraid she could hear it.

"It's done, Aggie. You did fine." She brought her hands to her face, pushing her fingers slowly along the skin.

"But . . . I was expecting bandages. How is it possible that I feel so good?" She then lowered her hands down to her breasts, where she prodded along the sides and pushed into her nipples through her hospital gown. "I can't notice much difference," she said. "When I stand?" Her voice was so desperate and childlike that Frank pulled in his lips and nodded just to see her smile again.

"Thank you, Frank." Then she put her hand on his wrist. Her fingertips were soft and warm. "Now, bring me a mirror, I want to see!"

"Aggie, why don't you just recover from the anesthetic first . . . and then we can have a chat about how things went in there?"

"Don't worry, Frank! I know there will be swelling and all that. I just want to see my new nose and neck. Don't deny a girl this pleasure!" She was being a bit flirty with him and he was afraid that maybe he didn't deserve it. Or that she would change her mind when—

A mirror appeared in Aggie's hands.

"Oh thank you, nurse!" she said. Frank narrowed his eyes at the back of the nurse's head as she walked away. Aggie turned back towards the mirror and upon seeing herself, her expression turned empty and expressionless. "I . . . I don't understand," she said, watching herself trace her lips over the words.

"Aggie, let me explain . . ." Frank began. "It's just that when I got you under and I was about to do what you wanted, well, something held me back. I think, perhaps, Aggie, that you were not meant to have these procedures. That maybe it would take someone like me to tell you that you didn't need it for you to actually believe that you are beautiful just as you are."

"You couldn't do it." Her statement was cold. She was still staring at herself.

"I'm sorry." Frank shifted uncomfortably where he stood.

"Do you know, Dr. Ganji, what it is like to know that you are going to be put asleep and cut open?" She looked at him. She wasn't smiling.

"No, Aggie. I can't say that I know that, but I do have a lot of experience with other women who are facing—"

"Do you know, Dr. Ganji, what it's like to put most of the money you have into a surgery meant to take years off your life . . . to give you a new chance, only to wake up and find that nothing was done. Nothing at all!"

"Aggie, please . . . I can assure you that this is for the better. I never would have forgiven myself if—"

"Oh, you're not going to forgive yourself all right," she said. "You're definitely not going to forgive yourself when you hear from my lawyer. When I slap you with a lawsuit so big that you'll be lucky if you're ever able to operate again." Her voice trailed out. There was a tear threatening to fall from her eye.

"Aggie, I'll make it up to you. We can try it again, really, if that's what you want."

"And if you can't do it that time? What am I supposed to do, just close my eyes and hope for the best?" She looked up at Frank and he too felt tears in his eyes.

"I don't know what to say, Aggie. This has never happened before."

"And it will never happen again, not with me." She raised her hand and wiped at the tears that were now making their way down her cheeks. She wouldn't look at him.

"Make sure you talk with the nurse about—" He stopped himself from saying the familiar words about follow-up care. She wouldn't need any of that.

"Just go, Frank."

He did. He walked back down the hall, the one he had covered with pictures he had taken of the spring flowers growing on the patio of his condo building. He kept his vision focused on the small space in front of him and on avoiding anyone else's gaze. He felt his breathing increasing with every step and his heart tightening as he closed his office door.

He sat down at his desk. He looked around the room, barely able to focus on the things he saw: his medical diplomas on the wall by the window, his "before and after" poster board of past clients. And on his desk, a framed photo of his parents — his father had the same menacing look of disapproval he always wore — and one of his cat that had died in the spring. Frank concentrated hard on his breath, willing himself to take at least four seconds of air and let it out for four seconds until he felt more balanced. He scratched at the hair on his knuckles, pinching his lips like he was a little boy who had just been scolded. Eventually, he picked up the hand mirror he kept in his drawer — the one he gave to new patients so they could examine themselves.

He looked into his own dark eyes. Like many of his patients, he too had crow's feet in the outer edges. His skin had grown less vibrant, his hairline receding. He wondered if perhaps it was time to get some work done on himself?

The phone rang. It was Frank's father, shouting at him before even saying hello.

"What's this I hear from your mother about you cutting down your hours at the clinic?"

"Hello, Father."

"It is unacceptable. There are only so many years, Frank. Only so much time for you to make a name for yourself, to establish your practice, to the make the investments in your future, in your family's future. This is not the time to be self-indulgent, lazy, distracted—"

"I'm not lazy, Father."

"It's just that your mother and I are concerned. We've seen how things can fall apart even when you think you have checked every box. You have to stay at it, son! You must fulfill your commitment to this job. Stay married to your job. There is room for nothing else!"

"I will make you proud, Father," he said to make him stop. "I will do everything in my power to continue to make you proud."

"Just do not cut down on your hours, Frank. Not one bit."

"I have to go now, Father. I have a surgery in ten minutes and I must prepare."

"Your mother sends her love, Frank. She is praying for you."

"I really have to go."

They both hung up without saying goodbye.

Frank tapped on his desk. *Snap out of this, snap out of this. She's only a woman.*

He brought his warm hands to his face and covered his mouth and nose, breathing in all he had touched that day. His thumbs traced up and down his jawline as he tried to remember the last time he felt loved — not a superficial, "thank you for fixing my face" love, but a real love that warmed him and nurtured him. It was, he had decided, not since falling asleep in his mother's arms as a child that he had felt that. He closed his eyes, took one last cleansing breath, and pretended to be there again.

Losing Him

Gladys needed a man like Harry to protect her from her own body. When they married, she was certain that if she could see past his pudgy tummy, then he would overlook her thick arms and wide hips; their acceptance of each other meant that they were each perfectly lovely in another person's eyes. They could spend evenings cuddled under two sleeping bags zipped together, eating potato chips and drinking cherry cola. They could dine at the all-you-can-eat Chinese buffet and shuffle home together in the dark. They could complain about their bodies in unison — how they were both so round and buckled.

But after nine years together, nine years of eating sundaes drenched in caramel, lying too long in the bed, and skipping the after-dinner walk, Harry's body staged a revolt.

Gladys found him naked on the floor of the bathroom. He had

fallen out of the shower, white soapsuds still dripping halfway down his back, thick black hair clogging up his ears and butt crack. When she found him he didn't seem to be breathing. She placed the flat of her hand on his soapy back, her fingers slipping as she stroked him. He was perfectly still and he looked blue, with some pasty white parts still under the folds of his skin where the sun never got in.

Gladys walked to the kitchen as fast as her round calves would allow her. She punched the numbers on the phone with her wet fingertips and told the woman on the other end what had happened. Then, she sat down on the floor beside Harry and waited for the ambulance. Her oversized parachute dress ballooned up around her. She decided she shouldn't move him, but didn't know how she could have. She stroked his wet hair and kissed him on the shaggy goatee covering his chin.

Harry's doctor said he was lucky to have made it to the hospital alive. Fat had clogged his arteries and his heart was barely pumping. Gladys only cared about the part of Harry below the fat — the part that used to send her flowers at work when she had a job at a government call centre, the part that laughed when she joked, comforted her when she was frustrated, and bought her the sweetest, most complimentary birthday cards. These were the only parts she wanted to remain intact.

With a deep swipe of his wrinkled brow, the doctor said Harry wouldn't have long to live if he stayed at his current weight of four hundred and ten pounds. Something drastic had to be done if he was going to survive. And of course, Gladys wanted him to.

Gastric bypass surgery — the name sounded ominous when Gladys first pondered it, sitting on a wooden bench outside Harry's doctor's office. As Harry had blood taken, she waited and said the words out loud. "Gastric," her mouth moving around the bloated, floating sound, "bypass," her clenched teeth barely letting the two syllables pass from her throat, "surgery." The more she thought about it, the more panic poured over her thoughts.

Three months later, when Harry was getting ready to go in for his operation, Gladys stood beside his gurney and looked into his marbled green eyes. "I love you, Harry, don't ever change," she said. "I am nothing without you." She took his plump hand in hers. Harry just nodded weakly and drifted off on a wave of narcotics.

It took him an hour to wake up from the surgery. Gladys waited in the yellow room with blue seats, crunching on a hunk of peanut brittle she had stashed in her purse and gulping down Mountain Dew from the buzzing vending machine in the hall — she always ate that way when she was nervous. When a small girl eating a banana stared at her with squinted eyes and crinkled nose, Gladys threw her a disgusted scowl. *Get your mom to teach you some manners*, she thought and sunk down further in her chair.

When they wheeled Harry back into his room, sticky bandage wrapped around his middle, Gladys stood by his side as he floated in and out of consciousness. On the outside he looked the same, but inside, she knew things were different. She put her ear to the blue, pulsing veins on his right arm, hoping to hear something familiar rushing through his blood stream. Lying motionless, he seemed more active than he had ever been. She squatted down on a slippery stool to relieve some of her own aching weight, her bottom flowing off each side of the seat.

After taking Harry home, his food portions had shrunk to barely noticeable: a tiny helping of vegetables, a miniscule blob of baked beans, and a smidgen of pork chop. His stomach was a quarter of the size it used to be, and Gladys's was exactly the same.

At first, she was excited about this new start for both of them. They had been overlooking their health for far too long. It was time for them to stop being overwhelmed by their heredity, their medical problems, and their lazy habits. She was sure that they could revitalize their bodies together.

She started eating smaller meals with Harry, but afterwards, she still felt hungry so she snuck extra helpings and heavily buttered rolls when Harry was downstairs watching evening television. After that, she'd find herself with the freezer open, just moving a spoon around the ice cream carton and eating until the top was smooth — then spooning the rest of the tub into her mouth. When Harry came up for bed, she'd have chocolate chunks ground into the grooves of her gums and sugar on her breath.

"Night, Gladys," he'd say on his way upstairs, and she'd hug him with her mouth closed, not allowing herself to smile.

"I'm so proud of you, Harry," she'd say. "It takes so much will power to do what you're doing. I wish I had it."

"Just be you," he'd say back, tapping her on the head.

Harry's wounds healed and he eventually started getting up before sunrise to take power walks to the community arena and back. The first time Gladys lifted her eyelids and found him gone, she felt like a cow sleeping too long in the pasture, waking up to find she had been abandoned. Her heart raced at the new space between them — a gap that seemed to be spreading with each pound that her husband lost.

Harry lost fifty pounds in the first two months after surgery. Gladys told him he looked great, and he gloated as he stuck his hand inside the waistband of his now sagging jeans. He lost forty-five more pounds over the next two months and on his urging, Gladys made some of the recipes his doctor had recommended: couscous with beans, egg white omelets with asparagus, and green salad with tuna. At each meal, Harry ate one small helping and Gladys ate three, plus an extra meal she had made for herself: usually hot dogs, pizza, or pasta with extra sauce. Five months after the surgery, Harry had lost one-hundred and five pounds, and Gladys had gained ten.

Ten months after the surgery, as Gladys sat in the La-Z-Boy putting a stitch in the elastic on Harry's green sweatpants to tighten them, he mentioned that maybe she should start walking with him in the mornings. "It would probably be good for you to lose a few pounds too — just look how energetic I feel!"

These were the words that Gladys had been dreading; the ones she knew were inevitable.

"Are you saying you don't like the way I look?" Gladys said, tears blistering in her eyes, her needle and thread dangling precariously in mid-air.

"I just wish we could get out together sometimes, unless you don't want to."

"You know that's not true!" Gladys shouted out.

"Fine. I can do it alone," he said, pretending to pout.

Harry had started taking his walks later in the day, when the bright sun and small-town gossipers were out to judge him. As Harry shrunk down to a thirty-eight waistline and a trim two hundred and forty pounds, people stopped staring and pointing at him.

In fact, he fit in like any other man out for a walk. Gladys watched him from the window as he skipped back up their cobblestone path, a smile stuck wide across his face.

"I've decided to sign up for a swing dance class," Harry announced one night, twelve months and one-hundred-and-sixty lost pounds after surgery. "It's time to see what this new body can do."

"But who will be your partner?" Gladys said.

"You, if you like, otherwise I'm sure they could assign someone."

"What makes you want to do this all of a sudden?" Gladys said.

"I just do."

"I hope people don't laugh. You know, because you're so small and I'm still so big."

"Just ignore them, okay, Gladys?"

"I'll try," Gladys said, although she knew that she was lying to him. She could never ignore the people who made fun of her — it went in too deep.

Turned out, Harry had talent as a swing dancer; he swayed, shimmied, and step-ball-changed around the floor while Gladys struggled alongside, stepping on her own swollen feet and knocking her large breasts against Harry's chest each time he swung her weight around. Out on the dance floor on the arm of her svelte husband, Gladys felt like a clumsy elephant being escorted around by a graceful giraffe in a green golf shirt. They had become two opposite creatures, and she danced with what felt like a hundred eyes glued to her butt cheeks. She flushed a bright shade of crimson and decided five times in her mind she would quit. She stayed because she still couldn't bear to see Harry dancing with any other woman besides her.

When it came time to practise the "lift" — where the woman spreads her legs and jumps up onto the man's waist — Gladys knew gravity would not comply. Kristi, the petite blond who was teaching the class, approached and asked if Harry would like to try the lift with her, because Gladys looked like she was getting tired. Although Gladys did need a break, she stood in the middle of the dance floor and drilled an imaginary hole between Kristi's pretty blue eyeballs. She thought about pushing Kristi to the ground and sitting on her until her skinny guts oozed onto the floor, but decided it was better not to draw any more attention to herself.

After another round, Gladys gave in and sat herself on the bottom bench of a row of bleachers in the studio. Panting heavily from trying to keep up with Harry, she watched as her husband of ten years smoothly lifted one hundred and five pounds of blond into the air. When Kristi's legs straddled his hips, Harry's face was wide with excitement, like he was on a Cuban vacation or had just won a new sound system for his car.

Later that night, Harry asked Gladys if she would like to spend some time holding each other naked under the sheets. They would turn the lights off, of course. She told him she was too tired from dancing. As Harry turned over to sleep, Gladys nestled her ear close to the back of his head, hoping she could hear what was going on inside.

The following week, she convinced Harry to go to dance class on his own. Through a fake grin, Gladys told him she had to take her mother out for dinner.

"The poor woman is so depressed since my father died. I'm sure Kristi will fill in as your partner."

"I'm sorry you feel that way," Harry said, but he agreed and left for class, his shiny black dancing shoes squeezed onto his long feet. Gladys went back into the living room and settled into their worn-out couch, fumbling behind it for the bag of salt and vinegar chips she had hidden the week before.

She told a lie like this each Thursday night for the next six weeks. Harry would ask her to go, but she would find an excuse not to and instead sit in their dimly lit family room. There, she watched cheesy sitcoms about perfect television families — the moms always with flat bellies and perky avocado-shaped breasts. By the seventh week, he stopped asking and instead shook his head at her every time he left the house.

In Gladys's absence, Kristi had been reassigned as Harry's dance partner. Gladys decided he deserved someone like Kristi: young and nimble with a smooth figure. When Harry asked Gladys if she could find time in her hectic schedule to come watch Kristi and him at the studio's annual swing dance recital, Gladys agreed but felt her stomach knot and tension squeeze at the base of her neck.

On the night of the recital, they didn't say one word to each other in the car on the way over to the studio. Instead, Harry whistled some tune Gladys didn't know and drummed his fingers on the steering wheel like he was going over his dance steps in his mind.

"That is so annoying, Harry," she said. "Can you stop it?" He stopped the tapping, but Gladys was sure she could still hear some quiet whistling coming from his mouth. She covered her ears like she used to do as a child when her brother made fun of her for not fitting into her clothes.

At the studio, Gladys once again sat in the bottom row of the stands and watched as Harry threw Kristi around the floor to the sound of big band music coming out of a silver radio on the windowsill. Squinting her eyes, Gladys imagined herself up there with him. She the one with the slim body and rippling muscles, her husband bringing her up in the air in front of the friends and family gathered in the stuffy studio. When Harry looked her way while spinning Kristi under his arm, Gladys slumped down. Waving to him feebly, she bit her bottom lip and looked to the floor.

When the final number was finished and people went to the other room for a reception, Gladys just sat there. She had been struck with a stabbing pain in her left calf during the performance and was still dealing with the ache. As she leaned forward to rub her leg, she could hear the laughter spitting out from the other room. She was certain she could distinguish Harry's throaty laugh and Kristi's high-pitched giggle. She imagined them reminiscing on their performance, hands resting casually on backs, eyes darting quickly down to check out each other's bodies. As tears greeted Gladys's eyes, she heard a loud *click* and the auditorium lights went out.

She sat in the dark, weeping for her failed marriage, the supposed benefit of a miracle operation, and the way her thighs squished out to twice their size when she sat down. She lowered her wide head into her hands and the tears flowed, creating muddy mascara rivers down her cheeks.

When Gladys opened her eyes again, Harry stood in front of her.

"Did you like the show?" he asked. She nodded, and tried to wipe the tears off her cheeks with her fingertips.

"I must look like such a mess," she said. "I had a pain, in my leg, that's all."

Harry took a step closer to her.

"You look wonderful, dear." He gently kissed her forehead and dried her cheeks with the cuff of his blue silk dancing shirt.

"Harry, I . . . I . . ." But she couldn't say anything that she didn't think sounded stupid. Instead, Harry pulled her to her feet and stroked her back. They danced together to the hum of voices from the other room, their faces lit by the red glow of an EXIT sign.

Gladys could feel Harry's breath on her neck as they danced. She smiled, and gave herself permission to finally sink deeper into her husband.

Possessed

I'm pretty sure my new heart hates me. It was supposed to be a gift. My wife and I cried when we got the phone call that I was going to have another chance at life. But now, I am getting the distinct feeling that this new organ beating inside my body wishes it were still nestled under the ribs of its original owner.

I first got this feeling when I was in the hospital after the surgery. I was sitting in my bed, watching TV and listening to the medication drip into my IV when I heard an unfamiliar voice inside my head. Not out loud or in a way that anyone else could hear but me, but I heard it just the same. The voice said one word: loser. The word surprised me when I heard it, but I knew right away that it must have come from the heart. For one, I had never heard this voice before the heart, and the deep tone of the word vibrating within my thoughts was exactly the way I would expect a heart to sound if it could talk. It surprised me that an organ could be so disrespectful, especially when it had just been through so much. So my next question, of course, was why does my new heart think I am a loser? That question could only be answered by the heart. Perhaps the guy who donated it to me was the opposite of a loser, a really cool guy, and now I was just a letdown.

I'm not sure how to tell my wife and son about this, or if I even should. They were both so very excited to see me after the surgery. Even at four years old, Cael still knew that this meant he was going to have his dad around for more soccer games, pizza runs, and rounds of Go Fish. His little face was so sweet in the hospital when he visited. He made me a card, drawing a picture of him and me with a giant red heart on the front. Inside, Margaret had helped him write, "I love you, Dad. Thanks for being you." How could I disappoint a kid after that? It would upset them both so much to learn that my new heart was displeased. They might even think I was crazy if I said that my new organ was out to get me.

Sometimes at night when I'm in bed, I actually think the heart is beating faster just to keep me awake — trying to kill me with exhaustion. And when I try to run on the treadmill that we've set up in the family room, my heart really slows down, making it harder for me to breathe because it hates me so much. I'm trying my best to focus on my recovery, so for now I have chosen to ignore the heart and hope that it will change its mind.

It was a bit surprising for me to learn that I needed a new heart. I'd always considered myself relatively healthy for forty-one. And so when I couldn't work out at the gym because of my laboured breathing and my doctor told me that he found a congenital heart disease, I was astounded. My heart problem had gone undetected for my whole life. Turns out that while everything seemed to be swimming along — job, wife, house, kid — just under the surface, I had a bomb in my chest.

Margaret was scared about my impending surgery, but not really for me — for Cael. She did not want him growing up without a father. She'd once said she'd take an ill-hearted me over no one at all.

I waited on the list for months, taking my immunosuppressants in anticipation. Then one afternoon, the hospital called to say that I needed to get there immediately for pre-op. They had found a heart for me. Everyone waited at the hospital while this unknown and foreign body part was inserted into my chest. When I awoke, Margaret was by my side. "It's all done, Kenneth," she said. "We have everything we ever wanted. We have you."

But now I can clearly see that we do not have everything. I've been home from the hospital for two weeks and this morning as I brushed my teeth in front of the mirror, I heard the heart again.

"I hate you," it said. Could it have been any clearer? When it said it, I felt it speed up, thumping away like it was punching me from the inside.

I've started pacing around the house at night to try and keep this thing quiet.

Margaret has been watching the way I've been acting and has decided to take me back to the doctor. She saw an episode of *The Dr. Oz Show* and figures my agitation and sleeplessness could mean that I am rejecting my heart, despite my having taken all my medication. She's made the emergency appointment with my cardiologist, Dr. Harpoon.

Dr. Harpoon's waiting room is white and tidy. Margaret takes me there, but then decides to wait in the car rather than pay for parking on the street. "I'll just keep driving around so no one can give me a ticket," she said. As I wait, I feel myself growing increasingly more anxious. This new heart is laughing at me from the inside now — a creepy, methodical laugh that rolls on and on. I'm trying to ignore it, read a magazine, smile at someone, and hope they will start a conversation with me, but it won't shut up. Finally, it's my turn to go in.

When I finally have Dr. Harpoon in front of me, I have a hard time speaking. With his stethoscope up to my chest, I ask him what he hears.

"Good rhythm," he says. "Sounds like everything is settling in nicely. You just need more time to totally accept the heart. Keep taking your medication."

"Doctor, I need to ask you an important question."

He nods.

"I know it's probably against the rules, or whatever, but do you have any idea who had this heart before me? I mean, what kind of person was he? Should he be someone that I should feel intimidated by, or—"

He starts shaking his head before I can finish my rambling

question. "I'm sorry, Ken. You know that information is classified. All I can tell you is that it was a healthy male who suffered a head trauma."

My heart is sad when he says that; I feel it through my whole body. That's when I realize that it's not so much that the heart hates me, but that it just really, really loved its old owner. But where does that leave me? Trapped.

"Just say a little prayer of thanks for the great gift of organ donation," the doctor says then. "One person's loss is definitely your gain in this case."

I get up and follow Dr. Harpoon towards the door, but stop as he turns the handle. I am sweating, my eyes feel buggy, and I am clutching my hands together.

"Doctor, please. I need to know . . ."

"Yesssss?" he says, turning around and looking at me over his glasses.

"Have you ever heard of a heart not working right because it is too attached to its former owner?" I take a short breath and a step away from him like I'm expecting him to hit me or something. I can't believe I've said it.

He pauses, looks inquisitively towards the ceiling, and then continues to turn the door handle. As he leaves the room he says in a low voice like a father scolding his two-year-old: "No. That is scientifically impossible."

As soon as Margaret and I arrive home, I go straight to our office and boot up the computer. I am certain that there must be another way to rid myself of the negativity spewing out into me from this heart.

So I google it: *demons, bad energy, spirit.*

And it comes up clearly in front of me . . . "Madame Grady, the voodoo lady. Ridding negative energy through voodoo cleansing." I copy the number onto the back of one of Cael's drawings and stuff the paper into my pocket just in case.

"What's that all about?" Margaret asks. She's standing behind me, looking over my shoulder and down into the computer screen. I scramble to press the Escape button on the keyboard.

"Nothing," I say like she's just caught me drinking a bottle of Scotch at the breakfast table. "I'm just surfing around."

"Voodoo, Kenny?" She's got her head tilted to the side, her lips pressed together, and her hand on her hip.

"I saw it in a movie last night, that's all. Is there something wrong with being interested?" I hear Cael's voice from down the hall.

"Mommy!" he yells. "I need you to get that down!"

"Well," she says, "Maybe you could think about being a little more interested in your son instead."

"Give me a break, Margaret."

"Isn't he the reason we did all this?" She motions to my chest and I bring my hand to my heart — afraid of what it might say.

"I'm not sure how much more of this strange behaviour Cael and I can take."

"I'll spend more time with him, I promise."

She tsks and leaves.

The heart thinks it's all hilarious, and I tell it to shut up.

That night, I don't sleep at all. I just lie there staring at the back of Margaret's head in the dark, thinking about how she doesn't deserve to have a husband who is agitated and tense all the time. After what she has been through with my surgery, and the way she stood at my bedside and fed me soft foods with a plastic spoon, she deserves me back one hundred percent. Cael does too. He needs a dad who can stop listening to the voices in his head long enough to take him to the park, help him with his homework, and make tiny forts out of blankets and couch cushions.

Thump, thump, thump, says my heart from inside me in the dark.

"I'm going to get you!" I find myself saying out loud. It wakes Margaret up.

"What did you say?" she asks groggily.

"I can't sleep," I tell her. "I'm going to get up for a while."

She rolls back over. "Whatever, Kenny. Just keep it down."

I sit in the La-Z-Boy in the family room without moving. I watch infomercials and bad movies and try to distract myself. I keep my hand over my chest and can feel my heart hitting my fingers from the inside like it's threatening to get out.

In the morning, when Margaret is taking Cael to school, I decide I have to call the voodoo lady — for their sake if not my own. I dial the number in a rush and the voice on the other end says she can fit me in that afternoon.

I tell Margaret I am going to the library to read up about the long-term effects of heart transplants, and she nods, even putting her hand on my arm and saying, "Do what you have to do to get through this. Something has to change here, Kenny."

"I know, Margaret. It will. I promise."

I take the subway to Christie Station and then walk to Madame Grady's house — a broken-down brick townhouse at the end of a sleepy side street. When I get to the door she is waiting for me.

"Well, hello there," she says from the doorway. She is only as tall as my chest, has huge red hoop earrings and pink lipstick that shines on her dark face. "So, you're the man with the broken heart," she says.

I am stunned silent by her question, and then squeak out, "Heart? How did you know about . . . ?"

"No worries," she said, grabbing me by my forearms and ushering me through the tall wooden door of the house, "'Tis just my intuition is all."

It is then that I have my first feelings of hope since the heart started calling me names. This woman, this voodoo priestess, or Madame, could have the power to make this organ stop bugging me.

I sit on the crusty orange couch in her living room and she at a small table and chair near the door. I begin to interview her like I would a new hire at work:

"So how long have you been into voodoo?"

"Oh, my whole life, dear. I was initiated in Haiti, where I grew up. Came to Toronto in 1972 to live with my Aunt Rhonda. She's gone now, crossed over."

"And so, you have good success with, you know, getting rid of bad energy and spirits and all that?"

"Ah, yes," she says as she begins laying out playing cards in front of her on the table.

"Do you have any references perhaps? Someone who can vouch for the work you do?"

But she isn't listening to me anymore. She is studying the cards on the table like she has my body sliced open on the table. A silence hangs between us for probably five minutes before she speaks.

"So, you've been ill," she says. "But you've recently received the help you needed to get better?"

"Yes, I had an operation a few months back."

"You seem well, but this operation, it didn't go as well as you planned?" She looks up at me, her eyes serious, her pink lips pinched together.

I feel tears in my eyes despite myself. I open my mouth to speak, but she raises her hand to stop me, her gnarled knuckles hanging in the air. Her eyes close then, like she is watching something on the insides of her eyelids.

"This heart. This new heart is not content."

I put my hand on my chest, hoping she isn't making it mad.

"You have to rid the spirit that is still attached to this organ."

Relief floods over me. Finally I am not alone. I have found someone, this little Haitian woman, who understands.

"Have you seen this before?"

She raises and drops her eyebrows. "I can fix for you. Two hundred bucks."

"Do you take Visa?" I ask instantly. To me, it is a small price to pay to get rid of the torment I am in.

"Yes, or debit," she says, hauling up her machine from her feet and dropping it on the table with a clunk. "Does your card have a chip?"

I hand her my card, press "yes" to the two hundred bucks, and sit back down on the couch while my receipt prints. "Will it take long?"

"That's not up to us," she says, grabbing my hand and leading me towards the back of the house. "It's up to the heart," she whispers as she pushes me into the dark.

Three hours later I find myself naked in a tub of sludge in Madame Grady's bathroom. Through the light from the candles placed around the room, I stare at my naked white knees, which poke up from the dark water. The scar on my chest leads down into the grime. The water is warm but my hair is wet and cold from the cleansing. I feel something brush up against my foot and realize that Madame Grady has thrown in one of the chicken heads that she had been beating against me. Despite the strange water in this strange place, and the peculiar ritual I have just endured at the hands of this small laughing woman, I'm still hopeful about what is going to happen next.

Madame Grady pushes the door open then without knocking. She stands with her bare feet on my pile of crumpled up clothes on the floor.

"You saying those chants like I said, Kenny?"

"Trying to," I say. "What you did back there . . . I think it might be working."

She smiles without teeth, her brown eyes crinkling in caution. "Just stay there," she says. "We'll know more soon."

When Madame Grady leaves me alone again, I close my eyes

and try to concentrate on the strange words that she had asked me to say. "Damballa, Damballa, give me the power back," I whisper into the air around me. The water is starting to grow cold and there is a smell of alcohol, raw meat, and unidentified herbs in the air. There is a pipe rattling somewhere in the house. The clanging seems somewhat ominous to me, an impending problem that gets louder as the minutes go on . . . *bang . . . bang . . . bang, bang, bang.*

That's when I hear it. My heart. It is laughing. Taunting me from underneath my ribcage, speaking its own chant: *Loser, loser*, it says over and over. *Get me out of here or I'm going to kill you.*

———

Madame Grady does not offer a money-back guarantee, but she does say that I can try again in a few months if it is still bothering me. She leaves me wet and smelly on her front porch, the cool spring air blowing right through my jacket to my raw and throbbing skin. I know I will have to sneak past Margaret before she smells me and make sure she doesn't catch a glimpse of the red marks on my back from where Madame Grady tried to batter this thing out of me.

I trudge my way back to the subway. My heart is still mocking me, which makes the situation seem even more pathetic.

What a bunch of bullshit I have gotten myself into.

It is clear that my heart is not going to give up and I know I can't wait another few months to try again. Something tells me that this thing isn't going anywhere until I figure out just how to make the heart happy.

I call Margaret on my cell phone and tell her that I'm going out with a couple of the guys from the bank.

"Okay, then," she says from the other end of the phone. "I guess I'll go ahead and feed Cael and put him to bed."

"I'll do it tomorrow, Margaret. I swear."

I walk around blocks and weave up and down alleys until the sun goes down and the stars and club-goers come out, but I still haven't escaped it. When I get back to the house, Margaret and the Cael are asleep — they're both probably tucked up in bed so sweetly. I close the door quietly and sit at the kitchen table in the dark. There is a rumbling in my chest. My heart? No, actually, I think I'm hungry. I find some Ruffles chips and crunch on them while hanging off the ticking of the kitchen clock.

Tick, tick, tick. Thump, thump, thump.

I can't stop thinking about it and can't undress myself from the feeling that something really bad is about to happen. I see a carving knife on the counter and momentarily think about plunging it into my chest, letting my guts flow out. But that's what the heart would want, isn't it? To end me.

This heart will not win. I go upstairs into Cael's bathroom and undress in front of the mirror. It's funny how by looking at me, people would think I was the same man I used to be before my operation. Except for this red scar down the centre of my chest, I might still be good ol' Kenny — always early to work, watches golf on weekends, takes his kid to Chuck E. Cheese's birthday parties, loves his wife enough to stay faithful. It could be the same old Kenny, but the more I look at myself, and feel the organ bouncing inside my body, the more I feel that I will never be the same. As long as this hateful piece of meat is inside me, I will never be the whole of who I was. A piece of me will always be missing.

I pull back Cael's ducky shower curtain, lean down to turn on the taps, and then let the water stream from the shower. I step in, pick up Cael's Johnson & Johnson soap, and squeeze some into my hand, rubbing hard on my skin. As I'm cleaning off, I'm hit with the feeling that I have to tell Margaret what is going on — now. It may be one in the morning, but she needs to know that if it's what's inside that counts, then, well, my surgeon has rendered me utterly worthless. She loves me. Maybe she can think of some way out of this.

I get out of the shower, towel off, and slip on a T-shirt and track pants that are hanging on the back of the door. I open the bathroom door, take a step into the hall, and before I can reach our bedroom, am struck down by a pain that feels like I have been shot in the chest. I fall to the floor on the hallway, clutching the place where the new heart lives, thinking that this is it . . . the heart has finally decided to try and get out of me.

Will it rip my skin open until I bleed?

Will it pound its way onto the carpet and leave me in a broken heap on the floor for my family to find?

I'm panicked and folded over in the hallway while the heart rebels inside me. Its voice is getting louder and louder in my mind. It's swearing, it's mad, it just . . . can't . . . take it anymore.

And neither can I. I stand up and run down the stairs, through the kitchen, and into my backyard. It's black except for one small light on our neighbour's porch.

"Ahhhhhhhh!" I yell, collapsing into the cool grass, my hands clutched to my chest. I try to escape the pain within by concentrating on the smell of dark soil. "I can't do this anymore!" I say to the heart. "But if I go, you go!"

I hit myself over and over in the chest, right over my scar. I pound on myself until I am too weak to even lift my arms. By the time my exhaustion has made it hard to stay awake, I have beaten myself up and the heart isn't saying anything.

I wake up. It's morning. There is something sitting on me. A small boy. It takes me a minute to realize that it's my son Cael. He's carrying a bucket and a shovel and asking me to play with him.

My heart is still inside my chest. It's quiet. It's beating like any man's would.

"You scoop up the sand and I'll make it into a castle," Cael says. I nod and look up at him, shielding my eyes from the morning sun.

"Is there any reason why you slept on the lawn last night?" It's Margaret. She's standing on the porch. I look up and see her still in her nightgown, her legs long and white, her red hair messy and hanging down onto her shoulders. She squints into the light and rings her hands in front of her. "Do we need to go back to the doctor, Kenny?"

"No, Margaret," I say, sitting up and looking at her with a serious, unwavering stare. I do a quick scan of my body, looking for any pain or tension. My skin is tender on my chest, but underneath feels okay for the first time since the surgery. "I think I'm better," I say. "I think it could all be over." I bring my hand to my mouth and breathe into it. I still smell like Madame Grady's bathtub, but there is a new peace inside me — a calm.

Cael is in his sandbox, pouring sand from a bucket and making a small pile. I stand up, steady myself by putting both of my arms out to the sides, and take my first tentative steps over to help him.

As She Was

HER MOTHER

I entered St. Michael's Hospital in a panic, thrust into an in-between world that cut me off from everything. The phone had woken me from a deep sleep, but for all I knew, it wasn't the first time it had rung. It intruded itself into my dreams and created confusion that gave way to the panic that comes from a 3 a.m. phone call. A phone call at that hour usually means one of two things: someone is hurt, or someone is dead.

I thought she was home. I thought she was asleep in her bed by then.

And soon, I stumbled down the hallway into the Intensive Care Unit, searching manically through the numbers beside each room, looking for the one they had given me at the front desk.

Her door had a sign on it — No Stimulation — and through the tiny window I could see that the lights were low inside. I pushed open the door, looking for my daughter's face. When I saw her, I screamed. My legs buckled underneath me and a nurse ran over and grabbed me by the arm, trying to help me up.

"It's my fault, it's my fault," I shouted into the trauma room. "I shouldn't have let her go."

"We're monitoring her cranial pressure," the nurse said. This was her only response to my shocked white expression. She tried to hide the pity, tucking it down with a bite of her bottom lip.

Rebecca was hidden within a spiderweb of tubes. They came out of her nose, her mouth, the top of her head. Her long brown hair had been shaved and she had a gauze bandage wrapped around her skull. She had blood smeared and dried on her forehead and in her eyebrows. Her eyes were closed. The only thing I could recognize were her hot pink fingernails; she had been painting them on the couch last night before she went out, stroke by stroke, like she was covering up a part of her.

"Is she, is she . . . ?" I stammered.

"She just came out of surgery. We'll know more when she wakes up," the nurse said, trying to smile.

That really pissed me off. "Wipe that pathetic grin off your face!" I screamed. "Can't you see my daughter is destroyed! There is nothing to be happy about."

I sat down beside Rebecca's bed, my mind jumping back and forth from devastation to denial. I held her hand, wiping at the dark bits under her fingernails with my own fingertips.

"Becky, it's me, Mom. Can you hear me? You must be starving.

I know I am. Would you like me to run to the cafeteria and get you something to eat?"

No response.

"Are you cold? Do you need a drink?"

Nothing. From my only daughter, nothing.

"Did you have a good night, dear? Did you have fun with Chris and Enid?"

The slow, deep sucking of the breathing machines, peppered with the sporadic and alarming beeping of the medical equipment around us was the only reply. She was silent and still like she was having the best, deepest, and most all-encompassing nap of her life. A nap, from which I feared she would never wake.

———————

I sat in the hospital cafeteria, watching an old man with a stubbly grey beard try to scoop squash soup into his mouth. Each spoonful seemed more painful than the next. Up to the mouth, then the old grizzled head tilted forward, then *sllllluuuuurrp*.

"Keep it down!" I finally yelled out at him. He looked at me, unfazed, and continued his painful snack. For all I knew, it was the first thing he had eaten in days, but I certainly didn't care. My head was aching and I wanted a drink.

Becky had been asleep for two days. This, they assured me, was to be expected after an injury like hers, but that certainly doesn't help a mother. Not at a time like that. I had been considering who I should call to come to the hospital — Mom and Dad were still in Vancouver visiting my aunt, my friend Vicki couldn't very well bring the two kids with her, and everyone else, well, I just didn't really want to deal with them at that point. I didn't want to explain anything; I wanted to keep this tragedy hidden, to keep her to myself as long as I could.

I did make a few phone calls.

I called Ray at the Gap, to let him know that Rebecca would not be in for any more of her shifts until further notice, and I called Chris's mom, Irene. I found the number in the phone book hanging in the hallway. The nurse who called had told me that Chris had been brought in too. A motorcycle? That was the part I couldn't believe.

"He's out of hospital," Irene said on the phone, and I felt my rage boiling in my pit. "Just kept him for observation really, and he's home."

"Mmm-hmm," I had hummed into my cell phone.

"He's been asking about Becky."

"I'll bet."

"I haven't gotten too many details out of him, but I know he feels really bad about what happened."

"Does he?"

"He says that things were so frantic when the ambulance arrived, he didn't even get to talk to her. Do you think she'll be home soon?"

"Hard to say," I said. "How do you define soon?"

"Like, within the next few days?"

"I don't think so," I said, my eyes sockets soaking with tears.

"Chris really is sorry, Candy."

"Tell him . . . that I want him to stay the hell away from my daughter."

Then, I hung up.

I made a third phone call the next night. This time to Chris himself. I got his number from Becky's cell phone (the police had brought me some of her things from the scene of the accident). I called him after watching the nurse change my daughter's breathing tube and put another new IV in her soft pink wrist. I called him after the doctor told me that I should start preparing myself for the worst. So I don't blame myself at all for being hard on him when we spoke. It was late. I was exhausted. I needed an outlet and he was it.

I wrapped my hand around the Styrofoam cup that was holding my coffee. The old man had finished his soup and left. The cafeteria was almost empty by that time. The dinner rush was over and it was too early for a late snack.

I would have always been by her bed if they had let me, but they shooed me out of the room every day at that time so the doctors could do their tests, try to gauge her responsiveness.

It killed me not to be in there. To leave her alone. I wanted her to know that I would always be by her side. But out of the room, I could feel my hope start to grow — hope that this might all be a dream, or that better yet, it was real, but it was almost over and she would wake up, get dressed, and come home with me. And that in another year, she'd be off to university like she planned —York, for social work so she could show her father just what he missed out on, and how I was able to do it all on my own, no problem.

I had a muffin on a white plate in front of me, untouched. It was old and crusty around the edges like it had been sitting out there most of the day. I stared at it hoping it would disappear, preferably into me so I would be able to live a bit longer. But only long enough to find out what was going to happen next.

I thought about how strange it was to be in here for so long, how it seemed to cut everything out and stop time — kind of like when you're at a casino, or a spa. It was silly that I was all alone at the hospital, keeping her injury a secret, hoping no one would find out. But I think that was my way of coping. If I didn't have to talk about it yet, then it wasn't real, there was still a possibility of this all reversing itself.

That maybe Becky didn't go out that night at all. Maybe she stayed home like I wanted her to.

"You don't own me!" she had yelled out. "I'll be fine to go to work tomorrow, Mother."

"Becky, get your sorry ass back in your bedroom."

"Why don't you worry about yourself for once," she had said.

I lunged towards her then, without ever making the decision to do it. I pushed her, hard, with both my hands on her small shoulders. She fell back and landed on the couch, looking up at me with those same blue eyes that had cried in my direction when she was a baby. She was hurt; not her body, just her feelings. And without saying anything, she grabbed her backpack and hurried out the door, leaving me alone in our apartment.

I let her go because quite honestly I had scared myself by doing that. And I have to admit that I was a little drunk at that point, but I only had a few drinks to unwind after work. And I can't really say why I didn't want her to go so bad. I knew that Enid would be there, and Chris, well, I figured he was harmless enough despite his mumbling.

"Ms. Foster?" It was a woman's voice, one of the nurses who had checked Becky's vitals that afternoon. She had come to find me.

I nodded at her, still clutching my coffee, not an ounce gone from the cup.

"Ms. Foster, the doctor would like to talk to you. Rebecca is waking up."

Rebecca was born in the bathroom of a McDonald's restaurant on the Danforth. It was 3 a.m., and I had just had a horrible argument with her father, Quinn.

I had never intended for her to come out of me in the bathroom. I was just hanging out there for a bit after fighting with Quinn, thinking that my stomach pains were because of him taking a dagger to my future, and not my labour. After all, I was not due to have the baby for another month.

No one really plans to have a baby at age sixteen. Well, maybe somewhere in the world, but certainly not in Toronto in the 1980s. So when I found out, it took me a long time to tell anyone. Quinn and I had only been dating each other for three months before it happened — and by dating, I mean, hanging out after school in a group of our friends and sneaking into the bushes on evening walks along the Don River. A baby was not really something I had factored into my grade ten year. My parents hadn't either, and when my mother finally guessed (after noticing how little I was eating and how tired I was), she lectured me, cried, yelled at me, and then gave me a hug and started planning. She wanted me to have an abortion, but I, being a strong-willed type who hated to even squash an ant under my sneaker, said I could never, ever do something like that to a baby. That I would never be able to live with myself afterwards.

So I decided to have the baby. I decided this before even

informing Quinn that he was going to be a father, that one of our late-evening grunt sessions had been much too productive.

At first, he seemed happy about it and said that I should have the baby.

Then, the next time he saw me, he tried to talk me out of it. Looking at me straight with his blue eyes, he let his sandy hair flow in front of his face as he shook his head back and forth. I didn't back down. I assured him that I was keeping the baby with or without him (and secretly prayed that it would be with him).

He seemed to come around, he really did. He got a job pouring Slurpees and mopping floors at the 7-Eleven by his house. He studied for his grade ten math tests in hopes of someday becoming an accountant. We had big plans to buy a house out in Scarborough. Just a small bungalow to start. I would get my GED, and he would finish high school and work at the gas station in the evenings. When he was finished with university I would go next. Both our mothers could babysit the baby on the weekends so we could have a date night. We still hadn't figured out how we would get the money to buy the house, but "these are just details," he had said. "Most important is committing to each other, and getting our schooling . . . The rest will come."

He never talked about marriage. I guess he figured that would come too, or I guess as a sixteen-year-old kid, he had really never even considered proposing to a girl. Even if his sperm had implanted into her egg.

Quinn was pretty serious about it all for the first few months after he found out about the pregnancy. Then, when I was six months and staying at home most weekends, he started to go out without me.

"Just for a quick game of pool," he would say. Or for a horror movie, or a drive.

As the months went on, I found myself alone on the couch most weekends. But I didn't really blame him. Who would want to spend his weekends with some pregnant chick with swollen feet? I wasn't worried. I knew that once the baby was born, he would change.

Then came February 11, 1983. I was eight full months pregnant. He wanted to take me out for dinner downtown. It was cold, windy, and I had wrapped my father's thick black parka around my belly, its fur-trimmed hood hiding most of my face when we walked outside.

I had ordered a Big Mac and fries with a chocolate milkshake, and Quinn had only had some nuggets and a Coke. After I had finished everything, and ripped the Big Mac carton into a million pieces on the table, he reached across and took my hand. And for a split moment, I thought he was going to propose.

"Candy, I have horrible news."

I pulled my hand away and crossed my arms over my belly. "What."

"We're moving."

"Me and you?"

"No, my family. My mom and dad, me, and my brother. We're moving up to Sudbury." Tears came spilling down my face in frantic patterns.

"But you can't, not now," I said, gesturing down to my belly.

"That's why it's so horrible," he said. "The thought of leaving you and the baby, why, it tears me up inside."

He was speaking like an after-school special and I hated it.

"But what about our house? Our plans?"

172

"I wanted that, I really did, but I'm just too young to not live with my parents. I don't make enough money."

His sudden sensibility enraged me, and I started talking really fast and loud. "You planned this! You told them to leave because you can't handle being a father."

He shook his head. "I'll come visit. I promise. I will still be a part of its life."

"Of her life!" I screamed, remembering the fuzzy sonogram I had brought home to him three weeks ago.

"I'm sorry."

"You're lying!" I screamed. "You're not going anywhere; you just want to leave me alone in this. You can't handle it."

"No . . ."

I stood up and then crumbled down onto the dirty floor of the McDonald's, my head buzzing with shock and disappointment.

"Candy, get up," he said, pulling on the sleeve of my black maternity turtleneck. "You look like a fool. It didn't work out between us, that's all. Things don't work out with people all the time."

I wiped my eyes, leaving black mascara on the side of my hand. "They don't work out because someone like you fucks them up!" I said, pushing him out of the way and running to the bathroom, sobbing and fighting to catch my breath.

I sat on the toilet with my pants still on and bent myself in half, letting my tears fall onto the greasy linoleum below. At one point, I thought I heard someone knocking on the bathroom door, but eventually it stopped. No one was coming back for me, for us. Quinn's parents were saving him from this — I knew that for certain. I could see his mother devising plans the second she got a look at my swollen abdomen. She may have nodded and smiled on the outside, but I knew that she would find a way to get her son away from this.

The light bulb above my stall started to buzz and flicker with every anxious moment that I sat in there. I could feel a sharp tightening in my guts, but was numb to any real pain. That was, until I felt Rebecca trying to poke her way out of me. In shock, I quickly pulled down my pants and underwear and squatted over the toilet, tightening up to ride the pain and soon, letting out the one long groan that pushed her slippery body into my hands. As I pulled her, bloody and crying into my arms, I have to admit, I didn't want the next part of my life to begin. I held her tiny body close to mine and waited one full minute before screaming out for help.

––––––––––

She was sitting up a little when I came in the room; the tubes were out and for just a moment I assumed that she was fine. That she was back and I could apologize for pushing her and go back to the way things used to be.

But as I came closer to the bed, I could tell that something was different — that something was missing.

It might have been that spark in her eyes that had disappeared, that little spot of recognition deep in her pupils that had always invited me in. Her head was pushed towards her shoulder, her wrist still weighted down with the IV and bent down awkwardly in front of her.

"Becks?" I said. "Are you all right?"

It was a horrible question to ask, almost an insult. With one look I could tell she wasn't all right.

She grunted at me, rubbing the back of her hand into her eye socket like she was fighting the urge to go back to sleep.

"She's going to have a bit of a transition as she wakes up from this," the doctor said. "Once she's settled, we'll do tests to uncover the full extent of the damage."

My head was pounding when he said that. My eyes wanted to shut and stay that way. My body smelled from so many days in the hospital, my bangs stuck to my forehead, my temples were aching, and the glare from the fluorescent lights sent stabbing pains into my eyes.

I felt my bottom lip start to tremble. "Well, what . . . the . . . hell . . . are you doing to help her?" I said (almost incoherently, and no, I had not been drinking this time, though I wanted to).

"We're keeping her hydrated and comfortable. She'll have another MRI in the morning."

In a huff, the doctor left me in the room with Becky, who was now clenching her teeth and shaking her head back and forth on her pillow. I put my hands on her shoulders.

"Stop, honey, stop it."

My voice seemed to trigger something in her. She stopped, looked up into my eyes, and spoke: "Mommy," she said in a voice that sounded like she was four again. "You came to get me."

When Rebecca was five years old, her father came to visit her for the first time since she was a baby, and for one of only a handful of visits during her entire childhood. We had just moved into our own apartment (the one Becky would grow up in), and Quinn had just moved back to Toronto to go to the cooking school at George Brown College. He wanted to be a chef, which was odd, because he had never shown much interest in cooking when we were dating, but that was five and a half years earlier. A person can change a lot in that length of time.

For example, me. Since he left me that day in the McDonald's, I had a baby in the bathroom, spent nine days alone in the hospital with her, then went home to live at my mother's house. I worked part-time at the neighbourhood grocer's and got my GED instead of graduating high school.

When Quinn arrived at my door unannounced, it was only the second time he had visited Rebecca — he had come once when she was six months old. His mother drove him down from Sudbury, and we — me, Rebecca, Quinn, and our mothers — had sat in my parents' living room for three hours. We watched as Quinn held her and looked for some sort of recognition in her eyes. It was easy to convince myself there was none. Quinn's mother had a lot of good things to say about their new life up north: the friendly people, the winter sports, and the cottage they had recently purchased. "It was the best decision for my family," she said. "Frank's job was at a dead end down here. Now, at the mine, he has a promising pension and good salary."

Mother only nodded — she was too proud to show any anger.

When it was time for them to go, Quinn stood in the doorway, rubbing a bit of Rebecca's baby vomit off his shoulder, while his mother quickly gathered up their belongings. "Quinn will be in touch," she said. "It's just so hard when he's so busy at school."

They left. And every year for the next five years we received a birthday card for Rebecca with a cheque for $200. I never asked for child support, which I see now was the wrong choice, but I couldn't bring myself to beg him for anything else.

Then came the knock on my apartment door. I was still unpacking boxes, plates and cups that had been wrapped in pages of the *Globe and Mail* that my father had delivered each morning. Rebecca was playing in her bedroom, colouring and making up stories with her Barbies: "Oh, you are so late for the party," one Barbie would say to the other. "It's almost not worth you coming."

"Candy," Quinn said when I opened the door. We were on the ninth floor, and he looked out of breath when I saw him, almost like he had walked up the stairs.

"What are you doing here?" In khaki pants with a carefully ironed white T-shirt, he looked older, his hair neatly trimmed around his ears. His face was clean-shaven and his jaw line was strong. I felt suddenly self-conscious of the torn, stained rug in the hallway and the boxes, clothes, and junk scattered on the dusty parquet floor in my living room.

"I'm here to see Rebecca," he said, like he was making a point. "I'm in town now, so I thought I could start spending time with her."

I hesitated, his offer coming five years late.

"Mommy, who's at the door?" Rebecca called from the bedroom.

"Oh, no one," I shouted to her, to which Quinn narrowed his eyes.

But then she was there, in front of us both. Her tiny torn sundress drooping over her right shoulder, her long golden hair unbrushed and flowing down her back, her face smeared with the chocolate bar we had shared after lunch.

"Rebecca, this is Quinn."

She held out her tiny hands to him, "Nice to meet you, mister."

He shook her hand and kneeled down to her level. "We've met before," he said to her. "When you were a small baby."

She smiled, then dragged her tiny fingers through her hair. "Did you think I was the sweetest baby you had ever met?" she asked.

"Something like that," Quinn said with a chuckle.

"So you did?"

They laughed together. And she invited him into her bedroom to meet her Barbie family. Her mattress was on the floor and I sat on it while they played, Quinn cross-legged in front of her, Rebecca talking so fast that her words slurred together. She stuttered when she couldn't find the right one. I stared out the window into the park below — there were families down there, playing together in the late summer sun. I imagined myself sitting with them, tossing balls, flying kites, instead of in this nondescript bedroom with Becky and Quinn.

"Hey, Candy," he said suddenly, handing me a small silver camera that had been shoved in his pocket. "Do you mind taking a picture of us?"

I didn't say anything, just held the camera up and snapped a shot. He was sitting on the floor, and she was standing up to the left of him, striking some sort of silly pose.

"Where you working now?" he asked me later when Rebecca was settled in front of our twenty-inch with a sandwich.

"At a bar. I'm a waitress."

"And who watches Rebecca while you're out?"

"She goes to daycare. My mom helps me pay for it."

"Don't you think it would be better if you looked after her all the time?"

Anger pricked me in the spine, but I ignored it. "Probably."

"And this place," he said, gesturing around. "Is this really the best environment for her?"

"It's all I can afford with no fuck'n child support," I said, crossing my arms across my tank top, trying to cover up my bra-less breasts.

"I mean, are there even any other children for her to play with her, and where do they play? In the hallways?"

"Quinn, I think it's time for you to go."

"When can I see her again?"

"Never. We don't need you."

"Candy, I have rights. She's my daughter after all."

"Find a lawyer, I guess," I said as I pushed him out the door.

He resisted a little as I closed the door in front of him — a little, but not enough to make anything different.

———

On the fifth day after she woke up, Rebecca's eyes rolled back in her head and she started to froth at the mouth. I held her until it stopped, even though the nurses told me to step back.

Speaking was much more difficult for her in the weeks after that, though she still tried her best to push out the words.

"Want juice, Mommy," she would say. "TV, please," she'd mumble, pointing up at the television set hung from the corner of her hospital room.

I tried a few times to talk to her about the night she got hurt. One, to say sorry for the fight we had, and two, to find out from her what really happened with Chris and Enid.

She had no memory of any of it. That, or it was not something that she could really comprehend anymore, given how she had become. She couldn't sit up yet, or move her legs very well, but she did have some good use of her hands. I even helped her write her name one day, just to show the doctors.

"Yes, she seems to be coming along," they would say to appease me.

"But is she . . . is she going to get better?"

"There are parts of Rebecca's brain that have been severely damaged in the crash. We really can't tell if other parts of her brain will take over, and for what. But . . . you should always assume she will make a full recovery, because it won't happen without your belief."

Nothing, it seemed, could happen for Becky without me during those days. I stayed at the hospital for four straight weeks, sleeping on the fold-down chair by her bed, eating from the vending machine, washing my body with the metallic-smelling water from the sink. As talk of her going home started to come up, I began to get scared. How was I supposed to go back to work with her like this? My boss had been kind up to that point, but I could only expect so much.

And that's when Quinn showed up.

It must have been my mother who called him, as she had been at the hospital off and on and could see how I was struggling. No doubt she felt he deserved some of this burden too, even seventeen years later.

He came with his wife, Debra, who was pregnant with their third child. Debra's eyes grew red when she first saw Rebecca — they had met only a few times before, and the most recent time was the previous summer when Debra and Quinn had invited Becky and I to a barbeque at their house in the Beach. I had convinced Becky that maybe it would be good to get to know her dad since she was getting older. When we got there, Becky refused to speak to either of them the whole time. She wouldn't look at Quinn when he offered her a soft drink. She rolled her eyes when Debra talked about her daffodils. The barbeque ended with their youngest child, Brittany, throwing up on Becky's canvas runners.

"I can't believe it," Debra said looking down at Rebecca in her hospital bed. "It's too awful."

Quinn looked upset too and reached over to Debra to help keep her up. Becky was actually looking pretty good that day — her brain monitor had been removed and she hadn't had any seizures that week. Plus, her hair was starting to grow back a bit, a low fuzz developing all over her head like a light brown moss.

"Rebecca, it's Debra and Quinn," Debra said. "Can you hear me?"

"She can hear you just fine," I said, annoyed. "She's just having a nap right now."

Becky's eyes flickered open, and when she saw them she smiled — wide and inviting. "Dadddd-yyy."

I had never heard her use the word "Daddy" in relation to Quinn. Despite the sentiment, he looked horrified.

"Is she going home soon?" he asked.

"Maybe," I said, taking a sip of a Diet Coke I had bought from the machine in the hall.

"And how are you going to be able to look after her in that apartment? Won't you need things to be installed, rails and stuff? Wait, can she even walk?"

"Please don't talk about her like she's not here," I said. "And no, she hasn't walked yet, but rehabilitation is scheduled."

"And are you prepared for this, Candy?"

"Can you ever be?"

Debra was sitting by then, her hand on her swollen belly. Quinn put his arm around her and rubbed her back.

"I have to go now, Quinn," Debra said. "This really has been too much exertion for me."

"Okay, yes, of course, Debra."

Quinn went over to Rebecca and took her hand in his. She started to sway her head back and forth on her pillow again, like she was trying to will herself to stand up.

"I'll come see you again," Quinn said. "When you're home. I'll come to your apartment."

Becky mumbled something and one side of her mouth turned up in a grin. Quinn walked away from the bed.

As he passed me on his way out, he leaned over and whispered in my ear. His breath smelled of vegetables. His voice was strict and made me feel like I had just misbehaved.

"Damn you for letting this happen."

"Fuck you, Quinn," I said, flicking his shoulder with my adhesive nails as he left. I really wanted a drink by that time.

I brought Rebecca home exactly two months after her accident. It was strange pushing her wheelchair down the hallway she had run through so many times. She seemed pleased to be going home. I opened the door to find the surprise that Mom told me about. My mother and father had purchased an electric hospital bed for her and set it up in the middle of the living room. Mom had bought a floral comforter for the bed and two frilly cushions to dress it up. I had told them not to come that day — that I had to learn to do this all myself. If I were them, I would have been relieved by that.

I pushed Rebecca's wheelchair across the threshold of our apartment. Inside it smelled stale and tinged with the odour of hidden mouldy potatoes. Except for the bed, it was just as I had left it two months ago. I had only been back a handful of times since that early morning phone call. And Rebecca, she hadn't been back since the night we fought when she had headed off to the party at Melanie's house. I had gotten that much out of her before she left.

"Home," Becky said when I picked her up out of her chair and placed her down on the bed. After getting her set up in the living room, I turned on the television and settled on an episode of *The Simpsons*. It seemed to entertain her well enough. I liked having her back where I could have more control over her care.

I went into the kitchen and opened the cupboard over the stove, laying my hand on the bottle I had half finished before I left. I took a swig of whiskey and looked at my tired eyes in the reflection from the range hood. *Where are her friends?* I thought. *They must all know by now.*

I took another swig and put the bottle back, wondering if I should call my boss at the bar or wait another few days until they tried to get a hold of me.

I kind of liked in-between moments like these, where one part of life was ending and another just about to start up again. There was possibility in that; something I hadn't felt much of since the first night I saw Becky in her hospital bed.

When I got back into the living room, Rebecca was asleep. Her mouth was hanging open and her breathing was heavy. I stared at her, thinking about how round and pudgy her face had turned since it happened — her lips almost swollen, her cheeks puffy like she'd just had her wisdom teeth out. When she woke up, I would spoon-feed her some creamed corn from the can, give her a sponge bath, and see if I could get her to walk a bit, sit on the toilet. I looked down and saw her bookbag from school, abandoned under the window where she had left it last. I glanced up out the window and saw it was snowing for the first time that year — soft flakes coming from everywhere, not giving a fuck where they fell.

I flipped off the television, trying to make things quiet for her. I noticed there was a clock still ticking on the wall inside the kitchen. I stood up, retrieved it, and removed the batteries so it would stop making noise. The silence left me wondering where we could go from here.

HER FATHER

The last time I saw her she wouldn't talk to me — that's the thing I always think about. I had driven downtown, parked in the underground lot under the Bay, and walked into the Gap, thinking that maybe I would be able to catch her on her lunch break, and that we could go talk for a while. That we could sit down in a food court or something and I could explain to her that Debra feels threatened by her — that's why she acts like she does. That she feels threatened because we have two girls and, well, Becky was like this strange piece of our family puzzle that didn't really fit. And if she didn't want to listen to me, I was going to hand her the picture of us from when she was little and remind her that I've been trying. For years I've been trying to figure this relationship out, and now it was time for us to finally get to know one another.

But I wasn't able to do any of that. I arrived in the store and all I achieved was a small glimpse of her little body — clad in jeans and a yellow top — running away from me. She saw me, yes, I could tell by the way her face changed when I came in the doors, but she hightailed it to the back of the store almost before I had reached the first racks of clothes. It wasn't fair for her to run away from me. I can't be held entirely accountable for the way my wife acts. When Debra is pregnant, well, she's so annoyed that she can't be bothered to filter what she says to people, which is unfortunate.

After Becky disappeared another Gap guy came running out straight towards me, as if he was sent. He was kind of a strange-looking guy in his twenties with a headset over a head of thick dark hair that seemed to dip down into his forehead where it shouldn't have. His nametag said "Ray," but he did not introduce himself. I tried talking to the guy, but he didn't seem like he really wanted to hear anything I had to say. Mostly, he just wanted me gone, which was extremely irritating — I mean, what does some Gap worker know about my life and whether or not I have the right to have a conversation with my own daughter?

It was frustrating. I tried to send her the message that I was sorry about the barbeque and I gave him the picture to give to her, but who knows if she got it or not. If I had known then that that would be my very last chance to get to know her as she was, well, you can bet that I wouldn't have given up so easily. Definitely I would have stayed and pressed that guy more to let me see her. I would have explained what it is like, as a father, to know that you have a daughter whom you don't know and who doesn't want to know you. I may even have pushed him up against the wall until he gave in.

When I got home from the Gap, Debra was in the yard with the girls. They were running through the sprinkler and screaming when the spray touched their naked skin. Debra was sitting on the deck watching them, her tired face grimacing. One of her hands rested on her round belly and the other reached down to rub her thick ankles.

"I tell you, Quinn. I can't take much more of this. I feel like a prisoner within myself."

I knew it was hard for her to have to be off work. She was a fundraiser through and through, and when she was away from the hospital, well, she didn't seem to know what to do with herself. It's not like she didn't enjoy spending time with the girls, but it wasn't natural for her.

"Only a couple more months, honey," I said, grabbing a hold of Brittany and hugging her even though I knew her swimsuit would make wet spots on my clothing.

"Daddddddyyyyy!" Victoria shouted, running in to say hello. "I missed you."

"So?" Debra asked with a sigh. "How did it go?" I shooed the girls back into the water spray and sat beside my wife on the deck.

"She wouldn't even see me," I said. "I'll have to try something else."

"Sometimes I'm not sure why you bother, Quinn. Why is it so important?"

"You have no idea, Debra. None," I said, annoyed. "What if Victoria or Brittany wouldn't talk to you? Or what if they took this baby from you before you even got to know him?" I said, patting Debra's belly through her sundress.

"That would never happen because I would never allow anything like that to happen."

I sighed and looked towards the house.

"I'm going to go change," I said. "I don't have to be at the restaurant until seven. I might lie down."

"Whatever," Debra said. She called out to the girls and they ran towards her, collapsing into a giant towel that she held in the air.

"But I need a break too, don't forget that." She leaned in, snuggling their toweled bodies.

"Just give me a few minutes." I walked in through the patio doors and into the kitchen. Sitting on the counter was another copy of the picture of Becky and me from when she was little. It sat there like it was waiting for me. I picked it up and examined it again. Me and my daughter: her smiling, laughing almost, and me, thinking that maybe, just maybe, this was the start of something.

I never would have predicted that at sixteen I would have gotten a girl pregnant. Never, because shortly before that I had my doubts that I would ever feel the need to go out with a girl at all. But Candy was pretty cool when we met. She liked to hang out with me and my friends, and soon, we found ourselves sneaking off together. That's all I thought it would ever be with her — a little bit of sneaking around, but things got serious pretty soon after that.

It's hard to know how to respond when your teenage girlfriend tells you she's pregnant. I was not prepared to give any reaction at all, so by default I pretended to be happy. That's how I'd seen people act on television when someone relayed that news: "You're going to have a baby! Oh my goodness, that's amazing news . . . congratulations!" It took a couple days for my authentic emotions to infiltrate that cliché.

I wanted to do right by Candy. I liked her — she was funny, and pretty, and all that. We all liked hanging out with her before she was pregnant: the way she would sneak cigarettes for us or tell the most hilarious stories about lame things her parents had done, well, that was really neat. But when she started to grow more and more round, and started talking about us living together, and all that, it got tough. I could only pretend so much. I was not ready at that age to tell some girl that yes, she was the one I wanted to be with forever and ever. To me, forever meant to the end of grade eleven and that may have been about all I could have committed to.

I can't remember the exact moment things changed in my mind, or what changed, but there came a day when Candy and the baby had fallen to the end of my list of priorities. And although I had told my parents what had happened, I stopped talking to them about it, instead just grunting when they asked how Candy's latest doctor appointment had gone and did we hear the heartbeat? I shrugged when they asked me if we had picked any names and shook my head when they wanted to hear our plans for the future. My plans for the short-term were to do my best to stop acting like an adult, stop playing house when it was not something I had chosen.

And then one morning, just like that, my mother offered me an out.

"Quinn," she said (I still remember the hollow, even sound of her voice in the kitchen). "Your dad and I have made a decision. He's going to accept the job that was offered to him at Inco."

"In Sudbury?" I stopped peeling a sticker off a banana and looked up at her.

"I'm afraid so, Quinn. We'll be moving. You and your sister too." Mom and I both stayed quiet for a minute, sitting with the news, testing it out. Eventually, I nodded and said that was fine and she asked me what about Candy and the baby? Her question held more weight than anything I had ever been asked at school.

"It's not my fault that we have to go," I said finally. "That's what I'll say."

"And it's true!" Mother said, leaning over the kitchen counter and looking towards where I sat at the table. "It is most definitely the truth. This will be a new start for you, Quinn — just what you need." She looked in my eyes so earnestly that it made me look away.

"Whatever, she'll just have to deal with it. Things don't work out between people all the time." I stood up and my mom told me she was sorry before I walked out of the room.

The thing I didn't know then, that I know clearly now, is that when a child is born that you helped to create, you can never forget about her. Not really. You can move to another city and send some money and keep promising yourself that you will visit, but each and every day after that baby is born, she will stay stuck to the perimeter of your thoughts. The thought of her will stay in your fingertips and rest in your cheeks when you smile. She will always be a missing part of your own body.

This is a hard thing to explain to people who haven't been parents, and a hard thing for a teenage boy to fully understand. Especially given the complicated nature of babies — the way they cry, and poop, and fuss — and under the umbrella of a strained relationship with the baby's mother. It was so incredibly awkward to be around Candy after I left her. It's like no matter what I said, or how nicely I acted, nothing could override what I had done. And that is exactly what kept me from Becky when she was young.

It wasn't until I came back to Toronto for culinary school that I started to let myself imagine what it would be like to be a part of Becky's life for real. It was still hard though, dealing with Candy, seeing how life had ended up for her and knowing the part I had played. And then I met Debra — with her sweet eyes and fancy purses — and for a while, I forgot. Or rather, I was able to put Candy and Becky into a drawer at the back of my mind. I convinced myself that there were some things that just weren't meant to be. Some things that were just mistakes. I married Debra, opened my own restaurant, had my two daughters, and thought that I had moved on with things. But having more children did not make me forget about Becky, in fact, it made me think of her more — want to know her. I craved it.

When Debra was pregnant with our baby boy there was this day late in July that I looked over at her lying on the sofa, her gigantic belly ballooning up in front of her once more, that I started to think about Becky again. How she was once this innocent little baby under her mother's skin, and how every little baby that enters the world deserves to know both her parents. That's when I decided to ask Debra, "So, hon, you know this barbeque we're throwing next week?"

"What about it?" Debra said. "The part where I go buy all the meat, and hit the beer store, and haul everything home, or the part where I clean up the yard and put out all the lawn chairs, or the part where I stay up late the night before making potato salad and hoping it doesn't get mushy?" She yawned and kicked off a blanket that was partially covering her feet.

"That's not fair, Debra. You know I'm going to help you."

"Okay, sorry." She changed the channel on the television to some talk show I had never heard of. I knew she snapped when she was pregnant; I wasn't worried about it.

"I was thinking that maybe . . . I could extend an invitation to Candy and Becky to come over." Debra didn't flinch or say anything. The girls were playing in the backyard. I could hear them shrieking to one another, their voices seeping into the house through the screen door.

"I'm not sure if I could handle having to interact with that woman," Debra said finally.

"I can't very well invite Becky alone," I said. "It's only fair that her mother comes with her."

"But why should she come at all?"

"Because. I'm her father and that's never going to change."

Debra sighed, looking away from me, stroking her belly. "I suppose."

"So I can?"

Outside, Brittany was crying and Debra hauled her wide mid-section up off the couch until she was standing.

"I have to go see to Brittany."

"So I can, Deb?" I said a bit louder.

"Yes, whatever," she said to me from the kitchen. "Whatever you like, Quinn."

That was all the approval I needed. I made the phone call to Candy (after letting the phone ring nine different times before she picked up), and remarkably she said yes, that they would come.

This made the barbeque like none of the other functions we had had before. It would be the first time I had seen Becky in years. It would be the first time she met Brittany and Victoria and saw my home. I tidied the yard myself: raking up some old leaves that had been forgotten about last fall, mowing the grass, hosing down some mud that the girls had smeared on the fence, setting up the lawn furniture so there would be seats for around thirty. I cleaned the kitchen while Debra napped, even though I saw enough of a kitchen at the restaurant, was sick of scrubbing sinks and counter-tops almost as much as I had grown tired of the smell of homemade salsa and bean and cheese burritos. I put every dish back in the cupboard and set out a fancy stack of paper plates I had bought at Costco. And I made a spinach dip, and some Thai spring rolls, and a date cake covered in toffee. I even cleaned the house, bathed the girls, and put fresh dresses on them, and by the time people started arriving that day, I was exhausted but optimistic.

Candy and Becky were among the last to arrive. By the time they rang the doorbell, the yard was already filled with our neighbours and friends from work — Debra's colleagues from the office and my two chefs, three waitresses, and their families. There were a lot of people gushing over Debra's belly, and the girls were playing horseshoes with some of the other kids.

I answered the door on the first knock. And when I opened it, there was Candy, standing thin as anything in a sheer top that showed her black bra underneath, and Becky, her hair tied back, wearing cut-off denim shorts, her arms crossed in front of her.

"Candy, hi!" I said. I think I was out of breath when I said it because I may have run from the family room to get there. Candy nodded.

"Quinn." I pinched my lips and looked at Becky.

"I'm glad you could come, Becky," I said, her face like a stranger's but with such familiar undertones. She nodded and looked over my shoulder into the house.

"We've just got some neighbours over and stuff," I said. "A few people from my restaurant. I've told you, right? I own a Mexican bistro at Yonge and Davisville."

"Yes, Quinn. We've heard about your fancy café," Candy said. Her arms were crossed in front of her now as well. "Do you have wine?" She took a step inside and I let her by. For a brief moment, Becky and I stood in the doorway together. My heart fluttered. I choked on my breath.

"I mean it, Becky. Thanks for coming," I said to her.

"Mom thought I should." She was curling a piece of her honey hair around her finger.

"I'm glad."

"I thought that this could be a chance for—"

"Becky!" It was Debra, sneaking up behind me like an unexpected predator. "Becky. How are you?"

"Fine."

"You remember my wife, Debra?"

Becky nodded.

"Becky, I'm so glad I had a chance to talk to you before you went out back. It's just that, your mom is out there drinking and I wondered if that's okay."

"Okay?" Becky asked.

"Yes, I know that your mother has suffered from a bit of a problem when it comes to alcohol and I wondered if you wanted me to cut her off at any point?"

"Debra, please!" I said. "Don't be rude."

"It's just that it must be horrible to live with someone who has that sort of problem, and I wondered if there was anything I could do to help."

"How about you just shut up," Becky said. "That would help me a lot."

Debra pulled away from us, fiddling with the yellow brace-lets dangling on her wrists, then turning and walking back to the kitchen without saying anything.

"I'm sure she didn't mean anything by that," I said.

"And you . . . Quinn . . . can just shut up too." Becky pushed by me and walked towards the backyard in search of her mother.

When a visit starts in such a poor manner, it takes a lot of effort to try to recover the mood. In some cases, nothing is enough, besides maybe a fresh start on another day.

Candy and Becky stayed for a while, but they sat together mostly, on a bench I had built into the deck near the barbeque. They talked to each other. I smiled at them as I flipped the burgers.

Debra talked to her work friends and my girls played in the grass for most of the time — only coming up briefly to inhale hot dogs without the buns and say hi to Becky as a result of my persistent prompting.

About the time that Candy and Becky stood up to leave was just when Brittany had downed an entire ice cream cone and cinnamon bun and was heading into the house to lie down on Debra's urging, but instead threw up the contents of her stomach onto Becky's sneakers. It was the perfect physical manifestation of how we had all been feeling about the visit. And when Becky was gone, I was already planning what I would try next — something more intimate, with just her and me perhaps. Little did I know that, in fact, I had messed up my very last chance with her.

———————

I didn't know how Candy could let what happened to Becky happen. Something in me wasn't surprised though — I expected bad things to happen as a result of Candy's parenting. That was part of the unease I had felt all those years as I went about my life, and Candy went about hers with Becky. It was a part of my punishment for being such a coward when I was younger.

Candy's mother was the one to call us. Becky's grandmother. She called us in the evening. It was late November. Debra had just put the kids down when the phone rang. I was in the dining room with the *Toronto Star* stretched out in front of me on the table.

"Quinn."

"Yes, who's this?"

"It's Janine. Candy's mother."

"Yes . . ." I was instantly uncomfortable. This was not normal.

"Quinn. Candy didn't want me to call, but it doesn't seem right. There's been an accident with Becky. She was hurt on a motorcycle, and well, I thought you should know. You are her father after all."

"Where is she?"

"They are at St. Mike's. Please, don't tell her it was me who—"

"I won't . . . thank you." I hung up the phone without saying goodbye, which shows just how messed up I was about what I had just heard.

Debra and I went over the next morning. It was terrible what we saw. I can't even talk about it to anyone, ever. No one wants to see his kid like that. I hated myself for what I said to Candy. I knew it wasn't really her fault but when there is no one to blame, well, you find someone, don't you? Plus, it was so incredibly hot inside that room, I couldn't even breathe.

When we were leaving the hospital, Debra weak because of her aching back and sciatica, I felt everything. Seriously: sadness, anger, regret, overwhelming despair. I felt it all, except happiness. There was no happiness involved.

"It makes you wonder though," Debra said when we reached the hospital parking lot. "What really happened that night?"

As she talked, I felt the air getting stuck in my throat, and my head moving in and out of dizziness. "I mean, what kind of mother lets her daughter go out on a motorcycle without a helmet?" I raised my hand in the air towards Debra whose head seemed to be morphing, her pregnant body doubling into two images. "Really, when you think about it, Child Services should have stepped in long ago."

"Debra . . . I . . ." My hand was still poised in front of me, my chest was rising and falling really fast by that time, and I could feel a decade's worth of anxiety burrowing its way through my skin, trying to get out. I thought I was going to self-combust.

"Quinn . . . honey . . . are you okay?" she said, though her words sounded hazy and slow. "You look a little white, dear, what's wrong? Why are you breathing like this?" I hated to stress Debra out any more than she already was, but believe me when I say that it was one hundred percent out of my control. I felt myself fall to the curb and I leaned my head between my legs, my palms pushing into my temples as if to try and keep my brains from exploding out.

"I'm going to get a doctor," Debra said, hobbling back towards to hospital. And when I was alone, well, that's when the tears started to fall. Tears like I had not cried since I was a child. Years of secret turmoil came loose and slid down my cheeks, as if that was the only way to finally break the pressure.

———————

After Debra had our son, Jack, she expected that things would get back to normal in our lives. I'd hoped it too, but even with the baby home and with our girls needing more attention than ever, I couldn't forget about the promise I had made to Becky in the hospital: that I would go visit her when she went home. On the day that Debra brought the baby home, Candy left a message on my machine. Her voice was strained and tired:

"Quinn, it's me, Candy. Lord knows you are the last person I want to talk to right now, but I just wanted to let you know that Becky is home, and for whatever reason she keeps asking about seeing you. Yes, I know it's kind of insane. Anyway, well, if you want to come see her, we're at the same place. That's all I'm going to say, really. I'm not going to beg you to be here, Quinn, because one, I don't want you here, and two, I don't need you. But Becky seems to. So bye."

I erased the message before Debra could hear it — she didn't need to be worrying about any of that, not now. I couldn't forget though. As I made the girls breakfast, and got them dressed, and read them stories, cuddled the baby while Deb took a shower, I couldn't get the image of Becky out of my mind. Of her lying in the hospital bed with an IV, her face all bloated, her head shaved. I couldn't get that Becky out of my mind no matter how much I looked at the faces of my three other children.

"So, I'm going to take the girls out for the day," I said to Debra one morning in the last few days of November. "You need a break."

"Whatever you want," Debra said. She was nursing the baby in the leather La-Z-Boy in the family room and wasn't really paying attention. "Why won't he just latch on, dammit?!"

"Do you want me to help you?"

"No," she said, annoyed. "There's nothing you can do, I just have to suck it up and keep enduring this nipple torture." She winced, and then we both smiled.

"I'll take them to the mall or something," I said. "I'll get them dinner."

"That would be nice, Quinn," she said, the baby now latched on and sucking happily. "Maybe I can get a little rest if he goes down."

"I hope so," I said, gently kissing the top of her head. "It will get easier, don't forget. Just like the last two times, it will get better."

"I may have to start giving him some formula," she said. "Just to give myself a break."

"Do what you need to, Deb. It's okay."

She smiled at me wearily.

"I'll go get the girls ready."

She nodded, leaned back, and closed her eyes as Jack nursed, and I headed to the basement to gather Victoria and Brittany from the playroom.

I didn't call Candy before I went over, which may have been a mistake. Honestly, I was trying to avoid another awkward conversation because I thought it might keep me away like it had done in the past — and I didn't want that.

"Why are we here?" Victoria said as we walked up to their high-rise. "I thought we were going to the mall?" She was holding her sister's hand. They were wearing matching striped hats with pink pompoms on the top.

"We're going to visit someone," I said. "Do you remember Becky who came to our barbeque in the summer?"

"The one who Brittany puked on?"

"Yes, her." At six, Victoria was probably old enough to understand that Becky was my daughter too, but I felt like I had to find my own place in her life before I could get my other daughters involved.

"Can we go to McDonald's after this?" Brittany asked, her cheeks reddened by the cool air, her hands clutching tightly onto her big sister's.

"I brought dinner," I said, pointing to the bag in my hand. "I'm going to make some mini pizzas for you girls and for Becky too."

They nodded happily and followed along as we entered the building. I looked on the directory and then buzzed the name Foster.

"Hello." Her voice was monotone and low.

"Candy? Candy, it's Quinn. I'm here to see Becky." There was a pause. The girls were playing with the locked door, trying to push or pull it open with their tiny fingers.

"You could have called?" She said it like a question — like she was asking me if perhaps things could have been different.

"I know," I said and waited. Candy buzzed us up and Victoria pulled the door open immediately. "We're in!" I said and smiled at them both as we travelled through to the lobby, Victoria running ahead to press the up button on the elevator.

"I wanted to do it!" Brittany screamed. "I wanted to press the button."

I grabbed her by the hand. "You can press the one inside, honey. We're going to the ninth floor." My heart was pounding as we waited. It had been years since I'd been there . . . not since Becky was little, but for some reason I still knew exactly where I was going. I thought about how I had chastised Candy for living in that place, but had a different perspective this time. This was the place that Becky had grown up in — the elevator that had carried her up and down on her way to and from school, the halls that surrounded her as she made her way home to her mother. And when I knocked on the door I thought it: this was the last place that Becky slept as herself.

Candy opened the door a crack.

"Is Debra with you?"

"She's at home with the baby. I brought my girls, if that's okay?"

She peered out at them, her face sunken like she hadn't been eating, and nodded.

"You can't stay too long. Becky will be getting tired soon."

"I'd just like to make you some dinner, if that's okay." I lifted the bag like it was a peace offering and she opened the door all the way.

"Sorry the place is such a mess. It's been a crazy couple days, trying to get her settled and all that."

I looked around. The place was a mess, and it smelled messy too, but I was not about to mention it.

"It's fine, Candy, really." I took off the girls' jackets and piled them on the floor by the front door. They stuck close to me as we walked into the living room.

"Is that her?" Brittany said, pointing at the hospital bed set up in the centre of the room.

"Yes, Brittany," I said. "But it's not nice to point at people." I walked up to Becky's bed, looking down at only the last moment. She was staring out the window. Her face was still swollen looking and her hair seemed to be a little more grown in since I'd seen her last. She was hidden mostly under the blankets.

"Hi, Becky," I said tentatively, not knowing what to expect. "It's me."

She opened up her arms and asked me to hug her and I did. Her hair smelled oily, like it hadn't been washed.

"I'd like to introduce you to Brittany and Victoria." I pointed to the girls, both of them clutching onto one of my arms.

"I know them!" she said, waving at them a little and making a goofy face by pushing out her bottom lip. They both laughed and eased up on me a bit, taking baby steps closer to the bed.

"Are you okay, Becky?" I said then.

She nodded and smiled at me.

"She's getting better every day," Candy said as she came into the room from the kitchen. "She walks around a bit. I'm helping her."

"That must be hard all by yourself?"

"I manage."

"Has anyone else come by?"

"My parents . . . the nurse. That's about it."

"Any of her friends?"

She paused, looking away, fiddling with her hair. "I guess they don't know what to say or something. I thought at least her boyfriend, Chris, and friend Enid would come. They were there when the accident happened."

"With friends like that, eh?" I said. She shook her head in disapproval and I looked towards the girls. They had their faces pressed up against the window and were looking down.

"Wow, Daddy, we are so high up!" Brittany said, pointing towards the window.

"You're not used to being in a big building are you?" I said to her. "Becky and Candy live up here!"

"Must be really neat." Victoria said matter-of-factly to Becky, who laughed a little bit and nodded.

"It's awesome," Becky said back to her.

"So, point me to the kitchen," I said, lifting up the bag a little. "I'm going to make some pizzas."

After we were done eating — with Candy feeding Becky's pizza to her and peeling off the mozzarella when it got stuck on her face — the girls got up on either side of Becky's bed and we turned on an episode of *The Wiggles* for them to watch. I went with Candy into the kitchen and started to clean off the plates with a dishrag I had found in the sink.

"You don't have to do that, Quinn. Dinner was enough."

"So you liked it then?"

"I have to admit that I would have expected something a bit fancier, what with all that culinary training, but the kids seemed to like it." She was smiling when she said this and I smiled back at her, a wall seeming to dissolve a bit between us.

"Thanks for letting us come over. I needed to see her."

"I know."

"And Candy . . . I'm sorry about the hospital, about what I said to you. I know it's not your fault — I was just upset. I was downright panicked to tell you the truth."

She picked up the last piece of pizza from a cutting board and nibbled on the corner of it. "It's okay."

"And for all of it, Candy, I'm sorry." I was standing very still with my hands by my sides like I was scared to move at all for fear of distracting her from what I had just said.

"We did just fine," she said. "We will do just fine."

"I can help you if you need it? Financially?"

"I don't need your money, Quinn."

"Then I'll visit. I'll come and take her out for a while, to give you a break." She put the half eaten piece of pizza back on the counter.

"Maybe when things calm down a bit."

"You just call if you need me. I want to get to know her."

"Even now?"

"Now more than ever." I finished up the plates and gathered my ingredients into the bag I had brought. "I guess we should be going, it's getting dark and Debra will be wondering where we are." Candy shrugged and threw the crust of her pizza into the garbage under the sink.

We walked into the living room where Dorothy the Dinosaur was singing enthusiastically about tending to her roses. Our girls, however, were all asleep.

For a moment, Candy and I stood side by side like a married couple looking in at our children. Becky's head was pulled back and her mouth hanging open a bit. Both Victoria and Brittany were sharing her pillow, their little faces smoothed out and serene. Brittany's little hand was resting gently on the sleeve of Becky's pyjama top.

"They're quite sweet," Candy said. "Your girls."

"They are all sweet," I said, letting myself sigh out loud and feeling whole for the first time since Becky was a little baby.

HER BOSS

Raymond. Raymond M. Bryant is my name, but most people will call me just a simple Ray. At least that's what I ask them to call me at the Gap where I work. I'm a manager. I have been working at Gaps since I was seventeen. I'm proud of how well I have done here — I've worked really hard to be a good member of the team, to fit in. I started out just helping people find turtlenecks that would match their slacks, and now I am proud to say that I am responsible for making up the schedule and also for closing up the store on some nights. This is huge.

I've never had a girlfriend. Before you start to judge me, you should probably know that despite how you might perceive me, I am actually painfully shy. I just push through it at work because I know what has to be done. But yes, I have never been romantically involved with an actual woman and this I attribute to how unsure I am of what to say to them. I don't think it's my looks really. I'm tall. And though I may have a few extra pounds around my midsection, I still have all my hair, and I don't have pimples, or anything like that.

So, as I said, I find it difficult to talk to girls/women. But there has been one exception. Rebecca. It was never difficult for me to talk to Rebecca. I hope you don't think that makes me a pervert or something, because she was only seventeen when she came to interview for a job on the floor and I was twenty-five. I really can't control the way I feel, and seventeen is legal age, right?

So anyway, the day she showed up it was a blizzard, and she was wrapped up tight in winter gear when she came through the doors. I remember watching as she stood there in the Winter New Arrivals and slowly peeled off all her layers and laid them over her arm: wool toque, long scarf, parka with fur trim.

And from underneath she emerged. Tiny, in slim-cut dark jeans and a red sweater, long sandy brown hair, blue eyes, and a sweet, sweet little face. I don't think that any other female has made me want to stare at her so much. But it wasn't just because I liked her outside. No, I think I could tell even in those few minutes, that what she had inside was just as delicious.

I feel bad for talking about Rebecca this way. I don't know what I'd do if she had noticed how I was watching her when she came in. Anyway, let's just say that I got a really good feeling from her, and when she spoke, well, it seemed to bubble out even more.

"Excuse me, I am here for an interview," she said to Judith, the girl we had hired to work ladies' wear. Judith raised her hand and motioned in my direction, and for a second, I wanted to just hide behind the hanging leather jacket rack. But I didn't. I put my shoulders back, tried to smile with teeth, and walked over to her.

Truth be told, I'm not the only or the main manager of my Gap location. It's a big important store right on Bloor Street, so, well, the real manager is actually someone else. And me, well, I'm a shift manager, which is just as important if you ask me. I'm the one who handles customers, and money. I also wear a headset. They don't hand over one of those to just anybody.

Rebecca's interview had been scheduled before Harry (the big manager, if you want to say) was called away to his aunt's funeral up north. I guess he forgot to cancel her interview before he left. I hated to turn her away — it was so cold outside and she had made the effort to come. When I reached her, I introduced myself and told her what had happened with Harry.

"Oh, that's too bad," she said. "I was really hoping to get this job."

"You will!" I blurted out, which was wrong. "I mean, you'll get another chance to interview, definitely."

I'll admit that as soon as I had seen Becky, I knew she was the one who was best, for the job that is. And I know what you're thinking. You think it was just because I had the so-called "hots" for her, right? No, actually, I just knew that her personality would go well with the rest of the staff. I knew it from the speed at which she unwrapped her scarf, and how happy her eyes looked when she talked to Judith. Her smile.

I think she could tell that I was a little nervous when I was talking to her about Harry and what had happened. When I paused, she asked how I liked working there.

"I get a sizeable discount," I said, which I wish I hadn't — *stupid*.

"I've been coming here for years," she said. "My mother and I always stop in when we're downtown, but we can't really afford to buy much. I was hoping that if I worked here, I could get things for less."

Her eyes were so hopeful when she said that. I could imagine her in the fitting room, trying on sweater after sweater and sliding her little legs into size zero jeans, letting out ooohs and ahhs when she'd found a pair she liked. I stared at her tiny little nose, turned up a little in a cute way, and her lips — the top one seemed to be a little fuller than the—

She cleared her throat.

"So when do you think my new interview time will be?"

"He'll be in touch," I said. "I'll make sure of it." I may have looked a bit too serious when I said this, but I wanted her to know that I was impressed with her — as a candidate that is.

"Thanks . . ." She looked down again at my nametag. "Thanks a lot, Ray. I guess I'll wait to hear from him."

I got Becky to fill out a new application and when Harry came back, it was sitting on his desk with a Post-it note from me: *Reschedule interview with this girl ASAP. Ray*

Turns out I was right — Rebecca made a perfect sales associate. After she started working it wasn't long before she was genuinely trying to help people when they needed it, tossing her hair over her shoulder and starting into some discussion about how the piece of clothing would really suit their body type and accentuate their positive attributes, or whatever. This was smart. I don't want to say that I couldn't think of a line like that, but sometimes (and I know this may seem hard for you to believe) things take a little longer to come to me. It's like I am standing just a few steps behind everyone, trying to see through the crowd. Even though I am tall.

Rebecca worked after school and on the weekends, and I soon found myself trying to come in for extra evening and weekend shifts — it was actually quite exhausting there for a while. When she went on break and I was there, I would take mine too, and always try to sit near her, and attempt to make conversation. The thing I liked most about Rebecca was that she never made me feel like the things I said were stupid. Even when I asked her what she was having for lunch ("It's a sandwich"), or if it was cold enough for her or whatever, she always answered me with a smile that was not at all condescending.

One day, she told me about her boyfriend, Chris, and that was really difficult. Now, I'm sure he is a great guy and all that, but it was hard to imagine Rebecca with anyone else. Imagine them talking, kissing, or whatever. When she talked about how pleased she was with him as a boyfriend, I just nodded and looked in the other direction. I didn't want her to see that I had instant tears in my eyes — it would have made me look so incredibly wimpy.

"It's great talking to you, Ray," she would say when she was done eating. And sometimes, she would touch me on the arm and smile before she walked back out to the floor. No one else really engaged with me like that.

I remember a day in the summer when Rebecca paged out to me over the Gap intercom.

"Raymond to the fitting rooms, Raymond to the fitting rooms." I melted, and then picked myself up and flew there in one second. She was hiding in one of the change rooms with her face in her hands.

"Ray, I need your help."

"Yes, Becky. Yes, anything."

"There is someone out there, who I do not, under any circumstances, want to see or talk to." She grimaced as she talked, looking more unsettled than I had ever seen her, and I wouldn't have been surprised if she had started crying right then and there.

"Who . . . who is it?"

"A man out there with brown hair, tiny glasses, and a blue button-up."

"A man with brown hair and . . ." I started to work it out — I told you I am a bit slow on the uptake — but she cut me off.

"It's my father, okay." She hid her eyes in her hand. "I hate him."

I wanted to ask her why, how could she hate her own father, and why was it such a big deal to see him, and what exactly could I do to help make it better for her? But instead, I walked out onto the floor, past the racks of jeans, and the new fall sweaters folded neatly, and the fragrance section, until I located a man of that description.

"Excuse me, sir. I think you have to leave now."

He was really surprised to hear me say that, and I probably

would have been too. I didn't care if I was putting my job on the line, or what Harry would think of me. I just knew I needed to do this for Rebecca — it was pretty much the only thing she had ever asked of me, aside from hiring her for this job.

"Umm, I'm looking for someone actually. She works here. Rather, her mother mentioned to me that she works here."

"Yes, I know who you are looking for. And she doesn't want to see you."

The man, despite his preppy-yet-macho appearance (perfect Gap model actually), seemed quite hurt when I had said that. He took his glasses off and rubbed his forehead with his hands.

"I've tried everything, man," he told me. "Her mother and her, well, it's been difficult."

"Yes, I know. I mean, I can imagine."

He started to look over my shoulder, like he was searching for her amongst the late summer clearance dresses.

"You won't find her, mister. She's hiding from you."

"Fine. You can't say I didn't try then, I guess. Just tell her I'm sorry about the barbeque. That I only asked her because it had been so long, and I thought that maybe we could become one of those modern families or whatever." I looked at him, unimpressed without knowing exactly why I was unimpressed. "And please, just give her this."

He handed me a picture. It was of the man, Becky's father, but he was a lot younger-looking. He was sitting on the floor with a bunch of partially clad Barbies out in front of him. And off to the far right of the photo was a little girl, a little girl whom I was pretty sure was Becky, smiling and posing with a feather boa around her neck.

When I gave Becky the photo, she ripped it up and tossed it into the staff trash can.

Rebecca's mother called me from the hospital shortly after it happened to her. The accident. She told me I was one of the only calls she was making because she wanted me to know why Rebecca hadn't been at work. I was glad she did. I had been going out of my mind when she didn't show up that Saturday. I waited by the front for her face to push through those doors and greet me like it always did. When she didn't show, I called her apartment. It rang and rang but no one answered.

At first I was angry at her, like she was skipping work maybe to be with that boyfriend of hers (the one I never thought or talked about), or that she had decided to quit and not tell me. But then I was just plain worried. In the staff room that week I had heard her talking to Angela about how she was going to a party that Friday, even though it was at the house of a girl who she wasn't really friends with. But that she (as I'm sure Rebecca always did) was trying to be the bigger person.

"It's all you can do, Becky," Angela had said to her. "It's not your fault she's fuck'n jealous."

Swearing always makes me uncomfortable, so that's when I stopped trying to pretend like I wasn't listening and actually didn't listen.

After her mom called me at work, I knew it must be really bad for her to be away indefinitely. She wouldn't tell me what condition

Rebecca was in, just kept saying that she hoped she would "be home soon." So that at least gave me some hope.

I had her address in her file and I vowed that if I didn't hear from her by Christmas, I would go out and find her.

When December arrived and I hadn't heard anything from her, I found myself standing in the lobby of her twenty-floor apartment building near Danforth and Victoria Park.

I had never been to this area of town before. I live at Bloor and Ossington with my parents — but I am planning to buy my own condo just as soon as the market improves.

I pushed the button beside her last name — Foster — and waited. A frazzled voice piped through, yelling, "What?"

"Umm, it's me. I mean, this is Ray from the store. I'm just here to check on Rebecca."

Silence. A black man with headphones opened the door ahead of me and held it.

"I'm coming up," I yelled towards the intercom.

As I stepped out of the elevator, I felt the jumping around of stuff in my stomach — it had been three months since I'd seen Becky, and well, I was excited. But another part, deep inside my brain, at the back, was nervous too. I didn't know what I was going to find. I'd heard that she had bad injuries, but that could have been anything from a broken leg to a shattered backbone.

I wasn't sure I wanted to know which one it was, but I knew I wanted to see her.

The door opened as soon as I knocked, flew inward to reveal a woman I recognized — frizzy hair, stained shirt, and too-tight jeans. This was the crazy drunk woman who had chased Becky down the street one day last winter. This was a woman to be avoided.

It's hard for me to talk about the day that it happened, mostly because Rebecca's boyfriend, Chris, was there, and well, I like to pretend that he doesn't exist.

He had come to pick her up after work, him and another girl that Becky knew, Enid. They were going out to a hockey game I think, at some local rink. And then they were going to go to have dinner at Casey's. I asked her all about it as she was walking out to meet them — hoping she would ask me to come, but geez, who was I kidding on that one. We met the kids at the front doors, so young-looking, and I thought, *Is this how young Rebecca looks too?* No wonder she wouldn't be seen with me outside the Gap.

"Ray, this is my boyfriend, Chris."

I avoided looking in his eyes, but held out my hand to him anyway. He shook it. He was tall and slim, with a black leather jacket and slightly pimpled skin.

"And this is my best friend, Enid."

Enid had dark hair, a prominent nose and was a bit taller and bulkier than Becky.

I felt a bit protective about letting her leave with Chris, almost like a big brother would feel about his younger sister. But I knew that really it was none of my business.

"Great work today, Rebecca," I said, tapping her on the back. She smiled and pushed into my shoulder with her fist.

"No problem, Ray," she said. And then she grabbed Chris by the hand and they left down Bloor Street.

I had no ill-intent, but I followed them for a bit. Just wanted to see that they got to the subway all right, and besides, I was going the same way. That's when they met the woman, the same woman who opened the door at Rebecca's apartment. She was dressed quite slinkily for the middle of winter, with some sort of lace top underneath a zip-up sweatshirt, and she had heavy eye makeup on: dark grey and streaky. She started shouting at Becky right away, right there in the street. Yelling about her lying and not coming home when she said she would.

I can't believe now that I never once assumed that this lunatic woman was Becky's mother. To me, there was just no connection that could be made between the two of them. No, I was sure in that instant, and even now when I think about it, that this was an insane woman who had flipped out and made Rebecca her innocent target.

I watched them for a moment longer, hoping that Chris would step up and protect her, but the woman was getting closer to her and grabbing her by the arm, trying to make her go in the other direction.

"Get off me!" Becky shouted, and that's when I knew that I had to step in. I came up from behind the woman without her seeing me, and, in one fluid swoop, cracked her on the head with my Gap satchel. She fell onto the sidewalk ice in a whoosh and slumped on the ground.

"Run, Rebecca, run!" I shouted to her, and although she seemed a bit too concerned about the crazy woman, Chris took her by the hand and she did go off with him and Enid.

I had hid around a corner and watched to make sure the woman was okay. She lay on the ground for a minute or two and before long, she was up, and stumbling back down the street. "Becky, Becky," she mumbled, which should have helped me identify her, but as I said, I'm a bit slow on the uptake.

So with this irritating memory in my brain, you can imagine how shocked I was to have this same woman open the door at Rebecca's apartment. Mind you, she'd cleaned herself up a bit, but it was hard to look at her and not see that other woman.

"Yes?" she said to me, looking like a mother who had been up with her newborn all night.

"I'm Ray."

"You're Ray?" she said, like she was surprised.

"Yes, do you recognize me?"

"No, not at all."

"Good. So, I just wanted to check up on Rebecca. On behalf of all her friends at the Gap."

This seemed to catch Rebecca's mother off guard. She looked from left to right, to left again. She rubbed her wrist with her hand and swiped at the inside of her bottom lip with her tongue.

Finally: "It's nice to meet you, Ray. You're actually the first one of her friends to show up here to see her. So you might as well come in."

The apartment smelled stale and medical. Without even looking for them, I could see dustballs in the corners of the floors and ceilings. There was a small pile of take-out food containers on the kitchen table. I wondered how Becky could stand living here, but as we turned the corner into the living room, I knew how.

She was lying down on a bed, pillows propping up her sleeping head. She was different, looked so much different than before. Her hair was short and wavy like a granny's. Her cheeks were rounder and she had a little double chin. She seemed much older than seventeen.

"Here she is!" Becky's mother announced, almost sadistically. Then she collapsed on the couch.

"Will she . . . will she know me?" I asked.

"Probably, but how the hell should I know," she said, looking out the window. "The nurse will be here soon, so if you want to wake her up, you can."

"Becky," I whispered, putting the small bouquet of carnations I had brought down on her bed. "Becky, can you hear me?"

She opened her eyes, scratching at her chin with the top parts of her wrist. Then, she saw me. Her eyes grew bigger.

"Ray!" she said, spreading her arms like she wanted me to hug her.

"Can I . . . ?"

"Be my guest," said her mother, who was curled up on the couch, staring out the window.

I leaned down and hugged Rebecca. She smelled like Vicks VapoRub and oranges, a nutty smell to her hair. Her arms were meaty but they wrapped round me. I let myself relax into her welcoming embrace.

"We've been worried about you at the store," I said into her ear. "No one knew what had happened to you."

She pulled away and looked me right in the eye. "I'm okay, Ray," she said. "I'm right here."

I stroked her hair, "I see ya, kid. I see ya."

Later, while the nurse was doing some exercises with Becky's legs and arms, I stood in the kitchen and talked with her mother. She had told me her name was Candy.

"It was touch and go for a while there, Ray," she said. "Initially she was on the respirator, then she was seizing. It was horrible."

I nodded, and took a sip of the drink she had given me — tap water in a glass cup. I was still trying to convince myself that Rebecca was now that girl.

"Will she get any better?"

"They don't really know, Ray. She's walking a bit now. That's something."

"Has she told you what happened?"

"She has no memory of it. I know that it happened on a motorcycle and that Chris was with her."

"Her boyfriend?"

"Well, not anymore, I'm sure. I haven't seen him yet, but it's probably for the better."

"Do you think this is his fault, is that why he is staying away?"

"Who knows." She looked down at the ground.

"I knew that guy was trouble."

As we talked, we shared a bag of Cheetos, each of us digging our orange fingers into the bag over and over. She offered me a drink of white wine then, which I refused as I am not a drinker — moreover, I like to remain in full control at all times.

"Don't take this the wrong way . . ." I said.

"Then I will," she said. "People always take it the wrong way when you start a sentence with 'Don't take this the wrong way.'"

"I'm sorry."

"What were you going to say, Ray?" When she said this, there was something about her mouth that reminded me of how Rebecca used to look. Somewhere under her hard and tarnished exterior was an older version of what Becky might have turned into. She chugged her wine out of a plastic cup from Canada's Wonderland.

"Do you really think you should be drinking, Candy. Now?"

"When else would you suggest?" she said. "I never leave this apartment, these nurse visits are the only break in my day."

"Maybe I could help you."

"Find more time to drink?"

"No, with Rebecca. Maybe I could help you look after her so that you wouldn't feel so overwhelmed."

She seemed surprised when I offered that and she put her cup on the counter and just stared at me. "She was right about you, Ray. You're a unique kind of fellow, but you have a big heart." It was really nice of her to say that. For a drunk lunatic mom, she wasn't half bad.

The first thing I helped Candy with was bringing Rebecca to the bathroom. "She'll walk a bit, and she's not that heavy," she said. "But it's so awkward for me, I'm not that much bigger than her."

"No problem, Candy, I would be happy to help."

"I would put her in the wheelchair but it's hard to get it down the hallway. Sometimes she'll stumble with her hand crutches, but other times, she just doesn't want to try. She pushes me away."

I went over to where Rebecca was lying on the bed. She was watching an old rerun of *The Cosby Show* and laughing a bit to herself.

"I'm just going to lift you up now, Becky," I said. I carefully slid each of my hands face-up underneath her, pulling her close to me in one slow movement. When she was in my arms, her head fell to the side and came to rest on my shoulder. It felt nice. I could feel her breathing on my neck.

She mumbled a bit and nodded while I carried her down the hallway and brought her into their plain, worn bathroom.

"Just put her in that chair," Candy said, motioning to a plastic and steel seat sitting in the bathtub. "I can help her have a shower if she sits in it."

I gently lowered Rebecca down, and she smiled at me and hummed something when I did.

"Thank you, Raymond," she said when I took a step back towards the door. Her head was leaning over a bit, almost like her neck was too weak to hold it.

"I guess . . . I'll go now," I said.

"I don't mind if you stay a while," Candy said. "You can wait in the living room. Have a drink if you want."

"Okay."

I walked back into the living room and sat on the edge of Becky's bed, just staring out into the park below. The snow had covered everything up nicely, giving a clean slate to every little imperfection.

From the bathroom, I could hear Candy's voice growing increasingly more frustrated.

"Becky, no. Becky, just let me do this. Do you want to be dirty? Do you want to get bedsores?"

Outside, a young boy was running over the icy sidewalk and sliding on his winter boots. He was laughing, which made me feel good. I remember doing that as a little kid — feeling myself come so close to falling, but struggling to stay upright and enjoy the ride.

"Becky, for Christ's sake, it's just shampoo. We can't have you getting all funky up top; you know how you hate greasy hair."

Below, there was a dog pushing his nose into the snowbank, trying to find something or other. Or maybe he was cold and that warmed him. Snow does have that power, doesn't it? Of warmth.

"Becky, that's it! I give up!"

Candy started to cry. I could hear her sobs seeping down the hall to where I sat. They were cascading, one leading into another, silence only between breaths.

I hurried back down the hall and found (luckily) Rebecca fully dressed in pyjamas and leaning up against the wall of the bathroom and Candy crumpled into a ball on the floor.

"You should go, Candy."

(Crying, sobbing, moaning.)

"I mean it. Get out of here for a while. I will watch her for you."

Her head popped up. Her eyes were red and puffy, her nose red. "Really?" She used her thumb to wipe some tears from her face.

Rebecca was just looking at us. Unaffected.

"I don't mind helping you," I said. "I'm not working today."

"That would be really nice of you, Ray," Candy said. "I mean, the nurse comes, and her father has stopped by but I don't want to have to bother him for help, he's got a family of his own, and well . . ."

"I don't mind, Candy, really. Go."

I helped Becky back to her bed and sat on the end of it staring at her. She pointed to the TV and I put on an episode of *Dr. Phil* for her. He was talking about child abuse, but Rebecca didn't seem to mind.

Candy said she would be home soon. That she just needed to get some air and could I feed Becky some sandwiches for dinner — the meat and bread were in the kitchen.

I said I thought I could do that and locked the door behind her after she left.

Rebecca looked so cute lying there on the bed. Still pretty, but helpless, like she was trapped inside herself.

I moved a foldaway chair to the side of her bed and sat in it. Next, I put my hand on her bare arm, almost by accident.

"Thanks for coming, Ray," she said to me.

"It's my pleasure." I started to rub her arm, which seemed to help her relax. Her breathing slowed and she leaned towards me.

"You're so beautiful, Becky," I said, like it had been bottled up in me for eternity.

"Thank you," she said, swatting at her nose with her fingertips.

"I've never met anyone else like you, ever."

She smiled and closed her eyes.

I don't like to talk about the Gap staff party that happened late last summer at the Hilton. In fact, if someone ever brings it up, I change the subject, or leave the room, which is usually easier.

The reason why is between Rebecca and me. I drank two beers

that night, which is unlike me. I was always able to talk to my colleagues when we were at work, it was part of my Gap persona I
took on, but it was more difficult when we were socializing. So of
course, I found myself talking mainly to Rebecca. She was the only
one who would listen to me rattling on about movies, and fan fic-
tion websites, and the like. I could tell that she wasn't really interested, but she always made a valiant effort. I think she knew that
these sorts of situations were awkward for me. She might even have
known that I only came there to see her.

She didn't bring her boyfriend, Chris, that night. I was glad for
that. And although she did spend some time talking to Angela, I still
needed to visit the snacks tray set up on the bar, as well as go to the
bathroom.

One time, when I was coming out of the bathroom, a guy
named Hudson stopped me in the hall by pulling on the sleeve of
my green cardigan sweater that Mom bought.

"Ray, buddy," he said. "You've really got to lay off that girl."

"I have no idea what you're talking about," I said, looking over
his shoulder to see if Rebecca was finished talking to Angela yet.

"She's not interested in you, loser," he said. "How come idiots
like you can never tune into the fact that some young chick would
not want you?"

"Stop it, Hudson."

"She just feels sorry for you, that's it." Hudson laughed and took
another swig from his beer bottle. He was never this cruel when he
nodded at me from his post in the men's jean section. I guess it's
alcohol that makes people want to act really mean; at least that's the
way I saw it.

Hudson's comments made me really mad, but I wasn't able to show it. I hate confrontation, so I just excused myself and went and stood beside the rack of tourist pamphlets in the lobby of the hotel, trying to shield myself behind a fake ficus tree.

"Ray, what's the matter? Did something happen?" It was Rebecca, poking her head through the tree branches. She had followed me. The entire front of my body warmed at the sight of her. "Are you okay?"

"I just needed a break, that's all."

"Did someone say something to you?"

"No, it's fine."

"Well, tell me who, because I'll give him a piece of my—"

I interrupted her by pulling her to me and planting my mouth square on hers. She pushed me away.

"Ray, what are you doing?!"

"I just, I thought . . ."

"Ray, it's not going to be that way, all right? Do you understand?"

I nodded.

"Say it, Ray. Say it so I know."

"It's not going to be that way."

"That's right. Now, I'm going to go home now. I'll see you next week at work." She leaned up with a jerk, shaking the tree so its plastic leaves bounced. I slid down to the floor and stayed very still until I saw everyone else leave.

———————————

Things were weird with Rebecca after the staff party. We still talked, but I could tell that something was on her mind, and she wanted to keep her distance from me.

And now, sitting with her in her living room watching *Quantum Leap*, as the sun began to set across the park, I felt like all of that was finally forgotten.

I asked if she wanted her sandwich now. She nodded "yes" and pointed down at her stomach. "Hungry."

I stroked her fingers with my thumb and looked into her eyes, trying to find her. *I like the new Rebecca*, I thought. I liked her even more like this. I ran my hand down her cheek and smiled at her. Then, I got up and went into the kitchen.

Later, when Rebecca had eaten and fallen asleep, I turned off the television and sat in the darkness with her. I started to imagine that Candy wasn't coming back. It was after ten o'clock and she had said that she would only be gone a few minutes. She had been gone for five hours by that time. I thought about what would happen if Candy had left Becky with me forever.

We would get married. Yes, I would marry her I think because truly, she is the only girl I have ever loved. We would work really hard with her and take her to lots of rehabilitation so that she would be able to walk down the aisle without crutches. It's not that important to me that she walks on her own, but I know that girls want to look perfect on their wedding day so I would want her to have that. After our honeymoon in Las Vegas, I would bring her home to my newly purchased condo. If there were anything she needed done, like special bars, or chairs, or whatever, I would do it for her because she deserves it. Except for the hospital bed. She would sleep in my bed with me. I would spoon myself around her while she slept, stroking her, telling her that it was all going to be all right.

And someday, with enough love and nurturing, Rebecca's brain and body would go back to how they were before the accident. She would become the old Becky, and one morning she would turn around in bed and say, "Ray, my dear Ray, you saved me. I'm back now, and together we can live our lives out as husband and wife. My mother not coming home was the best thing that ever happened to me."

Rebecca gurgled in her sleep. Her hands twitched slightly in the darkened room.

"It's okay, Becky. I'm here, I'm here," I said, rubbing her arm again. I felt my mind start to race, my underarms start to sweat. And then finally, to my relief, I heard Candy's key turn in the lock.

HER BEST FRIEND

It was cold that day, just after Christmas, and for some reason I decided that I would go to the Eaton Centre and do some shopping. It had been ages since I'd done anything like that — not since the accident — and I was just desperate enough to think that looking at new shoes and trying on fuzzy sweaters might actually make me feel like myself again. I was going to take the subway downtown, so I bundled up, walked to the end of the street, and started on the path that would lead me through the park to the overpass and into

Victoria Park Station. I was wearing the purple toque that Mom had given me for Christmas. It was itchy as hell, but the cold that day was biting, so I didn't even care how ridiculous I looked.

They were coming towards me on the path, pushing her wheelchair. It had been just over three months since Melanie's party. When I saw them, I gasped a little bit and felt some tears in my eyes. I think I swore inside my head too — or maybe even out loud.

Becky was slumped to one side in the wheelchair, resting her head on one of those neck pillows you use when you're travelling. She was dressed in an orange snowsuit with a fur-trimmed hood, yellow hat, the knee-high black boots we bought together (I have the same pair), as well as a pair of ski gloves she had perched in front of her face, fingers to the sky.

Becky's mother was walking beside the chair, looking down at her. And behind the chair, holding the handles, was that guy from the Gap. It was that weird guy, Ray. The one who hit Becky's mom that time she was drunk.

My first instinct when I saw them walking towards me was to look away, and I did. I looked down at the ice on the ground, pretending like I was trying to avoid falling on my ass. When they got closer, I heard Ray say, "It's nice to get her out, Candy. She's been cooped up much too long." That made me look up at them, and they were only a few strides away at that point. Becky's mom was nodding, and Becky was staring straight ahead like she had just been struck in the temple by a bat. She had short furry hair sticking out around the sides of her hat. She looked nothing — at all — like my best friend.

"Enid?" Becky's mom said then. I stopped walking, rubbed my

bare hands together, and considered running off. "Enid, what are you doing here?"

I looked both ways. The park was empty except for snow-trimmed trees and forgotten footprints. The sky was clearing, the sun peeking out from behind the fluffy white clouds. I took a deep breath and decided to speak. I owed them both that. "Mrs. Foster. Hi."

"It's been a long time since we've seen you." She was frowning and stroking Becky's head then, and Ray was leaning over, pulling up Becky's ski gloves to cover the strip of skin that was showing.

"I know. I'm . . . I'm—"

"Becky has missed you."

I looked down at her. Her eyes were wider than before. "Enid, it's you!" she said in a childish voice I really didn't recognize.

I squatted down in front of her like I did when my baby cousins came to visit. I opened my mouth, afraid, and told Becky that I was glad to see her too.

She nodded and I stood up. Ray seemed like he was kind of ignoring me at that point. He was fiddling with the zipper on his jacket, swaying nervously from foot to foot. He was kind of an ugly guy, with huge black eyebrows that nearly joined in the middle and big ears that pushed out from his face.

"Why is he here?" I asked, gesturing at Ray like he wasn't there at all.

"He's helping me, helping us, is all," Candy said.

"At least someone's been there for her," he said to me and I grimaced in response and felt my heart pound.

"Why don't you just fuck off, Mr. Gap-boy," I said.

"Enid!" Mrs. Foster said.

"This has been hard on me too, you know!"

With that, I started to run, not to the subway, but the other way through the park towards the Danforth. It was my intention to run as far away from that situation as I could. As I ran away, I heard Becky's mom yell something after me. It sounded an awful lot like "But you never even came to see her!"

At the end of the park, I turned my head to look back at the group of them — tiny and jagged like a warship floating along the horizon.

The truth is that I did go see Becky in the hospital right after the accident happened. Of course I did. I didn't tell anyone, not even my parents. I just said I was going out for a while to try to sort things out in my head, and of course they didn't care.

I took the subway and a bus to St. Michael's. I asked at the front desk where Becky would be and was informed that I was right on time for visiting hours. I took the elevator up to her floor. I got out. I found her room and I went in.

Becky's mom was asleep in a chair, stretched out over the arm-rest with her limbs dangling. And Becky was asleep in the bed beside her. It was awful to see her. Here was this girl who I had always envied for being so cute, and slim, and attractive to every boy, laid out in a way that made her look like she was roadkill waiting to be picked up. Her head was shaved except for a couple tufts here and there and she had an awful stitched-up gash on the top of her head. She was wearing a white hospital gown; tiny tubes and wires stuck out from under it everywhere and needles poked into her skin. There was no blanket on her and her bare legs were twitching a bit on the white bedsheet when she slept.

This was Becky now. Becky and me, this was us.

I was standing just inside the door and was surprised by how hot the room was — it smelled like an old lady's bedroom in there too, which was gross. I took a step towards her bed. I had every intention of putting my arm on hers, shaking her awake, and telling her that I was sorry it had taken me a week to come. That I was scared she would be mad at me — that her mom would hate me for letting this happen to her.

I had every intention of doing that, but I felt stuck. Just stood there staring at her chest rising and falling, wondering who was going to wake up if I woke her. Then, without opening her eyes, Becky's mouth opened and a sound came out.

She said, "Mommmmmmmy." She moaned it actually, like a toddler calling out for her mom in the night. That sound, that wasn't Becky.

"Can I help you?" someone said from behind me. I jumped a bit and clutched my Louis Vuitton purse like someone was trying to steal it. I turned to see that it was a nurse. She was dressed in a pale blue pant and shirt set with sneakers, her hair tied back in a messy way. "It's time to check Becky's vitals. Are you a friend of hers?"

I panicked. "No, no," I said, shaking my head. "I think I'm in the wrong room. I was looking for, for, someone else."

"Okay then," the nurse said, pulling at her ponytail. "If you'll excuse me." She pushed by me and walked towards the bed, placing her hand on Becky's forehead gently, adjusting the tube in her arm that connected to the bag hanging on the tall pole beside her. She turned to look at me again because apparently I hadn't moved. "If you ask at the desk, they can tell you which room you need."

"Yeah, okay. Thanks," I said. I took a step backwards towards the door, still looking at Becky — trying to take her in. Becky's mom moved a little bit in her chair and that's when I turned and bolted from the room, almost like I had never come in the first place.

On the way home I thought I was going to burst from the pressure of it. Instead, I turned myself numb and walked back into my house like nothing had happened. Mom and Dad were both there, sipping wine with their dinner. They asked me where I had been for so long and I told them it was none of their business.

I could feel my mother staring at me from the table as I took off my shoes.

"Maybe we should take her to talk to someone," she said to my father.

"I'm right here, you know!" I yelled at her. "I can hear you when you made snide comments."

"Enid, that was not snide," my dad said. "Your mother is worried about you is all."

"Yeah, right," I said before I stomped my way upstairs.

"We'll keep your dinner warm for you!" Mom shouted after me.

———————

That night before bed, Mom came into my room. I was listening to a Mariah Carey CD on my stereo, just sitting on the bed staring at my hands.

"Can you turn that down please, Enid?" Mom said, sitting

beside me. I did. "I think we should talk about Becky. About what happened the night she got hurt."

"They took Melanie's dad's motorcycle," I said without looking at her. "That's all. They made a stupid choice and now I guess they have to pay." I was doing everything I could to keep in the shakiness I felt in my stomach and brain. I swallowed to try and make myself forget about crying.

"I know this must be hard to deal with, having your friend in the hospital." I didn't say anything, couldn't. "But you've got to stay strong now, okay? Send Becky every bit of strength you can muster and I'm sure she'll be able to fight through whatever it is she is facing."

I nodded, squeezing my lips together so nothing would come out. Mom gave me a quick hug and stood up to walk towards the door.

"Maybe you should go visit her, Enid?" she said with her hand on the door handle. "I'm sure she'd be so happy to see you."

"Yeah, maybe," I whispered.

"Just remember, no one could have predicted or prevented this. I'm just glad you are okay."

That did it. I could feel the waves of blackness rolling through my body, wanting to make me scream that it *was* my fault. That I *let* her get on that bike and that if it wasn't for me, Becky would be totally fine. But I didn't. I held onto all those gross feelings until Mom was out of the room, then I turned up the music and let them loose into my pillow. I cried so hard that I didn't even feel like I was in my body anymore. Instead, I was floating up near the ceiling, watching myself losing it down below.

I had been getting through the days in a numbed state since that night at Melanie's party when I realized that Chris and Becky were not coming back. I began going through the actions of my life — brushing my hair, putting on my makeup, going to school — but I couldn't feel anything that was happening to me. Not really. And at night, when I finally was alone inside my room, that was when I could be in myself. That was when I could feel the weight of the ugliest emotions crushing me.

That whole last night with Becky was like an old nightmare that always felt fresh and never let you forget it. Even though I know it was Chris's fault for being so stupid as to actually take the bike, I knew that as Becky's best friend, it was also my fault for suggesting such a thing, and for not doing anything to protect her.

We were ten years old when we met, which seems like the beginning of time when you are nearing the end of high school. Me and my mom were walking our new dog, Lucy, in the park. Lucy was a Maltese terrier and Mom gave her to me for my tenth birthday. We were sitting on the grass, on one of the quilts my grandmother had made, throwing the ball so Lucy could bring it back to us. It was summertime, warm, and I remember I had walked there in bare feet even though Mom didn't want me to.

I saw a lady sleeping on the grass, curled up in a ball beside a tree. And near her was ten-year-old Rebecca reading a copy of *Charlotte's Web*. Interested, I started to throw Lucy's ball in her direction, and it hit her foot. She looked up, smiled, grabbed the ball, and started to come over.

"Now look what you've done, Enid," my mom said. "Why do you feel the need to bother people?"

"I just thought . . ."

Becky's face beamed when she handed us the ball. She was so beautiful, and I think I instantly admired and resented it.

"Your ball," she said.

"Thanks. I'm Enid."

"Rebecca."

"Thank you, Rebecca," Mom said. "Now hurry along back to your mother, she must be waiting for you."

Becky's mom was still sleeping on the lawn. She was wearing a sort of Chinese robe thing, which was a little odd, and her hair was matted and tousled.

"My mother is not waiting for anything," Becky said. "She's asleep."

"She must be tired," I said.

"She's upset because my father said he was going to take me on vacation next week, and he's backed out. His wife is going to have a baby."

"Your dad doesn't live with you?"

"I only see him every couple years or so," she said. "I think he's scared of me."

"Bummer."

"Not really." She leaned down and stroked Lucy's ears. "Nice dog."

"Would you like to play with us?"

"Okay."

Luckily my mom had received a call and was chatting on her new cell phone about some sort of social engagement she was arranging, and more important, what the placemats and napkins would look like.

I showed Rebecca how I had taught Lucy to shake a paw. She giggled at the light little dog hand in her palm. She showed me how if you looked up at the trees and spun around, then everything seemed to blend together into one big swoosh of green. We fell on the ground together, laughing.

That's when my mom grabbed me by the hand and said we had to take Lucy home for a drink.

"I live in that apartment building there," Becky said, pointing up towards the buildings that overlook the park. "On the ninth floor."

"Becky, get back here!" Her mother screamed from her place on the grass. She had woken up.

"I'll meet you here, tomorrow at 3 p.m.!" I screamed.

"Enid, we've got a function tomorrow," my mom said.

"The next day then!"

"Okay, I'll try to get here," Becky said.

We never met up that summer, or the next. In fact I had almost forgotten about Becky completely until I walked into my very first grade seven class at junior high and there she was, sitting in the front row in a pink button-up shirt with her tiny hands crossed on the desk in front of her.

We bonded instantly. By the end of the first week of school we had created our own secret language made up of symbols. It was Becky's idea. Each letter of the alphabet had a corresponding picture, and each common phrase had a symbol. We would write notes and pass them to each other in class. If someone else had opened up our folded-up foolscap, they would have thought it was a page of doodles and scribbles, but for Becky and me, every note made total sense.

Hi ♥ *(Becky), meet you in the* □ *(bathroom) after this class. Have some* ☺ *(news)!*

☼ *(Enid), I can't wait to hear! I will bring* © *(cookies) to snack on.*

After school we usually went back to Becky's apartment because her mom was already at work around that time. We'd braid each other's hair, weave friendship bracelets out of strips of plastic (to stay on our wrists as long as we were friends), and watch game shows like *Jeopardy!* and *Wheel of Fortune.*

When either of us had a problem — for example, when my mom forgot about my ballet recital, or her mom drank too much, or a boy I liked made fun of my nose — we would listen to each other when we talked, and it didn't even matter if we cried. It was great having that for so many years.

In grade eleven Becky and I got expelled from high school for three days. It was a misunderstanding really. We never meant to cause any damage, just have a bit of fun.

We were in the girls' bathroom, bored, between classes, and I mentioned to Becky how funny it would be to turn all the taps on full-blast in the sinks.

"Yes, I guess," she said.

"Let's do it," I said to Becky. She was leaning into the mirror above the sink, putting lip gloss on her perfectly plump lips.

"No way," she said.

"What could happen, really? Water comes out, water goes down. It will make a loud sound and someone will come in."

"We'll get in trouble," she said. I had already started turning the taps.

"Becky, live a little will ya?"

When we ran out of the bathroom, we ran straight into a girl with frizzy dark hair and braces.

"Hey, watch it!" this girl Melanie screamed, dropping the textbook she was holding.

Becky leaned down to help her, but I yanked her by the shoulder of her shirt.

"C'mon Becky, let's get out of here!"

She followed me as we ran down the hall towards the cafeteria, the roar of the running water pushing our legs to move.

Mr. Simpson found us in the corner of the caf and brought us to the office. No doubt Melanie was the one to rat us out. Apparently, the sinks were so plugged with toilet paper that the taps had flooded the floor before anyone could shut them off.

The air inside the principal's waiting room that day was thick with guilt and boredom. We waited alone until Mrs. Carey was ready to see us.

"I'm sorry, Becky," I told her. Her eyes were red like she had been crying and her cute little striped T-shirt was untucked.

"Why, Enid? Why do you make me do these things?"

"I guess I wasn't thinking. I thought it would be cool and funny."

"Next time, leave me out of it."

And then Chris walked in. It was the first time that either of us had ever seen him. He was the new kid back then because he had just moved here from Winnipeg. He was tall and lanky, but in a good way. His hair was a bit shaggy, but not like he had slept on it, more like he had strategically arranged each hair that morning. He had one of those sexy half-smiles that I like and he gave us one when he walked in. Then he sat down and pulled out a copy of that semester's assigned book, *Heart of Darkness*.

"What are you in for?" I said to be funny.

He looked up from his book, a little bit like I had just interrupted him, but in a cute way.

"Just got to fill in some forms. I'm new here."

"Oh, we know," I said.

"Why you in?" He had put his book down on the table beside him, which I saw as a good sign.

"Flooded the girls' bathroom," I said.

"And you?"

Becky looked up and bit the inside of her mouth a bit. "Same. Flooded girls' washroom."

"Wow, you girls are badass," he said and I laughed, trying to look at him right in his blue eyes. He avoided my gaze, but I didn't see it as a bad sign.

Neither Becky nor I had had much experience with boys. Sure, we'd had people we liked, and I even made out with some guy at a house party in grade ten. But neither of us had ever had a boyfriend — something I wanted to change.

I somehow managed to keep my punishment for the sinks from my parents. They were never around to get calls, and I was not giving them the note — I could fake my mom's signature better than anyone. We spent the days of our expulsion in Becky's apartment. Her mom was away, visiting friends she had in New York State, which was great. We had an amazing time lounging around on her velour couch watching soaps, and practising our makeup in the tiny, plain bathroom. Her place was small enough that it almost felt like we could own it ourselves. In fact, I almost wished we didn't have to go back to school at all.

I talked about Chris a lot during those days. How he was the perfect height for me, exactly a head taller, and how it would feel so perfect when he leaned down to kiss me in the hallway. How everyone would look.

"It sounds great, Enid," Becky had said. "He's cute, that's for sure."

"Thanks, Becky," I said. "I'm so glad you think so."

When we got back to school, that girl Melanie, the one who had ratted us out about the taps, was stuck to Chris all the time, draping her arm through his and stroking his back while they walked. But when they passed us, I would always cross to say hi to him.

"Oh hey," he'd say to me with a little wave.

At the end of November, there was a dance at the school. I remember standing in my bathroom, straightening my hair, arranging my dangly necklaces and putting powder on my nose to try to make it look smaller. I had on a black shirt that was a bit sheer, with a lace bra underneath and a jean skirt with black tights. I met Becky at the subway: she was wearing a pair of jeans and her white winter jacket with the furry hood.

"Enid, you look like you're freezing!" Becky said when she saw me.

"It's worth it to look good . . ."

She laughed and put her arm around me on the way down the escalator.

Chris and Melanie were two of the first people we saw when we walked through the gym doors. They were sitting together on the bleachers. She had her arm around him and he had his hands in his lap like he was uncomfortable. *Perfect*, I thought. When he saw us walk in, he stood up, said something to Melanie, and started walking across the gym floor. It was dark and there were red lights flashing. Some Nickelback song was playing.

"I'll let you talk," Becky said and walked the other way. I just stood there, breathing heavy and feeling the beat from the song bouncing in my chest.

"Enid, hi," Chris said.

"Does Melanie mind you talking to me?" I said with a smile, raising my arm to point at Melanie on the bleachers.

"That's just it," he said. "I don't like her."

"You . . . don't?" It was starting to feel kind of dreamlike at that point, and I fiddled with my bracelets to relieve some of the tension.

"I kind of wish she would leave me alone."

"She's psychotic," I said, looking into his eyes.

"And well, this is a bit embarrassing but . . ." A slow song came on: "Leaving on a Jet Plane" by Chantal Kreviazuk.

"Don't be embarrassed. It's fine," I said, tossing my hair a bit so he could see my new butterfly dangly earrings.

"I think your friend Becky is kind of cute."

Later, in the girls' washroom, I splashed water on my face for a full ten minutes, willing myself not to cry. Everyone was telling me that Becky was looking for me, but I wasn't ready to face her yet. I took four sharp breaths through my nose and thought, *Be strong, Enid, you can do this.* I left the washroom and stood at the entrance to the gym. There was another slow song, and soon, things began moving in slow motion as well. I could still see them through the dark — Becky and Chris in the middle of the dance floor, deeply kissing in time to the music. And across the gym from me, wearing her frumpy floral dress and staring at them from the other side, was Melanie. We looked at each other for a split second, each of us sharing the same pathetic look that said: *That should have been me.*

Becky stopped kissing, looked up, and saw me. She pulled away from Chris and started running towards me in the dark gym — seemingly in slow motion. I turned around and headed for the door, opening it to let some light from the hallway illuminate a corner of the dance floor. She put her hand on my shoulder just as I reached the outside door.

"Enid, wait!"

"What . . . what, Becky? What could you possibly have to say?"

"I wanted to ask you, is this okay? Me and Chris? Do you still like him?" I turned and looked at her. Her tiny waist, button nose, and sweet complexion seemed to be walls between us, putting her one place and me in another.

"I'm not sure how you could do this," I said.

"I swear, Enid. I didn't plan this. It's just that I've started liking Chris lately. It didn't have anything to do with you."

"It has everything to do with me." When I said this she looked down at the ground and crinkled up her little eyebrows like I had really hurt her. "But it figures that he likes you; of course he would."

I turned away from her then, feeling the inches between us multiply as I walked away.

After the dance, Becky and I didn't talk for a while. When I saw her in the hallway holding hands with Chris, I would zip around the corner or down a set of stairs. She tried to get my attention in class but I ignored her. She called me at home but I told my mom I was too tired to talk. The one time I accidentally picked up the phone, I told her that I needed some space to get used to how things were now, and she said that was fine, that she would wait for me. Christmas and the Millennium New Year's passed without us getting together like we usually did.

The first time we really talked was on her birthday the following February. I went over to her apartment with a gift pack of MAC cosmetics. We sat on her couch, looking out into the park. Her mother was at work until ten.

"You know, I never would have hooked up with Chris if I'd known how upset you would be," she said.

"It doesn't matter, Becky. I don't like him anymore."

"Are you sure?"

"I'll let you be my friend still."

"Thanks, Enid." She leaned in to hug me and I allowed her to, although my body stayed stiff and formal.

Later that month, she got her job at the Gap. I think it was her mother who pushed her into it, now that she was seventeen. Personally, I was never a fan of the clothes at the Gap — too preppy and generic. I much preferred Le Château or some of the more obscure places in Kensington Market. But I pretended that I thought her new job was really awesome anyway. From then on, she always invited me when she and Chris went out somewhere — even throughout the summer — which probably annoyed Chris as much as it made me feel like a third wheel. But she tried. And looking back, I'm glad to have had that time with her.

I don't think Melanie ever forgave Becky and me for taking Chris away from her — even though he was never really hers. He didn't seem to care, saying, "Just 'cause I'm new doesn't mean I don't have a choice in who I hook up with."

Becky would always giggle after Chris talked. She seemed to find everything he said really, really, funny. That, or he was just really good in bed or something.

So when Melanie invited us all to her house party that September, none of us really wanted to go. First of all, Melanie had hardly any friends and didn't drink as far as we knew. But the fact that she would go out of her way to invite Chris, Becky, and me, made the whole thing seem weird.

"Is she going to poison us?" Chris suggested.

"Maybe she wants to kidnap you and keep you in her basement," I said.

"We should probably go," Becky said. "After all, she was one of the first people you met here . . ."

Chris agreed with Becky, because well, she was Becky. We went. The three of us went to Melanie's party. It sounds so ominous saying it like that.

At first, the party was fine. About ten kids were piled into Melanie's parents' narrow living room. There were tacky paintings of fruit bowls and horses on the walls, and some seriously outdated coffee tables and plaid couches. We were just sitting there, listening to music, drinking beer, and doing vodka shots. Melanie's father was not home, which meant that maybe it could actually have been a fun night. Even when Melanie started telling everyone about her father's motorcycle and how it was so awesome and expensive to try to show off. Even when one girl puked in the kitchen sink. I still thought that maybe, this might turn into a party we would remember — in a good way.

But then Melanie told us that she wanted to show us all a little slideshow that she had prepared on her laptop. She projected it onto the wall using one of those fancy projectors.

A song started playing. That one that goes, "I'm an asshole-y-o-leo-leo." Then, up on the screen, pictures of Chris started flashing by. Melanie must have taken them herself. There was Chris at his locker, eating a hamburger in the caf, holding Becky's hand in the hallway, looking stunned as he stood up from the water fountain.

Chris looked at Melanie as if to say, "Really?" but didn't say anything. He took another vodka shot.

"Melanie, that's just mean," Becky said. "You're being a bitch."

People were laughing now. The photos were on a loop and so was the song. Melanie had her hand over her mouth, like she was trying to hide her smile.

"Let's get out of here," Chris said. He barely seemed like he cared. He was too cool to let a girl like Melanie make a fool out of him.

Me, Chris, and Becky went out back. We stood on the cement driveway that almost filled the entire yard. Chris took out a cigarette and held it between his long fingers.

"Really, why does she have to be so immature?" he said.

Becky flicked a lighter and raised it towards Chris, and he put the cigarette in his mouth.

"Don't let it bug you," Becky said. "Life's too short."

Chris took a long drag of the cigarette while Becky lit it. He turned his head to blow the smoke away from Becky's face. Then, he put his hand around her hip and pulled her closer to him.

"I've got what I want," he said.

"Can I have a drag?" I asked to interrupt them. Chris handed me the cigarette and I sucked the smoke down.

He smiled as I handed it back to him, his face seeming to light up in the dark. It was then that I looked towards the garage at the end of the yard.

"Hey, you into motorcycles, Chris?" I said, pointing at the garage. He shrugged. I walked over and tried the door, and to my surprise, it opened.

"Enid, you shouldn't go in there, babe," Becky said in her usual way.

"Just to see . . ." I said, walking into the garage. It was pitch black and smelled like gasoline and Trident gum. I could feel Becky and Chris behind me.

"Turn on the light, Enid," Chris said. I felt along the wall until I found it, and then flipped the switch.

The motorcycle was perched in the centre of the room, silver and chrome polished to perfection. It had a small polishing rag laid across its handlebars and some tools spread on the floor around it.

"Cool ride," Chris said, draping one leg over the side and coming down on the seat, cigarette still in his mouth. Becky rubbed his back while he pretended to lean into corners and cascade down hills.

"Let's get out of here now, Chris," she said.

"Just wait a minute," Chris said. "I used to ride motorbikes in Winnipeg; I could tear the streets up with this."

Chris was slurring his words a bit, and so was I for that matter, which is why, I am surprised by what I chose to do next.

"Maybe you could use this," I said. The key. It was hanging by the door on a hook marked "Keys."

"No way it's that simple," he said, grabbing the key from my hand and putting it in the ignition. With a push of his heel and a turn of his wrist, the motorcycle revved up.

Becky took a step back as I knew she would do. "Chris, really, get off the bike. You're going to hurt yourself."

He pushed her away a little, which kind of made me happy, and so, I moved in and flung my own foot over the side and sat down behind him. I could smell his cologne on his T-shirt, that, or it was his deodorant.

"I'll go!" I yelled out.

"Enid, stop it," she said in her non-drunk way. I swear that when people aren't drinking (Becky never did, on account of her mom), they are in a whole different dimension than us drinking people.

"This will show her," Chris said. "How do you think Melanie will feel to look out her front window and see us zooming by on her father's bike?"

"Fancy!" I said, feeling more excited about the possibility of putting my arms around Chris's waist.

"Chris, you've been drinking," Becky said.

"Hardly," he said, revving the motor a bit.

"Not too much," I said. "She'll hear you."

"Grab your helmet, Enid," Chris said.

I got off the bike and reached down to pick up the helmet, a red one with a lightning bolt. I scanned the room. There was only one. I held it in my hand, listening to the hum of the motorcycle's motor.

"Give the helmet to Chris!" Becky said. "It's too big for you anyway."

I looked down at the helmet, and then at Chris. I gave it to him and he put it on his head, snapping the strap closed under his chin.

"Awesome!"

He looked so handsome wearing the helmet, even when his face was hidden under the tinted visor.

I took a step towards the bike again, and felt Becky's hand come up in front of me.

"No," she said. "I'll go."

"Fine, Becky," I said, like she was taking something else away from me. I stepped out of her way.

And that's when she got on the bike behind him, sliding her little arms in around his stomach, resting her cheek on his back. "If he's got to do this, I'm going with him."

"Just a quick ride, Becks," Chris said. "Just to see the look on Melanie's face. We'll be back before you know it."

"Just go," Becky said.

I put up the garage door for them. The bike sputtered a couple times before it really got moving, but soon, I watched them roar down the driveway and out onto the street. Becky didn't even turn to say goodbye.

I waited for them for a couple minutes, then a half hour, then an hour. I waited there, sitting on the grass beside the driveway, feeling drunk and increasingly paranoid about what might have happened to them. Finally, I decided to go back up to the house.

I knocked on the back door. There was loud music playing from inside. I knocked harder. Melanie looked annoyed when she finally opened the door.

"What are you crying about?!" she shouted at me when she saw me, her springy hair flying out from around her head. I hadn't even noticed I was crying. "He deserved it, Enid," she said. "He is an asshole."

"It's not that," I said, wiping my eyes. "I'm just worried about Chris and Becky."

"I thought you guys left ages ago."

"We did."

"What's going on?"

"Listen, Melanie, I'm trying to tell you, okay? Just shut the fuck up."

There was a blast of loud music from the living room — something heavy metal that I would never choose. Some kids were yelling to each other about something.

"Get out of here!" she said. She moved forward to push me back out the door. I threw my arm up towards her, almost like I might punch her, but then let it drop down again. I left, and as my shoes scraped across the driveway that led to the street, I yelled out at her like I was screaming an insult, "You might want to check on your dad's motorcycle!"

As I turned to walk down the street, I saw the yard light go on in their backyard, but I didn't turn back to explain anything. Instead, I walked hard and fast. When I got to Main Street, I started to run, which was difficult in my heels, north towards Chris's house, thinking that I would knock on his front door and see if they were there. Maybe they had ditched the bike and gone home? Maybe they were making out in a park somewhere, the bike parked under a tree. It didn't take long to learn the truth. The flashing lights were easy to see, and the sounds of policemen talking into radios made haunting little echoes in the night.

There wasn't much left at the scene at that point, just a bunch of people in uniforms standing around measuring stuff and picking up little pieces of metal from the sidewalk. The motorcycle was lying on its side, the front of it smashed into a red Canada Post box. All the little polished parts were sticking out everywhere. There was a helmet on the ground, abandoned, and just beyond it, under a streetlight on a patch of grey sidewalk, a puddle of blood, still fresh like it had just dripped out of her perfect body.

Becky didn't come back to school that September, or November, or December. I'd hold my breath as I walked down the hallway each morning, thinking I might see her or that someone else could be waiting to ask me questions about the accident.

I'd see Chris sometimes, but never had the guts to talk to him. In fact, I avoided him, secretly worrying that he would call me out on it all. Tell me everything was my fault.

Once Melanie came to talk to me about it at school — asked if I had seen Becky yet. She still seemed pissed off so I refused to talk to her, just shook my head and scowled at her. When she asked me if Becky was going to be "retarded" now, I told her that was really rude and to stay out of my life. That it was all her fault anyway.

"Oh yeah, it's my fault my dad is never talking to me again," she said. "I didn't make them steal his motorcycle."

I just walked away.

Sometimes at school I couldn't stand being numb anymore and I would just go into the bathroom stall and cry — letting my body lean against the side of the metal cubicle, holding my breath if someone walked in, blowing my nose into those rough squares of toilet paper from the roll. When it was all out, I would close my eyes and make up this fantasy about Becky. Like: I hear someone walk into the bathroom, so I open the stall door and it's her. She looks exactly like she did before — her hair is hanging down on her shoulders in the same way, the thin leather belt she used to wear is looped up around her waist. She comes over to me and puts her arm around my shoulder, putting her forehead near mine. She says then that it wasn't my fault she got on the bike — that she made her own choice — and she says that everything is going to be better from here on out. That she's cured. It was only after a fantasy like that could I force myself to go back to class, clinging to the feeling that maybe tomorrow she would be back for real.

———————

I felt bad about running away from Becky and her mom and Ray that day in the park. It was my chance to make everything better with her, and I totally screwed it up. After I left them, I just ended up wandering around the Danforth for a few hours like I was hiding out. I had a coffee, checked out some cheap shoes at Zellers, and sat on a bench watching the people go by.

The next week, I decided I needed to call Chris. If anyone could understand what I was going through, it was him. He answered his cell phone like I had caught him in the middle of something.

"Chris, I think we need to talk," I said.

"About what?"

"Have you been to see Becky?"

"Not yet."

"Are you planning to?"

"Listen, Enid, I don't need you giving me a hard time about this too, okay?"

"It's not about you, it's about her."

"Goodbye, Enid."

He dropped my call. I remember feeling sad for Becky that Chris was being such a jerk to her when she needed him the most. I never would have expected him to act this way, but maybe I didn't know Chris that well at all. I thought about how I would feel if some guy ever did something like that to me. That was the day I decided that I would go visit Becky for her birthday. That she needed me, now more than ever.

———————

February 11, 2001. Becky was turning eighteen. I knew I had to be there. I bought her some makeup like I usually did: a new mascara, blush, and a pink lipstick. I wrapped it all in tissue paper and put it in a small pink gift bag with a butterfly on the front. I added a card; on the front it had a picture of two chimpanzees with their arms around each other. Inside it said, "Happy Birthday from one monkey to another."

I didn't tell Becky's mother that I was coming. It was too embarrassing to call, and I was terrified to know what she had been telling people about me.

"Enid, didn't even come to the hospital . . .

"Enid ran away from us in the park . . .

"Enid is a selfish, self-centred, superficial little bitch!"

I pushed it all out of my mind. This was about Becky now. It was time to make up for every way I had let her down in the past, and I wanted to deal with it face-to-face.

At the front door of her apartment building I avoided the buzzer and snuck under someone's arm. I went right up to the ninth floor.

I stood outside the door for a while before knocking, remembering the smell of rubber and fish frying from when Becky and I used to hang out there. There were days in early high school where we wanted to go in, but she was so nervous about how her mom would be that she had to stand outside for a long time before opening the door. Most of those times, her mom wasn't even there.

That day, it wasn't her mom who answered the door when I knocked. It was that guy, Ray, from the Gap.

"How can I help you?" he said to me slowly, eyeing me up from my suede boots to my fur-trimmed parka.

"I'm here to see Becky."

"It's her birthday today," he said.

"Why do you think I'm here?"

He looked very suspicious of me, and I tried my best to look the same towards him. I mean, who he did he think he was taking over Becky's life like this? Just when I was sure that he was going to push me away, I heard Becky's mom coming up from behind.

She looked good. Her hair was done and she had red lipstick on and a little blush. She was wearing a white blouse and there was a glow to her cheeks that I hadn't ever seen.

"Enid?" she said like a question, to which I just nodded, because well, it was pretty obvious that I was there.

"I'm sorry," I said on instinct. She sighed, shook her head a bit, and then let her lips turn up in a smile.

"Come in." I stepped into the apartment, my body moving through my own exhaled breath.

Their apartment was different. Brighter. There was a new kitchen table with a glass top and a fresh bouquet of flowers in a vase. The walls had been painted, yellow and creams. And there were new coloured area rugs and throw cushions.

"It looks really good in here, Mrs. Foster," I said, trying to distract us from what was really going on.

She snorted a little air from her nose in a bit of a laugh. "I get a discount at the Bombay Company. Ray helped me get a new job there and he's also helped around the house. He has a real flair for design and stuff."

I glanced at Ray who was looking down at the floor sheepishly.

"He sure seems to," I said.

"He's been a great help with Becky, Enid. We've both been lucky to have him."

We walked into the living room. Becky was sitting up on the couch, sucking on a lollipop. Ray quickly ran over to her, grabbed her hand, and whispered in her ear. He stood up again and she looked up at me.

"Enid!" she said like not a day had passed since we talked. "It's my birthday today!"

I sat down beside her. Her cheeks were rosy and her eyes wide. With her winter clothes gone, I could truly see how much weight she had gained. I put the gift bag in her lap.

"I brought you this, Becky."

She tore open the bag and started to try to peel open the plastic around the pieces of makeup. "Mom, can you help me with this?"

I reached over and took the blush and mascara from her hands, trying to find evidence of who she was behind her eyes. I peeled the makeup packages open.

"Will you put it on me, Enid?"

I looked up at Becky's mom and Ray, who were standing over

us. They both nodded, so I turned the top off the mascara and leaned down towards Becky's face.

"Make me beautiful," she said to me.

I smiled, steadied my hand on her cheek, and applied the mascara to her lashes in tentative strokes.

"And now the other things," she said, pointing to the blush and lipstick. I put them on for her, and when it was done, her mother brought a mirror from the bathroom and we let her look at herself.

"It looks great, Becky," I said.

She asked me if I knew what time Chris was coming over. Ray let out a loud tsk and shook his head.

I told her that I didn't know. That it was hard to tell with him sometimes.

Her mom rushed over to her and stroked her hair. "You don't worry about that now, Becky. You just worry about getting better. Maybe Enid would like to have some cake with us."

I nodded and watched while Becky's mom and Ray supported her as she hobbled over to the table. There was a cake, round with white icing, that said, *Happy 18th Rebecca*. Becky sat at the table while we all stood around her. Her mother lit a single candle and we sang "Happy Birthday to Becky." I sang louder than I had at any birthday party, probably in my whole life. I sang with the sweetest, warmest voice I could muster, and inside, I was feeling exactly the same way.

HER BOYFRIEND

I'll admit it. When I saw her on the ground, I was pretty sure she was dead. That I had done a horrible and selfish thing, and the one person I wanted to be okay — who would have been okay if it wasn't for me — was gone.

But she wasn't dead. Despite the blood, and the way her body was crumpled up, she was very much alive. By the time I thought to stand up and go to her, to hold her, it was too late. They were putting her into the ambulance. I thought I heard her moaning, but I can't be sure. It was so late, and dark, and if it wasn't for us, the street would have been entirely quiet. The guy was putting something around my neck, "to stabilize it," he said and it was really pissing me off. "I'm fine," I told him. "I don't need some crappy thing choking me out." The ambulance sped away then, leaving me. I still felt a little bit buzzed from the party. The motorcycle was wrecked. So was the mailbox.

They left a lot of her blood on the ground when they took her.

I took the breathalyzer while I was still on the stretcher. I chomped down on my bottom lip afterwards, biting hard, drawing some blood of my own. "To the hospital first," the officer said after checking my alcohol level and crinkling his eyebrows.

As it turns out, I was fine. No bones broken, my head protected. I hadn't flown off or anything. Not like Becky. Plus, I was wearing the helmet.

I had no sense of how much time had gone by between the hospital, the police station afterwards, and when I went home. Was it until morning? Was it a couple days? I didn't ask Mom when I woke up at home, even though she had been with me through it all.

"Chris . . ." she started, sitting on the edge of my bed.

"Leave me alone, Mom."

"I'm wondering . . . how did you even know how to drive it?"

"I drove dirt bikes on Uncle Tom's farm, you remember, that summer I went up there with Dad."

"I remember." Her face was solemn. Serious. Like she was waiting for me to tell her something really tragic.

"How is Becky?" My throat was hoarse and my head was pounding.

"I don't know, Chris. I don't know how Becky is." She had tears in her eyes.

"She's going to be okay," I said. "She's going to be just fine. I can feel it."

"For your sake, I hope so," she said. "Now just concentrate on making yourself well. You've got a court date coming up . . . DUI does not do much for your record, young man." She leaned in and kissed me on the forehead, like I was five years old again.

"She's going to be just fine," I said again.

"Sleep, Chris. Get some sleep."

"She'd never leave me," I said as she shut the door.

Moving to Toronto from Winnipeg was hard. The worst. I mean, I had everything set up out there: friends, sports, school. And then everything got screwed up when Dad got a new fancy job at a wireless phone company in Toronto. I swore at Mom when she told me — called her something I don't care to repeat here. My brother Richard was nineteen and my parents said he was allowed to stay by himself, move into university residence. I wanted to stay there by myself too. I even asked a few buddies if their families would mind putting me up, but in the end, who was I kidding? I was still only sixteen, and until I was able to live alone, I would be moving to Toronto with them.

The first nights in the new house were terrible. It was tiny, and old, and smelled like the leave-behinds of many other families. My room was at the front and I could hear noise from the street sometimes: couples arguing, passing buses pinching their air brakes, and the general stompings of feet on the sidewalk. At that point, I was pretty much convinced that this was going to be it for me — being alone and awake through long nights in a place I didn't belong. But then I met Melanie, pretty much by accident.

She was walking by the house one day in the summer before school started and I was sitting outside listening to Rage Against the Machine or something with my CD player and some earbuds. I remember thinking that she looked pretty geeky with her rolled-up jean shorts, braces, and fuzzy hair. As she passed, she looked over at me and tripped on the sidewalk, falling over herself. I laughed, which I think she took as me trying to communicate with her in some way. I wasn't. In fact, the first things she said to me I didn't even hear because of the music. I told her I was going to Danforth Secondary the next month. Turns out that we would be going to the same school. And knowing someone else who went there, well, I guess it made me feel a little bit like I fit in — even though she obviously didn't.

Melanie wasn't cute or anything, but I agreed to go with her to get a coffee sometime. She drank hot chocolate, not black coffee like me, but I have to admit, she was kind of funny. The way she talked about some of the other kids at school as being "stuck up so high," "drugged out beyond caring," or "into no one but themselves" well, that was pretty true I found out. So in those days before school started, Melanie became something to do when I didn't have much else. I'd had enough of her by about the second week of school, but of course she had probably fallen deeply in lust with me by then.

It was so different with Becky.

Becky was cute like a model in a magazine. And the things she said were funny in a way that made you like her more and more with every word that left her face. She never made fun of other people. I could tell that from the first day I met her in the office that she was someone with an extra special spark. At first, I don't think she noticed me at all — it was her friend Enid who always talked to me. Soon, Enid and Melanie seemed to be dogfighting over me like I was some sort of chew toy. And while they were busy fighting it out, I was watching Rebecca Foster.

Her bangs hung over her right eye a bit, and she would shake her head to push them back. She did this quite a lot and it only made me look at her more. She wore the tightest jeans over her tiny hips, but I was not complaining. Her skin, I could tell it was soft, even before she let me touch it. Her eyes were like headlights, leading me to her.

The night of that fall dance was my first real chance to get Becky alone. I asked her to dance and she followed me out. She put her hands on my shoulders and I wrapped mine around her waist. We smiled at each other, giggling at how uptight it all felt.

"Thanks for dancing with me, Becky."

"It's my pleasure," she said. "You look very nice in your blue shirt."

I pulled her a little closer. When the song ended and another slow one came on, I just leaned in and started kissing her. She didn't make me stop until Enid saw us, at which point she went flying from my arms, leaving me standing there like an idiot, but I didn't really care.

Enid left early so Becky and I took the subway home together. Somewhere right before Vic Park Station she said she'd go out with me. She was only my second girlfriend. The first was a girl named Tara in Winnipeg, but that had only lasted a couple weeks until she dumped me for some guy on the Junior B hockey team. It only took me a few days to get over losing Tara, but Becky, she got stuck somewhere inside me from that first time we kissed, and I knew right away that it would take forever to get her out.

In those early days, we could not get close enough to each other or stay there long enough. In the hallway at school, at her apartment, in the park outside her house, my hands were usually trying to make their way into her pockets, or around her waist, or cupped around the back of her neck. And there was nothing like feeling her arms around my chest, her tiny fingers in my hands, or her warm lips on mine. Like lightning between us: and that was just when other people were watching.

When people weren't there, things got more intense: make-out sessions in her bedroom, hands groping, kissing that seemed to go on for hours.

One month after the dance, we spent a little longer in her bed than we had in the past — and even took off our clothes, got in between her rainbow sheets, and let ourselves keep going. I felt instantly grown-up after it had happened.

"Guess I should call my mom and tell her what I've done," I said and she laughed, stroking her hands through this tiny patch of hair in the centre of my chest.

"Let's just keep this to ourselves," she said. "It's better that way."

"You're probably right. No reason to get people all—"

"Hyped-up!"

"Exactly." I kissed her on the mouth, noticing again that we were actually naked under the blankets.

"Never leave me," she said then.

"Where am I going?"

"I mean it, Chris. I've waited my whole life for you. Just stay with me, okay?"

"Of course," I said. "This is it for me, lady." And I meant it. And when she told me next that she loved me, I couldn't bring myself to say those cheesy words (I never did), but I kissed her, and hugged her, and stroked her face, and I'm fairly sure that she knew that time, and the times to come, that it meant I loved her too.

We celebrated the New Year's of the millennium together, and even though we just hung out at her apartment watching bad movies, I'm glad we did.

"Welcome to the future," I said that night at twelve-o-one.

"You're going to have to leave soon," she told me.

"But why?" I pushed closer to her on the couch. I could hear people clunking in the hallway and a couple fireworks popping in the park outside.

"It's my mom, she might be on her way back now."

I moved back from her: "So? We're not doing anything wrong. Yet . . ." I squeezed the bare skin on her little hip.

She stroked my face, looked into my eyes, and smiled. "You're so cute."

"And you . . ." I pulled her closer and nuzzled her neck.

"Chris, no. I don't want you to have to meet her. Not yet."

She must have had some sort of an internal detection system because by that point it was too late. Someone was already fiddling with the lock.

"Well, what do we have here?" a voice shouted out. It was Becky's mom.

I turned to see her. She looked nothing like Becky — none of the sweetness — and was dressed skimpier than any mother should, but maybe that was for her job.

"He's leaving, Mother," Becky said, pulling me up by my arm.

"And this is . . . ?" Becky's mother said.

"I told you. Chris. Remember?" She looked at her mother like *Please don't embarrass me*, and then at me like *Just get your butt to the door.*

I stood up and, in an effort to diffuse the situation, said, "Happy Millennium, Mrs. Foster."

And in response, Mrs. Foster burped. A large, long foul-smelling burp that bounced around the room and vibrated her hair-sprayed bangs.

"Sorry about that," she said.

"Mother, please."

"You're the one who was alone here with a boy this late at night. What kind of message do you think that sends?"

"He's leaving," Becky said again, pushing me towards the door from behind.

"Well, I should hope so—" Mrs. Foster tripped and landed face-first on the laminate.

"You're drunk, Mom," Becky said.

"I am not drunk," Mrs. Foster said as she stood up, but her nose was bloodied a bit and it had dripped down onto her lip. She wiped at it with her bare arm. "I'll have you know that I have been waiting tables all night, and they would not appreciate if I was drinking."

"Whatever, Mother," Becky said. I was putting on my boots and coat at that point.

"Perhaps it is you who are drunk, Becky," she said as she went into the kitchen.

Becky took me into the hall with her. It smelled like beef and curry, and the carpets were caked in fresh mud and slush.

"I'm so sorry," she said.

I held her and told her that it didn't matter. I didn't give a shit about who her mother was.

It was early in 2000 that we started to make a plan: we would get Becky away from that apartment, away from her mother.

"You just don't understand what it's like to live with her," Becky told me on the day we decided. "When she's happy, she's fine. But she's mostly so depressed all the time because of her drinking, and that just makes her want to drink more."

"It sucks," I said to try to make her feel better.

She told me that she blamed it all on her father. That if he had never left them when she was a baby, then maybe her mother wouldn't have to work such a crappy job to support them and maybe she would be happier with her life. This usually made Becky cry. Then she would start talking about her father and how he was trying to force himself into her life these days, just because it suited him.

"I don't know what to do, Chris."

"If you want to see him, do it. If not, tell him to piss off. It's your life!"

"I know that it's important to know my father, but I'm still so angry at him for leaving us."

"Well then, fuck him."

"Yeah, I don't want to see him."

"Then don't."

"And I don't want to live with my mother anymore."

"Then you don't have to."

She hugged me, relieved. "I'm sorry I'm so screwed up."

"You are not."

"Just my parents are." She was smiling a peaceful sort of smile that didn't seem to match what she said.

"So how did you turn out so sweet?" I asked her.

"Sheer determination," she said.

It seemed perfectly reasonable to think that Becky and I could have found our own apartment and moved in together. She landed her job at the Gap really quickly (which was not surprising to me at all). I was also able to find a job pumping gas at a full service station on the Danforth. It was only for a few hours a week and it scared the crap out of me to have to lean into the windows of strange people's cars, but I was willing to do it for her. Once we saved the money, I would just have to convince my mother and we'd be off to start our life together. That was how it was supposed to go.

———

Mom was the one to find out Becky was still alive. She got a call from Mrs. Foster two days after it happened. She was still at the hospital. Mom told me Becky was alive, but that she was not coming home anytime soon. I told Mom that I planned to go over to the hospital to visit Becky the next day. But later that night, *I* got a call.

My cell phone rang during the night, three days after I came home. It must have been around 2 a.m., and believe me, a cell phone ringing at 2 a.m. is not soothing to the soul, especially when you are hopped up on Tylenol 3s.

"Hello," I said in a quiet voice. My bedroom was dark, and my mom and dad were asleep. After I said it there was a little part of me that expected to hear Becky's sweet voice answer back in her regular singsong way. It didn't.

"Christopher?" The voice seemed far away and crackly. "This is Candy, Becky's mom."

"Mrs. Foster . . . I . . ."

"Don't say anything, you son of a bitch."

"Excuse me?"

"All I want to say to you is that I never, ever, want you anywhere near my daughter, ever again."

"But . . ."

"I know it was you driving that goddamn motorcycle. You did this!" I couldn't say anything. My heart was thumping under my T-shirt and my breath seemed like it was stuck in my ribcage. "You hear me, Christopher?" she continued. "You come anywhere near my daughter and I swear to God I will rip your heart out."

"I hear you."

And then she hung up. I was by myself again in the dark, struggling to get air into my lungs. I could hear footsteps down the hall and realized that my mother had gotten out of bed.

"Chris, Chris?" she said, coming down the hall. "Are you okay? Is everything okay in there?"

"It's fine, Mom. Go back to bed!" I threw my cell phone to the ground and lay back down, pulling up my comforter around me. It was the same comforter I had had since I was a kid, black with tiny stars and planets on it. I put it over my head and tried to escape — feeling the crushing pressure like gravity bearing down on me.

I wondered if Becky's mom was drunk when she called. She sounded like she must have been on something. So I didn't go see Becky after all. My thinking was that to avoid getting clobbered by Mrs. Foster, I would wait until she was well enough to reach out to me. But of course, I didn't know if that would ever happen, which was what made the situation was so intensely messed up.

I told my parents that I changed my mind and I wasn't ready to see Becky. That we had had a fight before the accident and I didn't think she wanted to ever talk to me again, especially after this. I just needed time to get better. I took the first few weeks of school off, but eventually there was nothing else I could say — they made me go back.

Being at school without Becky was like missing an appendage or something. No one talked to me much in those first weeks back. They ignored me mostly, probably out of the awkwardness of not knowing what to say, which I didn't mind. Melanie tried to make conversation a few times, but I didn't really say much to her. Don't get me wrong, I said sorry about her dad's bike, but beyond that, we were done. Whatever friendship we had was gone when she made that fuck'n slideshow.

Life moved at a slow and painful speed. I went to school every day, fidgeted my way through classes, and wolfed down lunchtime sandwiches by myself. As I said, people mostly left me alone, which was fine because, except for Becky, I'd never gotten to know anyone since I moved. Not really. And then eventually, I started to hear things. Rumours about Becky and what people thought had happened to her.

"She's a vegetable!" I'd hear randomly as I passed people in the hall. "They say she's lost the use of both legs and one arm."

Enid and I had seen each other in the hallways at school, but she usually looked the other way when we passed and I did the same. Then during Christmas vacation she called me on my cell. I couldn't talk to her. What was I going to say besides I should never have let Becky get on that bike without a helmet? Then in mid-February, she cornered me in the hallway, outside my biology class. Enid was different somehow, looking into my eyes seriously like she was trying to see inside me. She put her hand on my bare arm.

"Listen, Chris. Listen to me."

"Okay fine, what?" I said.

"Chris, I've seen Becky."

"And . . . ?"

"Chris, I think you have to go see her too. I mean, she deserves that."

"Yes, but she deserves more than me."

"It's time to see her, Chris."

"What do you mean?" I said in a whisper, like I didn't want anyone to know.

"She's gone, Chris," Enid said with a bittersweet smile. "The Becky you knew is gone."

———————

Becky was the one who thought we should go to Mel's party. She's always been nice that way, thinking good of people who most thought didn't deserve it. It was big of her to want to hang out at the house of a girl like Mel.

Becky and Enid both came over to my house that night to get ready.

"Who do you think will be there?" Enid asked. She was sitting at the desk in my bedroom, using a tiny mirror to put on eyeshadow. I was lying on the bed, reading a *Motocross* magazine and really not worrying about it much.

"Oh, I don't know. I'm sure there are some people who would want to go," Becky said from her spot on the floor beside my bed. Her thin shoulders were leaning up against my bed, and if I reached down I could stroke the top of her head.

"Becky, you don't have to pretend you like her!" Enid said.

"She's not that bad," she said. "What has she done to any of us, really?"

Enid sighed loudly. She put her makeup bag away and flopped on the floor beside Becky. "I don't even know why I'm making an effort," she said. "It's just Mel-an-ie's house."

"Let's get this over with then," I said. I fished a mickey of lemon vodka out from under my mattress, held it up in the air like I had just caught the winning fish, and tucked it into the waistband of my jeans.

"Really, Chris, do you have to drink tonight?" Becky asked.

"Loosen up!" Enid shouted to her as we left my bedroom and pounded one after the other down the stairs.

"Now, Christopher, be careful," my mother said as we put on our shoes and jackets. "You have no idea how I worry. Don't take any risks or anything."

"Mom, we're walking to Melanie's house. It's like two streets down. I think we'll be okay."

And as we left, Enid, Becky, and I all laughed.

The slideshow was cheesy, but also cruel considering I never did anything to Melanie besides not wanting to date her. It was a relief to get outside to the backyard. I'm not sure if we were planning to stay or leave at that point. We had escaped into a strange sort of party limbo that I was too buzzed to really understand.

I've always liked motorcycles, but I'd never sat on one like that before. I could see why Mel's dad was so obsessed with it. It was perfectly polished and impeccably placed. It was that buzzed guy, not me, who got on and decided to start 'er up. And it was some other person entirely who let Becky get on the back without a helmet.

I can still feel her arms around me as I drove down the driveway and out into the street.

"Just drive past the house," Becky said in my ear. "Just show Mel and then go back."

"Yeah, yeah," I said under the sound of the revving motor. "Go back, yeah."

Truth was, at that moment I was vibrating on my own as much as the machine was. I suddenly came alive within my revenge, my excitement over the bike, and the feeling of Becky snuggling into me.

Just to the end of the street, just around the corner, and back.

Before I knew it, I was heading north on Woodbine and Becky was hitting me on the back with her fists.

"That's it! That's it!" she was saying, "Go back, Chris!"

It was kind of cute at first, the way she was putting up a fuss. I think I might have even laughed at her because of it, which didn't go over well.

"You *are* an asshole!" she screamed at me, and I told her to be quiet. That I would go back, that I would turn around right at the next intersection.

"I'm serious, Chris. Turn around now and go back."

I couldn't believe how easy it was for me to drive the bike. Maybe I'm a natural or something, though I doubt I'll ever get on one again. I turned the thing around like she wanted. I was starting to feel a bit sick at that point, and quite honestly, was ready to put the bike back in the yard, collect Enid, and walk home. I might even have convinced Becky to stay with me that night, to have sex with me under the covers of my bed. To feel her breath on me as we slept. Yes, there was a chance that the night could have ended up that way, but instead this happened:

We were turning onto Main Street towards Melanie's house. One more turn and we would have been back there. But as I went around and relaxed the throttle a bit, Becky whispered once more into my ear.

"I'm hating you right now," she said, and it was enough to make me turn around, make me look into her eyes as we made the corner. My hesitation caused a wobbling in the bike. I clutched the hand-brake to try to correct it, but it only made it worse. The bike jerked us from one side to the other, our torsos swaying with it. But it was no use, the force of the bike's motion was too strong for me to fix. I lost control, driving up onto the sidewalk. The bike hit the mailbox with a horrid crunch, pushing Becky and I forward. I fell over with the bike, getting trapped under it, losing consciousness after. And Becky . . . Her body hurled through the air in a dramatic arc that dropped her hard onto the waiting concrete. I still remember the awful thud her body made when it landed.

I hate to think about what Becky thought of me in those last seconds before she was changed forever. It's hard to think that those feelings of hatred for me are still trapped somewhere within her damaged brain.

It was after Enid came up to me in the hallway that I knew I had to see Becky. Fuck what her mom thought. I needed to do it, especially if things were as bad as Enid had said.

I wasn't looking forward to having to listen to how pissed Mrs. Foster was about me and the motorcycle. It was a memory that I was trying to push from my mind. No one wants to feel that crappy all the time. Besides, I'm sure she had driven drunk before — the way she drank.

It was after I heard Enid say those words, "The Becky you knew is gone," that something changed inside me. I was overtaken by a dreaded thought that had been lurking, waiting for me for the last six months. This was not about being haunted by the depression or guilt, or even about wishing things had happened differently. It was a very real feeling that Becky was never coming back, and that in order for me to go on, I needed to see that for myself.

I started to feel really sorry for Becky, being stuck with her mom twenty-four-seven. I remember thinking how depressing it must have been for her to be in the tiny apartment day in and day out with nothing to do, no one to talk to except Mrs. Foster. But then I wondered if maybe the new Becky even noticed, or cared. It was hard to think about things like that. I didn't know whether I should be destroyed at losing her or hopeful to get her back. That was tough.

Then the next Sunday morning, from the darkness of my room (the blind was down as usual), I dialled the number of Becky's apartment. As the phone rang, I looked down at my bed, imagining the times that Becky had lain there — her white arms flung over her head, her hair dusted across her face.

"Hello." It was a strange voice. A guy's voice, which caught me off guard. I opened my mouth but the words stuck to my lips. "Hello," he said again, more impatient this time.

"Becky," I said first. "I mean, Becky's mom. Can I speak to Becky's mom?"

"May I ask who is calling?"

"It's Chris. Becky's . . . Becky's friend. And who is this?"

"It's Ray." I scanned my memory for any Rays I knew. "From the Gap. You remember me. I help out with Becky quite a lot now. I'm always here with her."

"Well, that's just great for you," I said, feeling confused when I remembered how Becky had felt sorry this guy, had tried to be his friend. I would not give him the satisfaction of asking him why he was there. "Can you just put Mrs. Foster on the line?"

There was a pause, and some muffles, and what sounded like some stomping. I almost hung up, but there was a tiny trickle of light shining in from the corner of my window, and for a second, I imagined that it was also shining on Becky's face.

"Chris. You have some nerve." It was Mrs. Foster. Her voice sounded clear and determined. Much more so than I had ever heard. I resisted my urge to hang up the phone.

"Mrs. Foster . . . I know what you said, but I'm just . . . um . . . I'm calling to see . . ."

"How Becky is?"

"Yes."

"Well, it's about time."

"But I thought you wanted me to . . ."

"I was upset, Chris, desperate."

"Okay, well . . ."

"I'm surprised you're not locked up."

"I went to court. I won't be able to drive for a long time."

"That's it?"

"It's been hard for me too, you know."

There was more muffling on the phone, and I heard the guy talking quickly and deeply in the background, like he was trying to make a point.

"So I guess you've heard what's happened to her," Mrs. Foster said.

"Kind of, but I wanted to know for—"

"Things are getting better every day."

"Will she ever be . . . ?"

"Who knows, Christopher. At least she has some of us who have been there for her."

This comment stung. I could feel my eyes twitching and my lungs shrinking, not to mention the continuous ache in my gut that had been there ever since they carted Becky away in that ambulance. I wondered for a second how I was supposed to make anyone believe that all I wished, every day, at every moment, was that Becky had been the one to put on the goddamn helmet. That I had been more sober, and less selfish, and that when the bike had crashed, I had been the one to have my head bashed in.

"I've been really worried," I said into the phone instead.

"We all have been," she said, and I thought about how strange it was to have a normal conversation with this woman.

"About that night, I . . ."

"It's Becky you should be talking to."

"Put her on the phone then."

"She's having a nap right now."

"I'll come see her then, tomorrow."

"Fine, for her. You can come to the apartment at lunchtime."

"Good. I'll talk to her then."

"Okay."

"Goodbye, Mrs. Foster."

"Chris?"

"Yes."

"She's missed you, Chris. She's missed you a lot."

———————

Truth was, I missed Becky too. More than I could express in anything that sounded like a sentence. There was also a part of me that was still holding out hope. Still thought that maybe I would show up at her apartment and Becky would be there, cute and well-dressed in Gap khakis with the same happy little smile she always wore. That maybe, she would have a bandage or something around her head, and I could comment on it, and she would put her hand to her forehead and make some joke about having one hell of a headache. And we would laugh, and she would say she forgave me, and we would kiss, and I would feel all warm inside and out like I always did. And her mom would say sorry she had to trick me on the phone, but that she wanted to make sure I came. And I would say it was no problem — that I was just glad to have Becky back, to be able to go on with things.

But I knew it would not go this way at all. And if I ever forgot the reality of the situation, for even just a second, there was always someone there to remind me.

Like the afternoon after I talked to Becky's mom on the phone. I left the house with my faded baseball hat pulled down, wearing jeans that had been wrinkled on the floor for a couple days and my green hooded sweatshirt. I walked down my front steps into the sunlight and was immediately freezing. I took a breath and watched the air turn frosty in front of my face, stopping to admire it like proof that I was still alive. My sneakers hit the sidewalk and I thought about turning back, about giving up my craving for a cigarette, but I kept going, my feet bouncing on the concrete, blowing into my hands to keep them warm. I was almost at the Bloor Variety Store when I saw him.

He was directly in front of me, holding a bag from Home Hardware: Melanie's dad. I had met him once when I used to hang out with Melanie, but I hadn't seen him since the accident and didn't particularly want to.

He stopped walking and stood in front of me with his legs parted and a scowl on his rough face. I was frozen in a surge of anxiety and immediately wanted to retreat back into the protection of my house.

"Well, look what the cat dragged in," he said.

I looked at the ground, trying to avoid his black eyes staring at me.

"I think we need to have a talk, Mr. Chris."

I took a step to the side, hoping he would just let me pass, but he moved his own body to block me.

"I think you owe me an apology."

"I'm sorry." I still wasn't looking at him. There was an ache in the centre of my chest that was threatening to swallow the rest of me up.

"You're lucky I didn't press charges, kid . . ."

"I said, I'm sorry."

He grabbed me by the shoulder and I flinched. "You should be ashamed of yourself for what you did to the bike — not to mention the girl. Have you no respect for anything sacred?"

"She was my girlfriend!" I screamed in his face. "Of course I respected her." I pushed his hand away until he loosened his grip on my clothing. And then I cocked back my arm and popped Melanie's dad right in the cheek. He brought his hand to his face.

"You little punk . . ." he started to say, but I turned and ran in the other direction as fast as I could. I didn't even check to see if he was following me. It didn't matter. I would have done the same thing either way.

I went straight into my room and stayed there for the rest of the night, even when Mom knocked on the door wanting to see if I was okay. I lay still under the covers of my bed, listening for the phone to ring or for Melanie's dad to knock on the door and expose what I'd done. But he never did. I fell asleep in my clothes, not even turning on the light after the sun went down.

The night was filled with hours of fitful dreaming.

At one point: I was running down a dark, empty street and there was a woman pushing a baby stroller towards me. I ran towards them, thinking that there was someone I was supposed to help. The woman looked up . . . It was Becky's mom, her eyes burning red against the black sky.

"Keep away from my baby!" she yelled and I looked down to see that it was Becky in the stroller — a miniature version of a full-grown Becky in a Gap sweatshirt. She was wearing a little mini motorcycle helmet. I reached out to her . . .

"Becky, it's me. Becky!"

She opened her mouth and started talking. "I miss you, I miss you, I miss you," she said.

"Stop it, Becky. It's me, Chris."

"I miss you, I miss you, I miss you" is all she kept saying.

"Becky, come with me. I can save you!" I tried to grab the stroller from Mrs. Foster, but she hit me on the side of the head with a bottle of wine.

"I said, stay away!" Mrs. Foster said. Becky started crying like a toddler, bawling and wailing.

"It's okay, Becky. It's going to be okay." I reached out to touch her, but her mom swatted my arm away. There were police sirens. We all stopped to listen.

"They're coming for you now," Mrs. Foster said. "They know what you've done." Then, some cops were there. They had me pushed up against a lamppost and were patting me down.

"They know what you've done!" a male voice yelled out, and I turned to see that it was that guy Ray from the Gap and he was wearing an oversized motorcycle helmet. "This is all your fault!" he said before he slapped down the facemask and started feeding Becky a giant baby bottle.

The cops were pushing me into the pavement. There was blood on the ground and they were putting my nose near it.

"Just admit it!" I heard another voice say. "You killed Becky!" I strained my neck to look behind me and saw that it was Enid yelling at me. Her dark hair was teased up around her face like some sort of bride of Frankenstein.

"Stop this!" I said.

"You're going down!" that Ray guy said and he and Enid started laughing, hard and loud, and they were hitting me in the back of the head when they did it. My hands were pinned behind my back. Their voices grew louder and I started to scream to get them to stop . . .

I was shot back from sleep, finding myself sweaty and tense in the dark of my bedroom.

"Chris? Chris, are you okay?" It was my mother's voice from down the hallway, and her footsteps.

"I'm okay, Mom!" I found the air to say to her.

She opened my bedroom door.

"You were yelling, Chris," she said from the doorway. "Are you nervous about tomorrow? Is that why you were in your room all afternoon?" I swatted my hand through the air, pulling up my comforter over me.

"No, Mother. I'm fine, okay? Please just go away. Leave me alone."

"It's going to be okay, Chris."

"I know. Please, leave."

"I'm just down the hall if you need me."

"Good night, Mom."

"Good night, Chris."

When the door clicked shut again, I knew. I could not be there anymore: not in this house, this city. I could not talk about this with another person, feel their eyes on me, their judgments. I could not

catch one more glimpse of my own mother's disappointment —
could not physically bear it for another minute.

I packed my bag before the sun came up. It was the ratty one I used
to use when I was on the track team at my old school. Pretty small
but it didn't matter. I would pick up the rest of what I needed later
on. As I shoved the last pair of underwear in, I had made up my
mind for certain: I was going back to Winnipeg.

There was this friend I had there, Jeremy, and I was pretty sure
that he would let me stay in his parents' basement, at least for a
while — until I found a job. I would call him as soon as I got off
the bus, and if not, I could always find my brother at university, or
head out to my uncle's farm. He would never turn me away when I
told him what happened. And if he was to say I had to call my mom
and tell her where I was before he'd let me stay? Well, I'd do it no
problem. In fact, I figured I would probably call her anyway when I
reached town. None of this was her fault. It was Dad who decided
we should leave Manitoba.

I got on my knees and reached down under my bed, waving my
arm around until I found it. I slid out the shoebox and opened it —
it was still stuffed with the money I had put there. It was everything
I had saved up for the apartment that Becky and I were going to
rent. I scooped up the bills in clumps and sorted them into a pile,
which I folded and stuffed into the pockets of my jeans. "You might
as well use it," I could imagine Becky's voice saying to me. "Go
ahead, Chris. Just take it."

"I wish none of this was happening," I whispered out loud to Becky like maybe she was sitting on my bed watching me. "I'm sorry I have to go." I flung my bag over my shoulder, looked around the room one more time, and opened my bedroom door as quietly as I could.

An early morning subway ride and crisp walk through the late February cold brought me to the downtown bus terminal just as the sun was rising. I went to the ticket counter and leaned up against the booth like I was going to fall asleep right there.

"One way ticket to Winnipeg, please."

The man behind the counter looked me over, pausing a minute before he spoke.

"You're going to have a bit of a wait, son. Next bus doesn't leave until 8 p.m." I looked at the clock behind the man's head. It was 8 a.m.

"What kind of sorry-ass schedule is that?" I yelled at him.

"It's Sunday, boy."

"Well, fuck me then, guess I'll just wait here on the ground for the next twelve hours."

"You'd better watch yourself or you're not going to get a ticket at all!"

I threw my money for the ticket onto the counter. The ticket guy took it and handed me the paper with the words, "Winnipeg Express. One Way." I put it into the pocket of my winter jacket, nodded at the guy, and moved away from the counter.

Mom probably wouldn't have noticed I was gone by that time. I'd been sleeping late a lot. But she'd notice if I didn't get up to go see Becky. I thought then that maybe I should have left a note, but decided it was better that I didn't let anyone talk me out of it. She'd be okay until tomorrow. I shut my cell phone off and put it back in my pocket. I would call her when I was there.

To pass the time, I went to the liquor store and bought a mickey of vodka without even being carded. I sat on a plastic chair in the corner of the bus station furthest from the ticket booth, cracked open the lid inside the paper bag, and drank the vodka straight from the bottle. Each sip stung but took me a bit further from where I was, which was a nice feeling. By 10 a.m. the station had filled up and I just sat there, sipping, and staring at the various bodies around me. There were parents with young kids bounding around with excitement about their bus rides, haggard old women who looked like they'd just smoked their last cigarette, and an old man with a walker who kept jumping every time they announced something, looking over his shoulder nervously and checking his watch. For all I knew, I could have been this guy. Or that little kid with the sucker that he kept pressing up against the butt-holes of the seat when his mom wasn't looking. That could have been me too.

At 11:30 I was sufficiently smashed and found myself singing along to that cheesy *Dawson's Creek* song as it sung out from a speaker above my head. People were staring at me but I didn't give a shit. I agreed with the song. I didn't want to wait for my life to be over, either.

When the digital clock on the wall read 12:00, I thought about Becky and her mom and whether they would have been waiting for me. I wondered if Becky would even have known I was coming, or if her mom would have kept it from her in case I didn't show up. I wondered if she would be sad. I hated to hurt Becky even more than I already had.

At 1 p.m. I went back to the liquor store to get another mickey of vodka. It took everything in me not to puke or fall on top of the guy who checked me out, but he didn't seem to notice. I just nodded at him like I was really tired and annoyed.

When I got back to the bus station, someone had taken my seat. The sight of her made me stop where I was, clutching my liquor bag.

Tiny, golden brown hair — this girl was an exact replica of Becky.

My heart felt as though it filled the back of my throat and I took a deep breath to try to steady myself. I looked at this girl hard and long — there was two of her, there was one of her, the image of her was morphing around in my vision, not letting me truly see her.

For all I knew, in the state I was in, this girl was Becky, and I so wanted it to be. There is nothing I could have wanted more at that moment than to have found Becky in that bus station and wrapped my arms around her.

"Becky," I said. The girl turned around. She was sitting beside another girl her age, who also turned around.

"Excuse me?" she said. She sounded a bit like Becky, but her voice was a little deeper, rougher.

"Becky, is that you?" I was almost going to cry at that point because I wanted it to be Becky so badly.

"Um, no." The girl turned and laughed with her friend. "My name's not Becky." I didn't believe her. My head was that fucked up that I thought she was just playing a joke on me. I took a step towards the girl and put my hand on her shoulder. The minute I did, every emotion I had felt since I first started going out with Becky seemed to bubble up inside me — the attraction, the love, followed by the uncomfortable reality of what I had done, searing pain of being away from her, and the horrible worry that I would never see her again.

"Get your hands off me, you creep!" the girl screamed, and that seemed to shake me out of it a bit. I took my hand off her. "Why are you crying? You're crazy!"

"Leave her alone," the girl's friend yelled. "She told you: she's not that Becky girl."

I dropped to my knees under the weight of what I had just felt, bringing the heels of my hands to my eye sockets to hide my eyes.

"Is there a problem here?" some man said.

"It's this guy! He keeps harassing me and calling me by someone else's name!"

"I'm sorry," I mumbled from where I lay on the ground. "I didn't mean to."

"And he's drunk!" the girl's friend shouted out. I felt someone grabbing me by the back of my jacket and bringing me to my feet.

"That's it," he said. "You're out of here." I looked around. Everyone in the station — including the two girls and the security guard who had hoisted me up — stared at me with disgust.

"But . . . I bought a ticket," I said in my own defense. "I have to go to Winnipeg."

"Not today you don't." The security guard pushed me towards the door that led onto Bay Street. "Go home and sleep it off."

The cold air from outside hit my face and I remember thinking how it felt kind of good, refreshing even. That feeling was quickly followed by a mouthful of car exhaust that turned my stomach. I hoisted my bag on my shoulder and tore across the street through the traffic, slipping on the icy sidewalk, but managing to reach the plaza on the other side. I found a public washroom and made it into a stall before the vomit started coming up. I covered the toilet with my own puke, heaving my guts until probably nothing else was left inside me. Then I started to cry again. I cried about the accident, what we went through, what had happened to Becky. Mostly though, I cried about the fact that instead of reaching out to help her, I was leaving her like I said I would never do. And then my vision started closing in and I passed out.

––––––––––

When I came to again I was laid out on the bathroom floor by the sinks and there were a couple guys standing around me.

"You okay, bud?" one of them said, kicking at my arm a little bit. "Do we need to call someone?" I opened my eyes all the way to see them. They were both in their early twenties with greasy hair and preppy shirts under brown winter bomber jackets.

"I'm okay," I said. "Can one of you help me up?" One of the guys held out his hand and pulled me to my feet. I felt like I had been hit by a cement truck and left alone on the side of the road for a few hours. "What time is it?"

The other guy turned his wrist and looked at his giant-faced watch. "It's almost six."

"Shit. I got to get home."

"You probably should," one of them said, and they both laughed. "I think you've had enough fun for a Sunday afternoon."

"Yeah, you bet," I said, combing my hair off my face and looking around me. "Have you seen my bag?"

"No, sorry," they both said. They were washing their hands then and checking themselves out in the mirror.

"But my money's in there."

"Hey, are you trying to say that we took your money?"

I shook my head. "No, no. It doesn't matter anyway. It's all my fault."

"There ya go," one of the guys said. They headed for the door but I tried to stop them.

"Do either of you . . . have change for the subway?"

———————

Luckily my dad wasn't there when I stumbled into my house at 7 p.m. He had left for a business trip that morning, probably thinking I was still asleep. But Mom was there and she was worried.

"Chris!" she said when she saw me. "Where on earth have you been?"

"I'm sorry." I sat on the couch in the living room, stripping off my winter jacket.

"I thought maybe you went off to Becky's apartment early but her mom called here looking for you."

"I couldn't go." I must have looked pretty pathetic because she sat down beside me and wrapped her arms around me. I nestled myself into her like I used to do when I was a kid.

"You didn't deserve all this, Chris."

I didn't cry. I was cried out. "Bad luck, I guess."

"I love you, Chris."

"Love you too, Mom."

———————

Turns out my mom had covered for me. She had told Mrs. Foster that I was down with the twenty-four-hour flu and could I come to see Becky next week instead? Mrs. Foster had agreed but said that Becky would be in therapy all week and that maybe it would do me good to come and meet her there instead.

Mom had said yes. That I would meet Becky on Thursday after her therapy session at the Toronto Rehab Centre. She gave me the address and the time, but I was pretty sure that I would have to find the nerve all on my own.

————————

Mom dropped me off at the centre a full ten minutes before I was sup-posed to be there. I was cleaned up, recovered, and for the most part, ready to do what I should have done the Sunday before. I got out of Mom's car and told her that no, I didn't need her to come in with me.

"I can do this alone. I have to."

"I'll be thinking of you, Christopher," she said before she drove away.

The industrial doors of the centre split and opened automati-cally when I stepped up to them, like they were inviting me in. I went to the front desk like Mom had suggested.

"I'm looking for someone named Rebecca Foster," I said to the woman behind the counter. "She's having therapy here today. I'm supposed to meet her."

"Well, of course," the woman said, her eyes warm and her smile welcoming. "I saw Becky come in just after lunch. She'll probably be in the client lounge now. It's this way."

"Okay, thanks." I looked down at the ground, making my way towards where she had pointed.

I didn't see Becky right away. Instead, I saw a lot of other people who I imagined had problems similar to hers. Some were in wheelchairs and some had walkers. They were sitting around, chatting and smiling. I was amazed by how happy people seemed to be.

"Chris? We're over here, Chris!" It was Mrs. Foster waving to me. She looked groomed and pleasant, more wide-eyed than I had ever seen her. I walked over to her.

"Mrs. Foster."

"Call me Candy," she said. "I'm not even married so I'm definitely not a Mrs."

"Sorry." I was biting at the inside of my lip trying to let some of my tension out, but then I took a breath and I stopped. "Where's Becky?"

"She's right over there, Chris. Sitting by the window."

Despite what her mom had said, it was not Becky sitting over by the window. I'll admit, she was wearing some of Becky's clothes, an old Gap sweatshirt, a pair of sneakers she used to wear in gym class, but the girl underneath them was different, just like everyone had said.

On first glance, it was her face that struck me the most. Her slim cheekbones had turned round and chubby. Her hair was short and puffy, a little less radiant. And her body, her body was heavier, and contorted in weird places, her arms and fingers sticking out at some bizarre angles.

I walked over to her.

"Becky?"

She turned towards me and smiled the biggest smile I think I had ever seen on her face.

"Chrissssss!" She was so excited that I couldn't help but smile back at her. "I missed you, Chris!" She opened her arms wide like she wanted me to hug her and I did. I leaned down, closed my eyes, and put my nose in her hair when I did it. She smelled different, but in that intimate space there were parts of her that were the same — like that sighing thing she used to do when we were close, she was doing it then. I pulled away and looked in her eyes.

"Becky, I'm sorry." I meant it. I meant it entirely.

"For what, Chris?"

"For not coming to see you. For the accident."

"Well, I don't remember anything about that, so it doesn't count."

"And there's something else I want to tell you."

"What?"

"I love you, Becky. I've always loved you and I'll always love you."

"I love you too, Chris." She hugged me again, only quicker this time, like a friend. "I want you to meet Ray!"

I turned around to see that guy Ray standing behind us, watching. He was wearing a blue button-up shirt and had those thick eyebrows that I always thought made him look scary.

"Hey. Hi there, Ray." He didn't say anything back, just nodded a bit.

"Ray is probably what you would call my best friend," Becky

said. "Well, besides Enid and Mommy. And well, you too, Chris." I smiled at her like I was appeasing a child.

"She's come a long way," Ray said. "You wouldn't believe how hard this girl has worked." It killed me that this guy was trying to provoke me, but mostly, it killed me that I didn't know how far she had come, how hard she had worked.

"That's great, Becky," I said. "I'm proud of you." I just stood there, staring at the point in Becky's chin, wanting to stroke her cheek like I always did.

"She's been really looking forward to your visit, Chris," Becky's mom said from behind us. "I told her it was her reward for doing so well at her physiotherapy today." I looked at her, narrowing my eyes, studying her face for a sign that she was just being friendly for Becky's sake, but I didn't find it. "Don't look so scared, Chris. I'm not going to bite you!"

Becky and Ray both laughed, so I did a little bit too.

"We're just glad you came," Mrs. Foster said and nodded at her daughter. Then, I turned to Becky again.

"So, what have you got planned next, Becky?"

"Well, first I'm going out for dinner with my dad, to his very own Mexican restaurant."

"Your dad? Wow."

"He has a tiny little baby — Jack."

"Nice."

"And tonight, Ray and I are going to go watch *Survivor*. And while we watch, we are going to eat strawberry ice cream with sprinkles on it."

"That sounds pretty awesome right about now," I said.

"It is, Chris. It really, really is."

She beamed at me and I reached out and grabbed her hand, feeling her pulse through her fingertips, looking out the window to where she wasn't.

ACKNOWLEDGEMENTS

Thank you to the Ontario Arts Council for their support and to everyone at ECW Press for being so kind and attentive, in particular: Jack David, David Caron, Crissy Boylan, Erin Creasey, Troy Cunningham, Sarah Dunn, David Gee, Jen Knoch, Rachel Ironstone, Ingrid Paulson, Jenna Illies, and my editor, Jen Hale, for her patience, intelligence, and all-round good nature. I also extend my gratitude to Natalie St. Pierre at the Humber School for Writers Literary Agency for all her efforts on my behalf.

I would like to thank the editors from *LICHEN* for being the first to publish "Spilt Milk" from this collection and to the folks at *subTerrain* for first publishing an earlier version of "Cross to Bear." Your belief in my writing was very much appreciated.

Once again, thanks to all my supportive friends and family for coming with me on this journey. A special thank you to my lovely mom for being an encouraging first reader and for loving me unconditionally throughout all the different phases of my life. I am *very* lucky to have you.

Finally, thank you to my two spirited children, for giving me access to so many new and interesting emotions, and to my equally spirited husband, for his love and friendship, and for always telling me when I'm being ridiculous.

ALLISON BAGGIO is the author of *Girl in Shades*, which was hailed by *Chatelaine* as "an immensely satisfying coming-of-age tale and remarkable first novel." Her writing has appeared in publications across Canada, including *Room*, *LICHEN*, *subTerrain*, *Today's Parent*, and the *Toronto Star*. She is a graduate of the Humber School for Writers and lives in Whitby, Ontario. Find her online at allisonbaggio.com.

At ECW Press, we want you to enjoy this book in whatever format you like, whenever you like. Leave your print book at home and take the eBook to go! Purchase the print edition and receive the eBook free. Just send an email to ebook@ecwpress.com and include:

- the book title
- the name of the store where you purchased it
- your receipt number
- your preference of file type: PDF or ePub?

A real person will respond to your email with your eBook attached. And thanks for supporting an independently owned Canadian publisher with your purchase!